The

Velocipede Races

Emily June Street

Elly Blue Publishing

Portland, OR

The Velocipede Races

© Emily June Street, 2014, 2015

This edition © Elly Blue Publishing, an imprint of Microcosm Publishing, 2015

A portion of this book was first published by Luminous Creatures Press, 2013

A version of the Epilogue was first published as "Winning is Everything" in *Bikes in Space Volume 2*, Elly Blue Publishing, May 2014

Cover by Caroline Paquette

For a catalog, write
Microcosm Publishing
2752 N Williams Ave.
Portland, OR 97227
TakingTheLane.com
MicrocosmPublishing.com

ISBN 978-1-62106-058-1
This is Microcosm #222

First Printing April 12, 2016

Distributed worldwide by Legato / Perseus and in the UK by Turnaround

This book was printed on post-consumer paper in the United States.

"Let me tell you what I think of bicycling. I think it has done more to emancipate women than anything else in the world. It gives women a feeling of freedom and self-reliance. I stand and rejoice every time I see a woman ride by on a wheel...the picture of free, untrammeled womanhood."
—Susan B. Anthony, New York World, 1896

Dedicated to all the cycling women of the world.

Acknowledgments

The Velocipede Races has been lucky enough to have two incarnations. Kim Street, Burr Snider, and Christine Kam-Lynch gave invaluable feedback on the book's first form.

Beth Deitchman, my critique buddy and partner-in-crime, proved instrumental at every step of the process, from reading early and late drafts to being the person I can call at nearly any hour to ask detailed questions about the project. I don't understand how other writers get by without a Beth.

Sandy Westin and Rick Smith offered feedback that shaped the changes found in this new edition of *The Velocipede Races*. Elly Blue—the world's first and only bike-publishing superhero— conceived and produced the book's second life with inspired aplomb. She deserves a cape and a custom velo.

Finally, a special kiss goes to Brady Wedman, who holds the space that makes my creative endeavors possible, and a hug to my dad for his support. He is *not* a track swaddy.

A Note About Language

Some of the words that exist in Seren do not exist on Earth, or may be used slightly differently than we might use them here. *Seren* is the name of the city-state where the story takes place, an imaginary combination of the prominent late 19th century cities of Europe and America. *Riesen* denotes the upper class of the city, the people who are born to privilege. *Velocipedes* are two-wheeled, human-powered vehicles similar to old-fashioned bicycles. The *keir* is a bicycle or velocipede race that takes place on a track, similar to the keirin race that developed in Japan in the early twentieth century. The first laps are paced to ensure all racers achieve a shared starting speed before the final sprint for victory begins. Finally, *manotte* is a uniquely Serenian slur used to insult a woman for behaving or appearing like a man.

I trailed in Papan's wake, keeping half a block between us as we passed the extravagant townhouses that bordered Vreeland Park. I couldn't imagine what Papan would do if he found me walking the streets unescorted, dressed like a boy in Gabriel's clothes. He'd surely have Maman lock me upstairs for the next year or so, or take a stinging belt to my palms. Or, more likely, marry me off to the first willing wastrel he could find.

I sidestepped a puddle and darted across Green Street. A crowd had gathered beside the park gates. A velocipede race at Vreeland's practice track had brought the crowd and Papan—not to mention me—out on this humid afternoon. I couldn't miss Gabriel's first qualifying race. Nothing, no fear of punishment or reprisals, could have kept me cooped up at home pacing the parlor in anxious anticipation with Maman. I had told her that my nerves for my brother had brought on a megrim and I needed to rest in my room undisturbed. Maman would understand the manufactured excuse, as she suffered that affliction frequently herself. I expected to be out for no more than an hour, and I could make it back home before she looked in on me if I hurried.

Papan entered the park and met up with two other men. I caught snippets of their conversation as I sidled along with my head down, taking care to make large steps that ate up space.

"Everyone's a rookie in this race," one of Papan's friends said. "Your son is racing, isn't he, Escot?"

"Should we bet on your boy?" the other one asked Papan. "Have you seen him race here at Vreeland?"

Papan had no answers for them. He'd never seen Gabriel race. Like most track swaddies, he spent the entire racing season observing the professionals at the Arena. There was no money to be made scouting the new talent coming up at the Vreeland practice track.

I knew the incoming talent well. I'd spent countless hours watching Gabriel and his cohort ride, longing to race myself, feeling the motions in my body with my entire soul twisted in a knot of envy that could never unfurl. Watching my twin brother compete was torture, but I kept coming back despite every danger—Papan's wrath, a ruined reputation, public censure, Maman's distress—because my vicarious pleasure in watching Gabriel was as close to racing as I could get.

Yet.

Papan headed through the gates with his friends, their dapper coattails snapping in the breeze, out of place at Vreeland where the dress code was casual. The early qualifying races took place at Vreeland until the wheat had been sorted from the chaff, at which point the track swaddies would return to their favored locale of the grand Arena.

I couldn't have gone to watch the race without dressing like a boy, and I couldn't have dressed up like a boy to watch the race without Gabriel's complicity. My brother permitted me to wear his clothes; he kept my secret and condoned my lies. I yanked at his jacket, making certain it covered my breasts, and followed Papan and the swaddies. They had begun to make bets. Though it was barely past noon on a Moonday, I suspected they had already been drinking. Papan had taken a shot of malt whisk directly after breaking his fast. He had offered a "good luck" shot to Gabriel and scoffed at his refusal, saying, "What kind of man are you if you can't handle a shot of malt whisk on a big occasion?"

Gabriel had gotten that hunted look in his eyes, the one I knew he couldn't afford right before a race. I had to bite my tongue to avoid snapping at Papan to lay off my twin brother. I'd learned from Papan's belt to keep my silence. Papan was deeply concerned about Gabriel's being a proper man and my being a proper woman, as if fitting his children into their prescribed boxes was his main duty as a parent. As if that would make up for all his own shortcomings.

I darted into the bleachers behind Papan and his friends, thinking about the past and how I had come to this deception.

My obsession, this love affair I had with velocipedes, had all begun on our eighth birthday. We had walked from the house together, Gabriel holding my hand, his palm clammy with excitement.

The new velocipede, a two-wheeler, red, shining in the sun, leaned against the gate.

Gabriel had given a great shout and launched himself at the new toy. It took him only a few tries to balance, and then off he'd gone, zipping around the yard.

My present that year had been a new petticoat. I'd wanted to ride like Gabriel, but even if the rules of the riesen class hadn't forbidden it, my new skirt would have hindered me.

Maman had stood behind me that morning, one hand on my shoulder as we watched Gabriel. Her fingers dug into my flesh the way the new petticoat dug into my waist. I thought at the time that her tension came from fear for Gabriel's safety.

Now I wondered if she had felt the desire coursing through me—the fierce longing born as I watched my brother on the velo. Maman had pulled me back. "Emmeline! Remember yourself, young lady. Show some grace and restraint."

But I couldn't hide my desires from myself. *That*, I thought, watching Gabriel as he rode unfettered out the gate and onto the street. *I have to do that.*

From that moment, all I wanted was to ride, a tainting dream that colored all the days of my confined childhood.

The velo jockeys lined up at the starting line. Papan and the other track swaddies sat closer to the track, but I knew the best vantage point—two rows down from the top bleacher—from long experience as a clandestine spectator at Vreeland. I scanned the row of novice jockeys to find Gabriel in third wheel position. Gabriel's coach, Mr. Kersey, held Gabriel's velocipede steady as Gabriel mounted it. The velo was not up to par with those ridden by the competition, and this disadvantage might cost him. Papan's financial situation had been on a downhill decline for many years—largely on account of his reckless gambling habit—and Maman had not yet found the funds to replace Gabriel's old model.

The top four jockeys in Gabriel's race would advance to the next round of trials. In a field of six riders, the odds were in Gabriel's favor. Even so, two jockeys would be eliminated. I interlaced my fingers in my lap and squeezed. *Please, don't let Gabriel lose.* The Escot family had pinned our financial hopes on Gabriel's success. To be a velo jockey was the only respectable profession a riesen man—who should not have to stoop to doing paid labor—could seek. In the stratified world of Serenian society, the Arena, the great forum for the velocipede races, was surprisingly egalitarian. Riesen men competed with commoners and even foreigners. The only criterion by which a velocipede jockey was judged was his record of wins, and winning earned money—money we desperately needed.

Gabriel had been working towards this dream for ten years, ever since that first red velocipede. He had put in endless hours of practice: calisthenics, riding a trainer indoors in winter, riding outdoors with Mr. Kersey when the weather was fine. I knew the muscle-burning pain of those training sessions. I had joined Gabriel nearly every morning, performing exercises in the secrecy of his bedroom: push-ups, handstands, squats, curls, stretches. We exercised diligently, and after, when Gabriel rode outside where I could not follow, I used the stationary trainer and a skipping rope in his room to build up the fitness of my heart and breath.

I kept hoping someday I would find a way to ride outside. Though I lived for my secret indoor sessions, they were paltry consolation prizes compared to the pleasure of a true ride.

A cheer erupted in the stands as the jockeys strapped on their helmets and pulled down their goggles. The six competitors dropped into their handlebars and put their heads down. The noise abated as everyone in the stands leaned forward to watch.

Bang! The starting shot fired. The jockeys surged forwards, forming a line as they descended to the bottom edge of the raked track.

I held my breath. The thrill of a keir-race never got old: the speed as the pack sprinted off the starting line, the anticipation as they spun through the park's battered old track. Watching a race made me want to sing and scream at once. My legs ached to pedal; my hands clutched my borrowed trousers like handlebars. God, I needed to race.

I'd raced in my dreams for years, perched atop a velo, the other cyclists packed around me so close I could count their breaths. I loved every second of that recurring dream, even the near crashes. Watching Gabriel's race only intensified my longing. But women, riesen or otherwise, did not jockey, not ever.

As the bell rang for the final lap, the jockeys sped up en masse, darting and swerving as they battled for the four top positions. The pack barreled around the final curve in such a tight formation I thought surely someone would fall, but like a flock of birds or a school of fish, they moved in fluid choreography, flying into the final straightaway.

The spectators shrieked and yelled and whistled. I burst up from my seat, biting my cheek as Gabriel pedaled furiously, head down, pushing beyond his neighbor and moving into second place.

And just like that, it was over. Gabriel had crossed the finish line second! My heart hammered against my ribs. He'd done it!

I dropped onto the bleacher and exhaled. Below, Papan cheered wildly as his friends smacked him on the back to congratulate him on his son's success.

I heard their conversation as I snuck down past them, my cap brim shading my face: "Your boy, Escot—he gave a good show!"

"He's got the right build for riding—slender, supple, and strong. He'd better work on developing his thighs, though."

"He seems a bit small for an Arena jockey, Escot. Better feed him up if he's to make it to the Arena. He needs to bulk up."

Papan's reply only twisted my heart with further envy. "Gabriel's got real potential. With a little more training, he'll come out right. Never fear, we'll make a proper velo man of him."

Papan had never seen potential of any kind in me. I had never been a proper daughter. I'd resisted the training of my governess and secretly defied the narrow rules that governed the life of a *riesen*, upper-class, woman. How I hated it all: the corsets, the mincing steps, the placid composure I was expected to display at all times. The boredom! God, the boredom: needlepoint, corsetry, flower arrangements, the art of conversation, the bruncheons. Feminine amusements had never interested me, and I could not bury my resentments. Maman and Papan both thought me a sullen, recalcitrant girl.

I could never be a perfect daughter, and Gabriel could never quite live up to Papan's expectations of him as a man. He and I were opposites in so many ways. I was edgy; Gabriel was calm. Gabriel deliberated every choice, even what flavor ice to order, for ages; I made my decisions in a flash and never looked back. He was cautious; I was impulsive. Gabriel accepted his lot in life as fate ordained; I railed against my place in the world. I thought God very cruel to house my more masculine impulses in female flesh, to give me the longing to race, but deny me the requisite anatomy to do it.

My legs trembled as I hurried away from the track. I needed to get home before Maman checked on me.

I got caught behind some spectators from the practice track, riesen swaddies with superfine coats and tall top hats. I couldn't dart around them so I had to slow down.

Then I saw what held them up. A familiar-looking woman with a folding card table spread with pamphlets: the notorious Lavinia Beau who campaigned for Serenian women's suffrage as well as other unpopular causes. She wore a simple white blouse, a long but serviceable skirt, and no corset.

"Damned radical!" hissed one of the swaddies, brushing her pamphlets into the dirt as he passed her table.

"Don't you need a permit for a booth in Vreeland?" another said. "We'll send the park managers after you. They won't approve of this." He picked up a pamphlet and glanced at it scornfully. "What drivel!" He ripped the paper in half and crumpled it in his fist. "Get back home where you belong, woman."

The last swaddy only spit at Lavinia Beau's feet before the pack of them moved on. She sighed heavily, sidestepped the spittle, and began to retrieve her papers.

I bent to help her, eyeing the inflammatory titles. *Rational Dress. Suffrage for All. What Does Equality Mean for Women?*

"Thank you." She smiled up at me. "Perhaps you'd like to keep those?" She nodded at the pamphlets I held. "Though it appears you've got your own version of rational dress all figured out."

I blinked, horrified that she had recognized me as a woman. "Uh, thank you," I muttered, stuffing the papers in my pocket. She'd tried to give me pamphlets at other times when I'd come to the park to walk with Gabriel, but he always steered me away from her, as though if I got too close her radical notions might taint me.

"Wait a moment," she called as I hurried away. "Miss, miss! You seem like someone who could help our cause—"

I broke into a run, fearing someone would hear her.

•   •   •

Gabriel had been all smiles for the two days following his successful qualifying race. On Mercenday he came running upstairs after his morning ride with Mr. Kersey and found me making the beds and sweeping, my usual chores now that Maman had let the last housemaid go. Maman never let me do chores that required hard work: "You already have such indelicate proportions, Emmeline. Your arms are too muscular and we mustn't let them grow any further." She also would not allow me to wash dishes or do laundry: "A lady's hands reveal all her secrets, so you must keep yours pristine and soft. What will people think if they see yours red and peeling?"

Gabriel stood before me, grinning. "C'mon, Emmy, let's go over to Vreeland," he exclaimed with uncharacteristic animation.

I dropped the sheets on the bed. "Vreeland? Now?"

He beamed and pushed his pale blond hair, so similar to my own, from his forehead. He still wore his cycling leathers, and old sweat made his hair stick straight up. He dug into one of his pockets and pulled out a coin. I leapt across the room to examine this rare prize. Gabriel and I never had any pocket money. "A guinea! Gabriel, how did you get a guinea?"

"I won my bet with Horace Barre," he said. "He said I would not qualify past the first race."

A little voice inside my head told me I ought to make Gabriel give the coin to Maman. We needed money so badly; every small bit mattered. A good daughter would place her family's needs above her own desires, would scold Gabriel for placing bets at all. After Papan's poor example, how could he? But a devilish idea struck me. "Oh, Gabriel, can we rent velos at the park?"

The rental slugs at Vreeland were the only place a respectable female could ride a velo—properly, in a dress, accompanied by a man.

Gabriel deliberated, staring at his coin as if the answer to my question might be written there. He bit his lip and turned the coin over and over again in his hand. "Fine," he said finally. "But you cannot tell Maman. You know how upset she would be to know we spent good money on something like this."

I didn't even grace that with an answer. Gabriel knew I would never tell.

The opportunity to ride even the slow rental slugs at Vreeland Park thrilled me—I'd been dying to try to balance on a real two-wheeler for years. Gabriel and I scurried toward the park with contagious glee, running through the gates in a very undignified fashion. I laughed with anticipation, even though my heavy dress made me fall behind. But when Gabriel had paid his coin for our rentals and pushed out the velo he meant for me to ride, I was disappointed. It had four wheels.

"Get me a two-wheeler, Gabriel," I cried, turning away from the monstrous slug he had selected.

"But women don't ride those." Gabriel pushed the quad velo at me. "This is the type that lets you ride with a your long skirt and petticoats." He gave me a warning look to silence the objections he saw lurking on my face.

I relented, fearing that Gabriel would curb our outing entirely if I persisted. The quad velo was so heavy that no matter how hard I pedaled, it moved only at a crawl. I scowled. I craved breathless speed, not this plodding amble.

Gabriel had rented a two-wheeled design for himself, of course, and he zipped around in circles, sweeping right and left on the wide path ahead of me.

"Do you like it?" he called over his shoulder. He meant the question sincerely, and I had to bite back the bitter words that wanted to escape my mouth.

"It's very slow." I tried to push the pedals harder to catch up with Gabriel.

"It's supposed to be slow," Gabriel explained. "You're supposed to look around and enjoy the scenery. Look, the tulip trees are in bloom." He pointed at the trees festooned with large purple flowers. I deliberately turned my velo and ran over the fallen blossoms in my path.

"Let me try yours," I called once we'd arrived at a deserted path. "I want to see if I can balance."

Gabriel pedaled back to me reluctantly. He glanced over his shoulder to check that we were truly alone.

"No one will see," I told him as I stepped down from the quad velo. Gabriel showed little excitement for riding the slug he'd rented me. He frowned as I tied up my skirts and mounted the two-wheeler.

Ah, now this was more like what I'd imagined! I wobbled at first, but I quickly picked up the trick of balancing. I'd spent hours visualizing riding, feeling it with envy lacing my blood while I watched Gabriel on the track. My body knew the sensations as if by instinct. I vaguely heard Gabriel calling as I took off down the path, but I ignored him. As I rode I experienced something that every velo enthusiast must understand: my physical self and my internal self became one. I breathed.

Gabriel caught up with me on the four-wheeler, huffing and puffing as he arrived at my side. "Emmeline, you've got to stop," he hissed. "Someone will see you!"

I stopped the velo and climbed down. Gabriel and I traded again, and I rode the slow quad back to the rental booth. That brief ride on the two-wheeler had set something free inside me. Unfettered and unmoored, I knew this first ride would not be my last.

I headed to Gabriel's room first thing the following morning, jostling him awake so he could do his usual exercise session with me. He often talked through his strategies as we worked out together. These early-morning lectures were the closest I ever got to coaching, and I drank up the information like water on a hot day.

I wanted to ask him about using cleats and racing pedals. All the Arena racers used them.

As I settled in to perform the exercises for my side belly muscles, I opened my mouth to ask, but paused. Gabriel would think the question implied a request to ride his racing velo. My secret taxed him. He hated to lie.

He should have betrayed me from spite long ago. Like any siblings, we had squabbles and feuds enough that he could have used my secret against me many times. Yet we had a silent sympathy between us. I did not probe into his worries, though I knew Gabriel suffered from anxieties about racing he would never reveal to Maman or Papan. And he did not shove me back into the glass box of propriety that confined a Serenian lady's life.

"I think Maman has a special breakfast planned today in honor of your success in the tryouts," I said to Gabriel as we both stretched on the floor.

"Then you'd better go back to your room and get dressed so you aren't late for it," he said.

I sighed and looked longingly at the indoor trainer beside his bed. There would be no time for me to ride it today.

I heeded Gabriel's advice and went to get dressed. It took me nearly half of an hour, and Maman had to come up to assist me with the corset. I couldn't tighten it sufficiently myself. Strapped into corset, bloomers, petticoat, boots, and a full-length gown, I made a perfect picture of a riesen lady. The corset held my body upright but made it impossible to bend in any direction. My ribcage, exercised by the vigorous breathing required in my secret sojourns on the trainer and perhaps naturally built for athletic endeavors—I took after Gabriel in physique—was far too broad for Seren's standards. Maman laced me horribly tight as a corrective measure. The constant, squashing pain of the corset disrupted my ability to move, breathe, and even think. I wondered if this effect was just as much the point of a corset as the slenderizing.

I took a seat at the breakfast table. Maman had prepared a rare treat of eggs and meat. Papan was nowhere to be seen, and I suspected he had not come home last night. A gambler lived in constant flux, swinging between the high of winning and the trough of loss. In either case—winning or losing—Papan often did not make it home by dawn.

Maman pasted a smile on her face, but I could see the pinch of anxiety around her eyes. She worried over Papan. "Open your packages, Gabriel." She pushed several parcels along the table to my brother. "They should help you in the next round of Arena qualifications."

I glared at the sacks enviously. Gabriel did not seem overly pleased about the gifts—he hated how much money Maman spent on his riding.

"How fine they are, Maman!" Gabriel exclaimed as he pulled a pair of bespoke riding cleats from the first parcel. "Where did you have them done?"

"Voronson's, of course." Voronson, the most renowned custom velo maker in the city, outfitted many of the Arena jockeys.

I gazed with ill-concealed longing at the shoes. They had a stiff grenadilla sole, shaped by hand to fit the curve of the jockey's foot. A specially-forged fixture was embedded in the wood, the cleat that kept the shoe firmly attached to the velo's pedal and allowed the jockey to spin with muscular backing through the complete range of the stroke.

The second parcel held a leather riding suit: breeches made to fit skin tight, a sleeveless vest, and gauntlets to match. Maman had also purchased a new helmet and goggles, essential for protection in the inevitable Arena crashes. The helmet was crafted from custom-shaped grenadilla and lined with lamb's wool. If Gabriel made the final cut for the Arena, one day it would be tagged with his race number.

Gabriel surveyed his presents and frowned. "It's too much, Maman. You've spent too much on me."

Maman shook her head. "Nothing is too much, Gabriel. You must be outfitted as well as the other jockeys, else how will you compete? You must have all the tools you need to win." She leaned forward, hands clasped so tightly her knuckles whitened. "Don't fail us, Gabriel." Steel lurked behind the softness of her voice.

Maman gestured us up from our seats. "Come, come, there's one more thing."

Gabriel and I followed Maman out into the overgrown front courtyard in a parody of that eighth birthday long ago. A new racing velo leaned against the wrought iron fence. Bright yellow, with all the latest track-legal innovations.

"Mr. Kersey assisted with the design," Maman explained. "It was cheaper to have him do it than one of the big makers."

Gabriel's excitement to ride the new velo was tempered by concern that Maman had spent too much and the pressure that put on him to perform. A jockey had no easy life, and Gabriel knew how desperately Maman needed the financial rewards of his success. Gabriel could not fail, and yet failure was the most common outcome for a velo jockey. The career was short-lived; it wasn't a matter of *if* a rider would crash, it was *when* and *how badly*.

"I want to take it for a ride." Gabriel let his excitement win. I paced the bottom stair with envy burning a hole in my stomach. I wanted to ride, too. Gabriel ran back inside to collect his new shoes, sliding them onto his feet and lacing them tight. He mounted the velo, snapped into the pedals, and took off in a blur of yellow, flying through the courtyard gate and onto the road.

I stewed in green hunger.

"Gabriel, be careful!" Maman cried as he swerved around an oncoming gas carriage. But he couldn't hear her, and he was already riding so fast he would not have stopped if he had.

Later that afternoon, Gabriel returned to the house sweating and gasping, a giant grin plastered across his face.

I sat in the drawing room, working on a bit of needlepoint I'd hunched over for weeks. My neck ached, and a headache crept from the base of my skull into my temples.

"You were gone forever," I told Gabriel, a dollop of bitterness flavoring my words.

"I met up with Manny Fitch and Horace Barre," he explained as he unlaced his shoes. "We raced up in the hills."

Manny and Horace were two novice riders also training to be professional velo jockeys—neither of them of the riesen class, but Gabriel's good friends nonetheless. They liked to pit themselves against each other; a competitive mindset was trained into jockeys as surely as the physicality of riding. Indeed, most experts would say the mental edge represented the most important factor in a jockey's success.

Though I could tell the result of the race by looking at Gabriel's face, I asked anyway, "Who won?"

"I did. And we're going out again tomorrow. A longer ride, farther out."

I threw down my needlepoint. "Let me come. I can ride your old velo."

"Emmy, you know you can't. You won't be fast enough, first of all. And second, what if you get caught?"

He would not chastise me, but he would not allow my rebellion, either. Serenian men believed themselves responsible for the behavior of their women. I batted my needlepoint onto the floor from the seat of the settee. "I have to ride out, Gabriel. I can't just ride in your room all the time."

Gabriel looked at me with surprise. "What on earth do you mean, Emmy? You can't be suggesting riding a racing velo *in public*! Imagine the scandal and backlash if someone found out. Imagine what Papan would do! It's bad enough that you dress in breeches and sneak around to watch the races at Vreeland. But riding like a man? You can't! You'd be lambasted, ruined, shamed! Look, tomorrow after I ride with the boys, we'll go to Vreeland. I have a few coins stashed away. We can rent touring velos."

I scowled. Gabriel's offer was well meant, but I didn't want to ride a fat, slow touring slug again. I wanted to try my mettle against the boys.

•   •   •

Gabriel's coach trained him only two times a week these days— that was all Maman and Papan could afford. The other days Gabriel rode alone. Knowing how my brother was vulnerable to long-term pestering, I took advantage. I whined, begged, and raged on a daily basis until he finally relented.

"Fine!" he barked one morning as he finished a set of sit-ups at my side. "Fine, Emmy, you can come today if you'll just shut up about it for an hour! Honestly, you never stop haranguing me. You're as bad as Maman!"

I sprang to my feet and hopped around Gabriel's bedroom with uncontainable excitement. *He was going to take me on a real ride. Outside! On a racing velo!*

Gabriel went to his dresser and opened the bottom drawer, pulling out a pair of leather riding breeches and a vest. He threw a pair of socks at me. "You'll have to wear my old shoes. They'll be too big, so you'll have to stuff socks in the toes."

Gabriel met me in the back courtyard where I had slipped off to change. He glowered as he examined my attire. "Good God, Emmy! If anyone were to recognize you, your prospects would be destroyed."

"Prospects? I don't have any prospects. You know that. Stop being a prig."

Gabriel shrugged and handed me his old helmet. "You know Maman wants to find you a husband. That'll never happen if you get caught. You'll be ostracized from good society."

The helmet was too big, but when I shoved the bulk of my hair up into it, it fit well enough not to slip.

As soon as we were mounted on the velos, my brother and I shifted our attention from everything wrong to everything right. Our bodies were satisfied with our choice to ride even if our minds had prohibitions, and we pedaled out from the back courtyard, me wobbling a bit as I accustomed myself to the novel balance of the lightweight racer.

Racing velos were as delicate as insects, with narrow frame tubes, nothing like the fat slugs Gabriel and I had rented in Vreeland Park. To reach the curved handlebars, I had to hold my body almost horizontal to the ground, my chest pitching forward, my belly upsucking. A racing velo pushes the body into an animal shape for efficiency. It was marvelous. I settled into the seat and grinned, letting my legs fly as I steadied my body.

Maman, if she'd happened to spot us out the kitchen window, would have thought she saw only Gabriel and one of his friends going for a ride.

• • •

How can I explain what it was like to ride a racing velo for the first time out of doors? You could only understand my exhilaration if you had experienced a long-term denial of your greatest desire. I had been forced to observe a thrilling game, but never been allowed to play. Suddenly I had a place on the field.

The air caressed my face. A mania captured me; as Gabriel and I pedaled out the city gates into the western hills, I let loose a yell, a shout of triumph and joy that reverberated in the pit of my soul. Gabriel rode faster. I matched him, keeping time with the rhythm of his legs. We moved together like a body and its reflection in a mirror. We did not need to speak to know which way to turn, when to brake, when to accelerate. We were the two halves of a whole, and riding was what we had been born to do together.

Gabriel took me high into the hills, testing me, leading me on a difficult ride for my first venture in the outdoors. I had to deal with the increased friction of road and wind, the new balance of the spindly velo. I knew exactly what Gabriel was doing. He thought he could make the ride hard enough that I would give up. He expected me to react to the challenge as he would have. He ought to have known better. The difficulty only galvanized me to succeed.

The descent back home sealed my addiction. Gabriel could have forbidden me further rides all he wanted, but after that flying, whirring euphoria of speed, I could not have been called off even with a threat of death. When we skidded into the back courtyard, my cheeks were tainted by a wild flush. In my borrowed clothes, I could breathe freely and completely; my limbs and ribs had ease of range, no restrictions, no horrible corsetry hemming me in, no rules narrowing my world.

I was ravished by the ride. I could not speak as I extricated my legs from the velo and untied my borrowed shoes. Gabriel gave me one desperate glance before he snuck inside to put the velos away. In that moment, he must have seen the force of my will: there would be no denying me more of this.

Thus began a new routine. On those days when Gabriel did not work with his coach, I would accompany him on whatever ride he had planned. Gabriel did not argue; I did not plead. We came into this consensus silently. He knew I would not be swayed towards more reasonable behavior; I knew if I ever asked for more than our usual outing he would refuse me. My need to ride pushed on him. He had no natural deviousness.

Most often we rode in the western hills for safety. Our primary concern was being found out, and out there we rarely encountered anyone. People would be appalled and outraged by my transgression, and Gabriel would be blamed for abetting it.

In addition to long hill rides, Gabriel still needed to engage in practice races at Vreeland to train for his next qualifying race, which would take place in three weeks. I snuck out with him to watch the practice races as usual, dressed in his clothing with my hair stuffed in a cap. Now that Gabriel had two velos we could both ride to the park.

"When can I try to ride on the track?" I ventured as we pulled up at the practice track.

Gabriel frowned. "It takes real skill to race on a track, Emmy. You can't just jump into it. Besides, the danger of being caught—"

"I've watched you race on the track for years, Gabriel. I understand the keir-race as well as you do. And I won't get caught."

"Watching's different than riding."

"I know!" I cried. "That's why I want to ride! I'm sick to death of watching."

He hesitated until he took a good look at my set face. "Fine. Fine, Emmy, but just this once, and just so you can see how risky it really is. And whatever you do, don't crash, even if it means losing. If you get hurt, we'll be discovered."

And so I found myself in third position at the practice-track starting line, mounted and snapped into the old velo with my brother holding the back of my seat in the starting line. Other jockeys were arrayed around me. Gabriel's hand shook as he held me in place.

The practice races at Vreeland Park were both casual and deadly serious. Jockeys gathered each morning to race. My palms sweated beneath the leather of my makeshift gauntlets, which I'd cut from my only pair of white kidskin gloves. Maman would have a conniption if I ever received a social invitation and needed to wear gloves, but that seemed unlikely, so I'd snipped their dainty fingers off. I would sacrifice far more to ride.

I ran through Gabriel's coaching litany in my head: *don't slow too much in the turn or you'll catch your outside pedal. Think of the curve as a straightway and accelerate into it. Don't pass low on the inside. Avoid contact with any other riders. No crashes!*

The gunshot fired; I took off. The dry track surface whizzed by as velo tyres swung into my periphery. I kept my head down and focused on the narrow picture of my handlebars and front wheel in motion. My rivals grunted and labored as they shifted and surged around me. I tuned them out. I knew nothing but the heady, precious moment. I raced like an animal, all instinct. The seconds passed in a blur of excitement, and before I'd even gotten the hang of the whole endeavor, I had crossed the finish line still in third place, not knowing quite what had happened. Gabriel wore an anxious smile, equal parts concerned and pleased by my success.

"You did well," he whispered as I came to a stop. I felt disconnected from the ground after the race, as if I floated several feet above the earth. "But I think we should get out of here before any of the other jockeys want to speak to us. You head out into the park now. I'll meet you at the eastern gate in a few minutes."

As I pedaled off on my own, I planned how I could ride in the practice races as often as possible. I needed more.

abriel's next round of qualifying races loomed, a frenzied week that would decide which jockeys would compete in the professional Arena. Only 42 jockeys would be selected from hundreds of hopefuls.

The morning of his next qualifying race, Gabriel sat on the lone settee in our sad, bare parlor, clutching a paper in his hand.

"Why are you up so early?" I asked. His blond hair stuck up in haphazard bunches, his clothing was wrinkled, and his socks didn't match.

He looked up from the paper with a queasy expression. "I couldn't sleep at all. Nerves."

I nodded. Of course he was nervous. This week would determine the course of his life. The fate of the Escot family also hinged on the outcome.

I wished I could take his place. Such pressures burdened me less. As Gabriel always said, I had nerves of steel. Poor Gabriel looked ready to buckle already. It was going to be a long week.

I sat beside him and extracted the paper from his hand. It listed the schedule of races for the day. Gabriel would ride at eleven of the clock, in the Arena this time rather than at the Vreeland track. I would not be able to go, even disguised, for it cost to enter the Arena, even for a qualifying race.

"Do you know the other jockeys?" I asked as I scanned the names of the others who'd ride in his race.

"One of them. Eddings. He rode in the Arena elite tier last year. He's the favorite, of course. I need to take second or third to progress to the next round." Gabriel's face was as white as the skin of my legs, which had never seen the sun in my eighteen years.

I patted Gabriel's knee. "You'll do this Gabriel. No one has such raw speed as you." Gabriel's great talent was speed. Control and strategy were his sticking points, which made it difficult to make good use of his speed, but I did not mention that. He needed confidence rather than criticism right now.

I watched Gabriel depart Escot House on his velo, pedaling alone into a morning that had never withdrawn its fog. I worried and paced in the parlor, wearing the dilapidated rug even thinner. I hated to be sidelined in the house.

Maman found me in the parlor. "What are you doing, Emmeline? I asked you to finish the edges of those handkerchiefs today."

The last thing I could consider in my state of heightened anxiety was sewing. "Oh Maman, I can't. Don't make me sit still, not with Gabriel's race on my mind."

Maman sighed. "Must you always be on edge? It is not proper behavior to worry so about an Arena event. It is unfeminine. You must learn to be more placid. How will we ever find you a husband if you do not display a soothing demeanor?"

"But Maman! It's Gabriel's race!"

She shook her head and waved a finger. "You two spend far too much time together. You are not children any more. Why, sometimes I look at your sun-browned face and wonder if you don't go out riding with your brother during the day!"

I froze in horror until I realized Maman only jested. "We like to go to Vreeland Park. Gabriel takes me walking. And Maman, you should approve—Gabriel has introduced me to several young men when we've been walking there," I lied, but I thought it would render Maman in a more lenient frame of mind towards my conduct. My relations with potential husbands always interested her. Shortly after my eighteenth birthday she had begun a campaign to get me married.

She sniffed. "Are they riesen, or at least gentlemen of means?"

"They are Gabriel's friends," I snapped. "Ask him."

Maman threw up her hands and left me to my pacing in the parlor. I suspected she was anxious about Gabriel's trial, too.

I peeked out the front window at short intervals, waiting to catch sight of Gabriel returning. The skies squeezed out a slight drizzle, and I hoped he would make it home before it began to pour.

As soon as I saw him I knew the outcome of the race. The tension that had twisted the corners of his eyes and the sides of his mouth had vanished. I ran out onto the stoop, ignoring the rain, and waved.

"Gabriel!" I shouted. "You did it!"

He shouldered his velo and strode up the steps. "I did!" He beamed. "I came in third." The relief on his face warmed my heart.

Buoyed by these successes, Gabriel got swimmingly through the next two trials, placing second and then third in his races to earn a spot in the pool of 100 riders who progressed to the time-trials section of the culling. Most jockeys found the time-trials more difficult than the races, but Gabriel was exceptional. His race anxiety disappeared when he was on the track alone, which enhanced his speed. He was one of the best time-trial riders I'd ever seen. He first had to perform a kilometer sprint in less than a minute and a half—a feat he could do with his eyes closed.

The second time-trial was more difficult; the final 42 jockeys selected for the Arena would be those who could post the fastest times in the kilometer. In the first test, Gabriel simply had to match the necessary time. In this second, he had to prove himself faster than more than half of the other competitors.

Gabriel left that final day of the trials a little anxious, but I had complete confidence in him. He was one of the fastest I'd ever seen at Vreeland, and most of the jockeys who entered the Arena trials, even the ones with years of professional racing under their belts, rode at Vreeland to prepare.

I waited in the parlor, Maman having given up on my help around the house during the week of the trials. I could not be induced to do anything while Gabriel's fate hung in the balance. *This is it*, I thought. *Gabriel is going to be a professional jockey when he returns home.*

Again, I saw it in his face immediately as he strode into the parlor. The emotion was not joy or elation but relief. Gabriel had been placed in the mid-tier competition group, a solid standing for a first-year Arena jockey.

As he threw himself sprawling onto the settee beside me, collapsing with relief and exhaustion, I had to curb that old envy that squalled in my gut.

•   •   •

Three months into the racing season Gabriel remained in the ranks. He had not crashed or been disqualified, but he had not showed in a single race or received a sponsorship offer. The strain in our household became increasingly apparent.

"I watched your race today," Papan said one night over dinner. He'd arrived home from the Arena triumphant, bringing home nearly sixteen marks of winnings.

"I know," Gabriel replied, stirring his potatoes around on his plate. "You won your bets."

"Do you know why?" Papan said, an edge to his voice. When Papan won he came home drunk; winning meant he had money to buy alcohol at the Arena. Maman only rarely permitted spirits in the house, and she could not restrain his excesses away from home. Our lives would have been much different if she could.

Gabriel frowned, recognizing Papan's slurry, antagonistic tone. "No, why did you win?" He set his fork down. Since the start of the season, Gabriel had been eating less. I wasn't sure if he'd lost his appetite because of nerves or if he needed to drop weight. Racing jockeys wanted all the weight they carried to be muscle. I ate carefully, too, though our limited diet offered few opportunities to be picky. It would have been nice if we could have had meat more often, for the protein helped build muscle, but most nights we were left to nothing but potatoes.

"I bet that you wouldn't place," Papan said. "Well, you and four others."

Gabriel flushed. "Glad to help you out," he clipped.

"I'd prefer to have it be the other way, son. Your coach says you're underperforming on the track, that your practice times are much better than the numbers you throw up in the Arena."

Gabriel went back to potato stirring.

"Well?" Papan demanded. "What is it? What's the problem in the races? What's causing you to ride like some lily-livered girl? Are you afraid?"

Gabriel winced at Papan's nasty tone, but, in typical fashion, he remained calm. "It's different, Papan. What do you want me to say? Races are different than practice. I'm still getting used to it." I'd never heard my brother sound so defeated. I had an immediate urge to put my hand on his arm, to comfort him, but I knew I'd have to wait until later.

I followed Gabriel upstairs after supper. He left his door open; he must have heard my trailing footsteps. I sat down on his bed.

"What is wrong, Gabriel?" I asked. He needed to speak to someone about his trouble with racing, and Papan and Maman would never be sympathetic.

"It's hard, Emmy." He leaned back on his bed, covered his eyes with one hand, and scrunched his face. "The crowd, the anticipation, the animosity of all the jockeys—it's hard. Everyone is so reckless. They ride like it's life or death and I—" he paused "—I don't want to get hurt. I'm too cautious. You have to be reckless to win. Reckless and ruthless."

"It's just because it's new," I said to comfort him. "You'll get used to it as the season progresses, like you said."

But Gabriel didn't reply.

My education had been neglected because of my family's financial situation. After my governess had been let go, Maman put me on a "reading program" in an attempt to cultivate me properly, selecting books that she thought would make me a well-rounded conversationalist.

"Witty and pleasant conversation is your best asset, Emmeline," Maman said. "Remember that you have no dowry, and your appearance is not all that it could be. You must charm a husband with your words."

I read the books Maman provided, but I read others, too. I liked the encyclopedia, for it gave me a window into the world beyond Seren. I hoped to discover a place where women could race velos.

I was saddened to learn from the encyclopedia that women elsewhere also led restricted lives. The women of Kelen wore links of metal around their necks to make them stretch as they grew. In Shomin mothers broke and then wrapped their daughter's feet in tight bindings to shape the appendages into a more "desirable" form. In a distant southern place girls were sewn together in their private regions in order to be considered of more value to men when it was time for marriage. Wealthy Aloran widows were expected to burn themselves on their husbands' funeral pyres. I came across no places where women had the freedoms I craved.

I flipped through the *Rational Dress* chapbook that I had collected from Lavinia Beau. How horrified Maman would be to know I supplemented my reading material with subversive pamphlets made by a radical woman.

"Medical studies show that corsetry squashes vital organs and leads to breathing problems," the chapbook read. "It is time for Serenian women to abandon garments of torture and breathe freely!"

Riesen women like Maman clung to corsets as markers of status and good breeding. Even though I would gladly have burned the confining garments, I knew Maman would never allow me to put them off. I could hear her arguments already: *lacing gives you a proper posture, Emmeline. How will you attract a husband if you run about like someone who cannot afford corsetry?* To Maman, wearing a corset showed refinement and taste. Corsets shaped the body into an hourglass figure. A tiny waist—so small a man could span his hands around it—a narrow ribcage, and breasts pressed up to appear larger than their natural size. All this was the height of feminine appeal—so I was always told.

I did not believe it. Maybe I was, as Maman said, "a perverse child who spent too much time absorbed in her own head." A perversity it may have been, but I could never accept the idea that corsets were anything more than nuisances, and it all came down to my obsession with velo racing: you couldn't *ride* in a corset, therefore, a corset was not the last word in beauty. What did *I* think was beautiful? Strength, power, efficient movement. Muscles and sinew. I wanted to look like a racer. I worked hard to lay down more muscle, to build my strength in secrecy at the expense of what others would consider my feminine appeal.

Corsets were difficult for me to escape, though, especially as the Arena season reached its midpoint and Maman focused more of her efforts on me. Since Gabriel floundered in becoming a moneymaker for the Escot House, Maman pushed me harder to find a wealthy husband who could support us. She angled for invitations to social events, which had always been rare given our financial straits. We were unfashionable because of our poverty. Maman's sister had married well, however, and, by importuning her, Maman procured us a few engagements.

"No more nonsense," Maman lectured. "You will comport yourself at these events with elegance and refinement as befits a girl of your birth. We haven't the leeway for any of your childish antics! For God's sake, wear your bonnet if you go out. You're almost as brown as your brother. I'm going to have to tell Gabriel he cannot take you walking in the park anymore."

"I'll wear my bonnet!" I cried, knowing that if Maman forbade our outings, I would not be able to ride in the practice races at Vreeland. I lived for my secret races.

Despite Maman's aims, I wanted nothing to do with marriage. I had other goals, goals that marriage would directly impede. Besides, I simply didn't hold with the notion that the only value I had was as a bride. Maman might want to leverage me on the marriage market, but I couldn't look at my own life that way.

Nonetheless, I humored Maman. She pushed me only out of her own desperation, though she had no guarantee that, should a man marry me, he would have any interest in supporting my family. It would not be his duty to do so. But marriage would at least get me off her hands, for I was one more mouth to feed, a burden more than an asset. I tried not to feel hurt. Mine represented the typical situation of a young riesen woman whose family had fallen on hard times. I could earn no money for the family independently, so my only value rested in my ability to catch a husband.

I comforted myself with the faith that Gabriel would make progress and get a sponsor well before I had to take any drastic steps.

Maman arranged for me to go to a bruncheon hosted by her sister. The event celebrated the betrothal of my cousin Helen to a Serenian business investor. The fiancé was not a riesen, but his considerable wealth balanced his lack of breeding. We were invited only because we were family and because Maman had begged. A number of eligible bachelors would be in attendance.

Maman came to help me dress. She was very particular about how I presented myself in public.

"Get up, Emmeline," she called as she breezed into my room. "You'll dawdle, and then we'll be late."

I'd already been up for hours, having snuck into Gabriel's room before dawn to ride the trainer and do my exercises, but I had returned to bed and pretended to be a late riser to hide my activities.

"Is Gabriel coming?" I asked. The bruncheon would be horribly boring without him, and he offered me protection from the other men. I did not like to make small talk, but Gabriel happily conversed on any topic with anyone. I could tag along on his jacket tails while he entertained people for us.

"No, he went for a ride with the Barre boy. Get up, Emmeline, what are you waiting for?" She shook out the dress she had selected from my meager wardrobe, a plain blue thing, but my best. "Once Gabriel gets a sponsor we'll get you a better dress," she said, mistaking my scowl.

I cared little for clothing. I'd rather put money towards a velo, but I did not get to make such choices. I scowled because I saw what my mother brought out with the dress: the horrible Whittler. I'd worn it only once since I'd received it, and it had been a miserable experience.

"Oh no, Maman! Don't make me wear that today." The garment was longer than a usual corset, extending all the way past the hips from just beneath the bust, and it had a serious architecture of whale boning that could be laced far tighter than most such devices, particularly about the waist. Hence the name. The Whittler, I'd been told by Maman repeatedly, was responsible for my cousin Helen's miraculous achievement of a thirteen-inch waist.

"Your cousin Helen wore the Whittler," Maman said. "And look at her now—engaged to Mr. Adon Voler, sponsor of *nine* budding jockeys and share owner in the Arena! I am certain with a little extra effort on your part, Emmeline, we can get your waist down to fifteen inches."

I glared at the Whittler—it was a ridiculous shade of purple—and made no move to don it, but Maman did not put it away. Her lips tightened, and she pulled my nightdress from my shoulders so that I stood in nothing but my sleeveless chemise and pantalettes. Her face wrinkled with displeasure.

"Look at you!" Maman cried, flicking my arm. "You ought to have been born a boy! You hardly differ in build from your brother! These arms! How can a girl have so much muscle on her arms? I asked you not to pick up anything heavy, and still the muscle grows. I don't know what to do with you. No man will want a woman who looks like a velo jockey! And your legs!" She shook her head despairingly, eyes closed to ward off the sight of my thigh muscle jutting out above my knee.

I pulled away, but Maman pressed in on me, holding up the Whittler. "Put it on!" she said, thrusting it in my face.

"I can't breathe in it," I argued. "I'll faint four times before the meal is over."

"And all the eligible men will be charmed by your delicate constitution," Maman snarled.

"Can't I just wear the regular one?" I begged.

"Emmeline, do you have any idea how much rides on your good marriage? This family depends on you. We must find you a rich husband, and if it gives you discomfort to do it, I expect you to be a strong girl and suffer in silence." Maman got very grim when she gave these lectures. I knew better than to push her.

Grudgingly I took up the blasted Whittler and pulled it over my head. While Maman worked the laces, I grasped the bed for balance, wincing as the bones clamped down on my ribs, the flesh of my waist squeezed, and the edges of the garment cut into my hips. It felt as though my mind got squeezed right along with my body when I wore a corset. I became duller, tamer.

Maman helped me into the dress, styled my hair into an updo of ringlets, and gave me her own pearl brooch to wear at my throat. By the time she finished, I looked like a typical riesen woman. My full skirt hid my too-strong legs; the billows of my sleeves covered my too-muscular arms, the rigid demands of the Whittler harnessed my too-broad ribcage into a more pleasing shape. I followed Maman slowly out onto the street to the rented carriage that would take us to the bruncheon. The Whittler would encourage me to sit still at the party and speak little, if at all. Again, I couldn't help but think the device might have been designed as much to silence as to shape.

Once inside the rented carriage Maman frowned at me. "Don't you dare bring up women's rights today, Emmy. It isn't a topic for polite conversation. I found those radical pamphlets you were reading, and I'll have you know I burned them, every one. You should be glad that I didn't tell your father you'd been reading such trash. He would have blistered your hands with his belt! And you without gloves to hide the cuts!"

I squeezed my spared hands together in my lap to conceal their trembling.

My cousin Helen and her fiancé stood on the portico of my aunt's East End townhouse with another man I did not know. Since my cousin's was the only familiar face at the gathering and Maman had abandoned me to my own devices while she went to speak with my aunt, I gravitated towards Helen, weathering the haughty sneer she gave me as I approached.

Helen had already benefited from an influx of capital from Voler. She wore a new dress at the height of fashion and a very expensive-looking jeweled brooch nestled in the froth of lace at her throat.

"Emmeline," she said, inclining her head and making her chestnut curls bob. "Have you met my fiancé, Mr. Adon Voler?" She spoke with pride, expecting me to envy her good luck in making such a catch.

I offered my shamefully ungloved hand—a sore point with Maman—to Voler, a man who dressed like a dapper track swaddy: well cut trousers with pressed creases, polished boots, and a jacket with tails. He kissed my bare hand with precisely the proper amount of flair.

Helen smiled superciliously. I grimaced back. I couldn't manage more than that while wearing the Whittler. Despite the pressure from Maman, I did not intend to find a husband. Marriage would crush my racing dreams as surely as the man standing across from me was crushing his cigarillo beneath his boot. He caught me watching his boorish behavior and looked sheepish.

As if to cover up his faux pas, the man held out his hand. "Cassius Everett," he drawled at me. I stared at his hand, wondering what I ought to do. Didn't he know riesen ladies didn't shake men's hands? Particularly as we both wore no gloves? Propriety demanded he wait for Helen to introduce us. Then I would be permitted to lift my hand—daintily, delicately, as if my arm could hardly bear the burden of it—and he was to capture it, relieve me of its weight, and kiss it airily as Mr. Voler had done.

I cast a quick glace at Helen and Voler. Helen looked horrified; her dark, shapely brows furrowed deeply, her wide brown eyes fixed on Mr. Everett's large ungloved paw extended between us.

Voler snorted and took a long drag on his own cigarillo, enjoying the other man's discomfort.

"Mr. Everett," Helen admonished.

Cassius Everett blinked at my pretty cousin, clearly bewildered. His hand still reached awkwardly in my direction. I felt a sudden pity for him. He didn't *know* the proper manners. I caught his hand with mine, a shock of skin on skin. Long fingers tightened slightly to cup my whole hand within his. I'd never shaken anyone's hand before—it was a purely masculine gesture— and I found that I liked it. I peeked up at Mr. Everett's face and saw that he looked directly at me with dark hazel eyes and a relieved smile lighting his face.

"How do you do?" I said.

"Very well, thank you!" He beamed. "May I have the pleasure of knowing your name?"

I secretly enjoyed his flouting of propriety, especially as it annoyed Helen so much. Voler seemed amused by his friend's ignorance of proper manners.

"I am Emmeline Escot," I said. "Helen is my cousin."

Helen sniffed. She didn't like to acknowledge her poorer relations, but what was she worried about? She already had her diamond from her rich fiancé. According to Maman's standards, she'd made it already.

I studied Cassius Everett more closely. His clothes were not so flash as Mr. Voler's. Oh, he'd tried. The fabric of his jacket was of the best quality, his boots were just as shiny, but the cuts were out of mode. It was as if he'd known only what the good materials were but none of the fashions. He looked as uncomfortable in his attire as I was in mine.

Voler murmured to Helen and then turned to Mr. Everett. "Helen would like to take a stroll in the gardens," he said. "Will you excuse us?" Helen looked relieved to be getting away. I was concerned to be abandoned with a man I'd only just met, but Maman had disappeared, and I couldn't very well just run away from Mr. Everett.

Cassius Everett remained silent as the others departed. I tried to breathe as quietly as possible, but it was hard to do, wearing the Whittler. I felt as though I panted like an overheated dog.

"Would you care to walk as well?" Mr. Everett finally said to break the awkward silence. "I hear Mrs. Finchley's gardens are superb."

I would have enjoyed a walk if I hadn't been wearing the damned Whittler. I hated feeling so limited. But it wasn't like I had never felt lightheaded before. Sometimes I rode so hard in a practice race that I almost fell over after crossing the finish line. I could manage a blasted *walk*.

"Yes, please," I said. "I like to be outside."

"As do I." Everett held out his arm, another faux pas. A gentleman offered his arm to a lady only at evening events, never at something so modest as a bruncheon. I did not correct him, instead taking his offered appendage.

Everett walked quickly, with long strides, apparently ignorant of how difficult it was for a woman to move in her clothing. His legs were longer than mine, and he had the build of a velo jockey, wiry and lean. His dark hair was sprinkled with grey at the temples and he had a few lines around his eyes, but, otherwise, I had no sense of his age. The expression he wore as we walked was pleasantly amused.

I could not move my legs very far with each step, and every time my weight shifted from one foot to the other, pins and needles stabbed from my soles to my calves in the squeeze of my boots. We made it to the hedge-maze before I had to pause. I clutched his arm and sucked air. My cheeks glowed red from embarrassment. Everett was obviously a vigorous man. My inability to keep up with him shamed and infuriated me. I could have run him around the maze if I weren't laced! I shook off his arm and turned to the shrubbery, pretending to examine the pink flowers that grew on it while I caught my breath.

"Are you well?" Everett asked as I gasped in short hiccoughs. *How embarrassing.*

"I'm fine," I snapped. "I just need a minute."

One of his broad hands came to the back of my waist. I turned in surprise at this touch—another thing a bachelor should never do to a lady. With the sudden movement, my head spun, my vision blackened, and my knees buckled beneath me. *Oh for God's sake*, I thought. Then the black world of the faint overtook me.

I woke with unbearable mortification as I stared up into a concerned expression on Cassius Everett's face.

"Thank God," he said. "I worried you wouldn't wake, and I didn't know what to do."

I coughed and closed my eyes.

"*Is* there anything I can do?" Everett asked. "Are you ill? Do you have the epilepsy?"

I sat up and realized the man held me in his lap. *His lap!* If anyone caught us we'd be completely compromised. Didn't he understand? I squirmed to get out of his reach, but his arms tightened and held me in place. I squirmed harder. If not for the Whittler I might have gotten free, but the corset restricted me too effectively. I subsided.

"I do not have the epilepsy," I bit out. "It's just this blasted corset my mother made me wear. I can't breathe."

Understanding dawned on Everett's face. Now *he* blushed. "I've been a boor, haven't I? This is all my fault. I was completely inconsiderate of your limitations. Voler is always telling me I need to remember that Serenian women are delicate and cannot move as briskly as I do. I'm sorry." His arms stayed tight around me. "Just rest for a minute. Breathe in through your nose and out through your mouth. It's more efficient that way."

"I know," I hissed. The very first thing Gabriel had taught me when we were climbing a big hill was how to breathe. All the advice in the world didn't help when strapped into the Whittler, however. I rolled my eyes. I was tempted to tell Everett to help me loosen my stays, but the thought of him seeing my dress unbuttoned was too humiliating to endure. Besides, if anyone saw, we'd both be doomed.

"Can you forgive me?" Everett begged. His eyes were friendly and warm, and they looked at me directly. I liked him and his ignorance of riesen manners.

"There's nothing to forgive," I said. "If I hadn't been wearing this corset, I would have been fine."

Discussing one's underthings was about as improper as conversation could get, but Everett took it in stride. "Then why wear such a thing?"

I snorted, though I secretly could have kissed him just for having the question. *Yes, I definitely liked this man.* "My mother insists. I do not have the correct shape for a woman." Again, I tried to pull away from him. Again, he held me back. *Bother!*

"I beg to differ," Everett said. "I think you are shaped quite perfectly."

"I'm wearing the damned corset," I cried.

Everett saw his mistake too late. "No—I mean—that is to say, I didn't mean—"

"Emmeline!" Maman called from behind the shrubberies.

Maman was not yet in sight, which meant we had a chance to disentangle ourselves. I made a powerful, desperate lunge out of Everett's lap, groaning as the Whittler dug into my flesh most uncomfortably. I felt as though I'd fallen and gotten the wind knocked from my body. Despite my valiant effort to get us into a less-guilty-looking arrangement, Everett held on, and he was strong enough that I did not escape his grasp. But I was strong enough that we did not stay put. So when Maman came around the bend of the hedge, she found us in an awkward position. I lay flat on my belly on the path, Everett's arms around my waist, with him half crouching, half lying over my lower half.

Maman's eyes almost popped from her head. "Emmeline!" she shrieked. Then she turned to Everett. "You beast!" she cried. "What have you done to my daughter?"

Everett moved as gracefully as an animal, releasing me and rising to his feet. I was much slower, hindered by the atrocious corset. He apologized profusely to my mother as I struggled, gasping, to my feet.

"Mr. Everett," Maman simpered, "apologies cannot rectify certain kinds of improprieties. There is only one honorable recourse to correct this terrible situation." Her face, as she spoke, took on an avaricious cast. Nausea joined breathlessness in my list of ailments. Cassius Everett couldn't be *rich*?

"Maman!" I cried, stricken. "It was an accident! I fell!"

"This isn't at all what you think, madam!" Everett said, not picking up on Maman's hints.

Maman lifted her nose. "Mr. Everett, I caught you *crawling* on top of my daughter. Whatever the reason, you must understand the damage. Her reputation and her virtue are the mainstays of her existence! The only action you can take is to offer for her!" Maman's voice steadily rose to a pitch of hysteria.

Mr. Everett blanched. His posture stiffened, and he brushed down his unfashionable but expensive jacket. "I hardly think that is necessary."

"Maman." I tried again. "He was only trying to help me. I—"

"And you!" Maman screamed, grabbing my wrist and pinching. "I'm ashamed of the daughter I raised! How can you disgrace your family this way?" She closed her eyes and looked so pained that my protests died in my mouth. Tears pricked my eyes.

"But of course I will offer for your daughter," Everett finally said, filling the awkward silence and looking from me to Maman. He appeared to think he was rescuing me from Maman's wrath. "We may proceed as you think it best, Mrs. Escot. You know more about these matters than I do."

"No!" I wailed.

Everett grimaced; Maman glared. "It is certainly more prudent to announce the engagement now. Someone might have seen the two of you together! And the less said about this unfortunate incident, the better. I will imply that I have been chaperoning the two of you throughout your walk and that my husband is already aware of the arrangement. My daughter is only eighteen, you know. Walking out with her alone was *most* improper, Mr. Everett."

Everett gave me a rather hard stare laced with suspicion. Now he thought I'd done it all on purpose to bring him to this point. I wanted to explain, but I was given no opportunity. Maman pulled my arm and brushed down my skirts. "Why don't you go back ahead of us, Mr. Everett? I would have a private word with my daughter."

Maman and I watched as Mr. Everett strode off through the hedge-maze, leaving a wake of dismay. Once he disappeared from from sight, Maman turned to me. "That was unnecessarily risky, Emmeline," she scolded, but she did not sound all that angry anymore. I had given her exactly what she wanted: a rich son-in-law. "But, oh, my dear, this is excellent, excellent! Cassius Everett sponsors many riders. You can sway him towards Gabriel! We might kill both our birds with one stone. Now, I think he might suspect what you did, so you must try very hard to placate him. You must be all that is proper during this engagement, do you understand? He is the type who would want a very refined wife since he lacks breeding himself." She dragged me back towards the party on the portico. I shuffled along with reluctant steps.

What a disaster. What was I going to do?

The sensations I logged about the announcement of my engagement to Mr. Cassius Everett were purely physical: the wretched clamp of the Whittler around my torso, the weakness of my legs, the ache of distress in my neck. Mr. Everett looked no more pleased than I. We did not say a word to each other while we stood side by side as my mother made the announcement of our engagement to the fashionable crowd at the bruncheon. Helen smirked; Mr. Voler looked very surprised.

I concentrated on getting enough air so I did not swoon again. I wanted to die. I needed to get home to consult with Gabriel. Maybe he'd know what to do about this catastrophe.

Maman, after congratulating me repeatedly on the way home, finally subsided into thoughtful silence. She no doubt planned how best to angle the engagement to her advantage. I left her to it.

As our rented carriage pulled up to the house, I wondered what Cassius Everett would think when he saw how truly impoverished we were. Our fence was broken in at least five places. We had no money for keeping up the lawn or the flowers that ringed the courtyard; everything was soggy and overgrown. A window in the front of the house had a long crack in it. The paint peeled on the trim; the front stair sagged as if it shared Maman's burdens. Inside was even worse. We had few furnishings: one settee in the parlor, one table for dinner in the dining room, single candles only in each chamber, never any gaslight.

Everett had met me as Helen's cousin, and he had every reason to expect we Escots to be as wealthy as the Finchleys. But Helen's Papan was not an inveterate gambler like mine. Where was Papan, anyway? I hadn't seen him in ages, which meant he was probably on a bad bender.

Maman floated dreamily into the house. Gabriel, back from his ride with Horace Barre and stretching in the front courtyard, looked up as I stalked through the gate.

"What's gotten into Maman?" he asked as he watched her enter the house. "She looks distracted. What happened at the bruncheon?"

"Oh, Gabriel. It was just awful. Maman forced Mr. Cassius Everett to offer for me after she found us in a—ah—a compromising position."

"Cassius Everett? Cassius Everett *compromised* you? How, Emmy? What do you mean?"

"It was all a mistake, an accident! We went for a walk, and I fainted. He caught me, and Maman found us and forced him to offer. He thinks I trapped him. Now he loathes me, and Gabriel— what am I going to do?"

"He offered for you?" Gabriel said. "So you're what, *engaged* to Cassius Everett? What a coup, Emmy! Congratulations! Why, this is stellar! He owns shares in the Arena! He sponsors jockeys!"

I glared at him. I had not expected Gabriel to take Maman's side in this. I needed him on *my* side. He was *my* accomplice. "Gabriel," I hissed. "If I have to get married, I'll have to give up my training!"

Gabriel nodded absently. "Yes, you will. It's for the best, you know, Emmy. It's time you gave it up, anyway. It won't go anywhere. It's not like you could ever race anywhere but Vreeland Park, and even then, it's so risky. We've been playing with fire, and it's got to stop. But this engagement is quite something! Cassius Everett! He's loaded. He used to be an Arena jockey, you know. He likes to sponsor young jockeys. I don't suppose you could, you know, put in a good word for me?"

"Gabriel!" I had always thought he saw my situation as I did. We'd been training together; we both had dreams of racing. I took mine as seriously as he took his. Now I understood that he never saw my aspirations in the same light as his at all. To him, my interest was a silly, childish dalliance. He'd never expected it to amount to anything. Like everyone else, he did not see *me*. He did not believe in my ability.

It was a devastating moment. For once, the Whittler served a good purpose: it prevented me from breaking down, for to bawl in such a device would be too uncomfortable to bear. Instead, I turned on my heel and went into the house.

•   •   •

For the first time in years, I did not get up to ride the trainer in Gabriel's room. Though awake at my usual hour, I did not want to speak to Gabriel; I was too upset. Sluggishly I rose and washed my face. I stared at myself in the tiny looking glass above the washbasin. I rarely evaluated myself according to the standards of feminine beauty. My concerns all revolved around how fast I could ride, how good my posture was on the velo, how strong my body might be. Only those attributes mattered to me. But suddenly, it had all been taken away. The standard I used to measure myself was useless—I'd never get to race *now*.

My velo riding had protected me from having to fully participate in the concerns of young women. But I knew as well as any Serenian lady what was considered pretty and what was not. My face was too narrow, the bones too prominent for true beauty. That came from my leanness. Because of my thin face, my other features looked too big. My eyes were an odd golden color that some might find pretty simply because it was unusual, but most people preferred blue eyes. My complexion would have been pleasingly white except for the tanning I took during my illicit outdoor rides. Maman always said I had potential to be beautiful, but not the discipline to realize it. That wasn't true; I had discipline, plenty of it, I just trained it on other dreams.

I splashed water on my face and patted it dry. I might be able to fake compliance with convention with the right hairstyle, a little rice powder, and the Whittler, but take away the accoutrements and it would be obvious I was no delicate flower. I was wiry and strong, muscular as only a boy should be. I'd never cared that I was too muscled to be thought pretty before.

It was tempting to do my usual calisthenics just for the comfort of routine, but I denied myself, instead walking to my armoire and pulling out my dingy blue best dress, and, of course, the dreaded Whittler. It seemed fitting to wear it again today, the first day of the rest of my life. I threw the garments on the bed for later, put on my morning gown, and went downstairs. As I passed Gabriel's bedroom I heard the familiar whoosh of velo tyres against the leathery resistance of the trainer.

Maman bustled in the kitchen, up early. She handed me a cup of hot water. I sipped it and stared out the window.

"Soon you'll enjoy coffee in the morning," Maman said, as if coffee were the pinnacle of a girl's pleasure. As if I could want nothing else.

I shrugged.

"Don't you get that way, missy," Maman said, reading my sullenness correctly. "You're a very fortunate girl, and I expect you to make good on this opportunity. He'll come to take you out today; I don't doubt it. I'll help you dress. We want you to look as pretty as possible. Wipe that peevish look from your face."

I suffered Maman's attentions, resigned. The day seemed unreal. My entire life had been turned topsy-turvy. Whittler well laced, blue dress smoothed down, hair in ringlets following Maman's ungentle administration of the iron, I sat on the lone settee in the drawing room and stared at the threadbare carpet. Everett would not be impressed with us if he actually did come to take me out. Maman seemed confident he would show; I was less certain. I'd seen how angry he was, thinking I'd trapped him. Today I meant to relieve him of the responsibility to marry me. Maman would be furious. Gabriel would be dismayed. But how could I go through with it?

Gabriel passed by the drawing room on his way out to the practice races. He always went to Vreeland Park the day before he had an Arena race. I could feel his nerves jangling already.

He poked his head into the drawing room. "Hey, Emmy," he said, trying to sound nonchalant and failing. "Are you going out with Mr. Everett?"

"If he comes," I said woodenly.

"Listen, tell him to come to the Arena races tomorrow. Tell him to watch me in the mid-tier race. You'll do that for me, won't you?"

I gazed at my brother as though he were a stranger. I did not reply, and Gabriel shifted his weight from foot to foot.

"Come on, Emmy. Don't be like this," he wheedled. "I kept your secrets for you. I let you ride with me. The least you could do is help me when I need it."

Gabriel always knew just how to get a rise out of me. "Oh!" I cried. "You! As if it's a debt I have to pay back!"

Gabriel glared at me. "It is. I've been good to you, Emmy, and you know it. Be good to me now. He can help us, your Cassius."

"He's not *my* Cassius," I hissed. "I'm going to free him of the engagement. I don't want it. He doesn't want it. It's ridiculous."

Gabriel swept into the room, anger radiating. "Don't. You. Dare. Goddammit, Emmy, this is the best chance we'll ever get. Don't you go mucking it up for the rest of us just because you're upset about giving up your little pleasure. This is reality, Emmy— you've been living in a childish dream for too long, and it's time you snapped out of it. Grow up. You're a woman. Women marry; they aren't Arena jockeys. I indulged you too long, and I'm sorry for it. But you owe me this. I'll say it because it's true. You owe me."

I wanted to cry. The world closed in around me, an ever-shrinking cage.

"Gabriel," I said. "I want—"

"No one cares what you *want*, Emmy! It isn't about what you *want*. Do you think I wake up every morning *wanting* to ride for ten hours a day? Do you think I *want* to sprint until I cast up my accounts or climb until my legs burn so bad I think they'll fall off? *Wanting* doesn't come into it. What I want is to lie around for two weeks and never have to step into the Arena again! I want to eat ice cream every day of the week and get fat! But it isn't going to happen. You do what you must. You do even what you're afraid to do. Now, pull yourself together and grow up. Stop being so damned weak-minded. All this whining and fussing—you'd never have made an Arena racer, anyway. Not just because you're a girl. *Because you're not good enough.* You can't compete at that level. It's too harrowing for a woman! Look at you, all this melodrama about marriage—you wouldn't last ten seconds under the strain of the Arena! You'd be hysterical. So shut up and suck it up, and do what you can for this family." With these devastating words, Gabriel stalked off to his ride.

Again, the Whittler prevented my sobs and I sucked down on my inner cheek. What I thought about as I waited in the drawing room was how, if there really was a God—and I had my private doubts—he was certainly a perverse creature to give us desires we could never fulfill. My brother wanted nothing but ease; I wanted everything he had, and we had no way to trade the outcomes of our lives to better match our dreams. What kind of creature made a world like that? I scrubbed the toe of my worn slipper against the carpet.

I heard the footsteps in the hall: Maman's determined shuffle accompanied by the harsh clack of well-heeled boots.

"Emmeline is waiting for you," I heard Maman say. "She will enjoy going to the park, I'm sure. She loves outings."

Cassius Everett and Maman stepped into the drawing room together. I watched Everett take in the room devoid of furnishings but for the rug, settee, and me. He looked impassive.

Maman chirped, as if we hadn't spent the entire morning preparing for this moment, "Look, dear, Mr. Everett has come to see if you would like to walk in the park. Isn't that nice?"

I nodded jerkily and found I could not meet my fiancé's eyes. I stood up as I stared at the carpet. It really was in awful condition, which was why we still owned it. No one had wanted to buy it.

Everett's arm reached out; I rested my hand on it. He led me to the front door.

"Enjoy yourselves," Maman simpered desperately. I wondered if she knew I planned to renege on the betrothal.

By the time we were outdoors, I'd reversed my position on Cassius Everett. When I'd woken this morning, I'd been resolved to end the whole farce of the engagement as quickly as possible. But Gabriel's little speech had slammed me mercilessly down to earth, as violently as my last crash on a velo. It didn't matter if I never married or not. I would not be allowed to race.

I wasn't good enough. That changed things. That made me think this might be the best option, this engagement. I'd liked Cassius Everett, initially, for all his blundering, unmannered ignorance and unfashionable clothes. He was not so priggish as most of the bachelors Maman had been pushing. If I married Everett, Gabriel and Maman would be happy, and maybe that was the best that could be said of my life: I'd made the people I loved happy. A true lady would have been satisfied with that, would even have concentrated all her efforts on just such an outcome. A woman had a duty to please her family.

Everett did not say a word to me. He kept our walking pace sedate, which I both loathed on principle and appreciated, since I was again at the Whittler's mercy. I soon realized it would be up to me to lead the conversation. Everett's silence indicated his anger.

"I'm sorry," I blurted. "I know you think I did it on purpose, but I didn't. I really didn't. I really did faint."

Everett cast a nasty little sideways glance that told me he didn't believe me. "Really?" he said snidely. "Really, really? Because if I lived in a house like that, I think what I would do, just as soon as I possibly could, would be to catch me a rich prospect out of it. I can't blame you; I just don't care for deceit." He sped up our pace as we came to the entrance of the park. I matched his steps as best I could.

My breath became labored ridiculously quickly. Everett gazed straight ahead.

"Whatever you think," I wheezed, "I'm sorry for what happened." Now would have been the time to free him from the obligation, but I found I could not do it. Gabriel and Maman were counting on me. To push away the chance would be weak-minded and childishly selfish, just as Gabriel had said.

Everett hastened his steps even more. The man moved like a rushing river; he did everything *fast*. I would have liked to see him race a velocipede, but he must be past his racing days. "If you speak the truth, do you think it pleases me? To know I will marry a girl who would not have picked me but for damning circumstances misinterpreted? It does not please me. It's not what I want from a marriage."

Well, I thought. *Welcome to the world of thwarted wants.* "What *do* you want?"

Everett pulled me to a small path that veered sharply to the right. My poor lungs were killing me.

"Honesty," he snapped. "A wife to trust. A woman, not a girl."

I flinched at the insult. I wasn't sure if he meant it in regards to my behavior or my appearance. Likely both. "I—I'm sorry," I said again, lamely.

"I take it," Everett said, "that you have no intention of setting me free from this?"

A part of me, raised up so well inside the box of Serenian tradition, reflexively longed to please him. I wanted to do whatever he wanted me to do. I opened my mouth and almost told him just what he wished to hear.

But no. That was not a good strategy. I would not come by another good catch so easily. Things could get so much worse for me. I needed to be sensible; I needed to think like Maman, like a grown *woman,* not a girl seduced by childish, impossible dreams. "No," I said instead. "I can't. I'm sorry, but I can't."

Everett scowled. He'd thought I would do it. I couldn't resist adding, "You know, it isn't entirely my fault. *I* tried to get free of you several times, but you wouldn't let me go. I tried to separate us before Maman arrived, but you held on."

"I thought you were ill. I was worried about you."

"I told you it was just the corset."

"And how is that corset today? Your waist looks just as small, and yet we're moving at my normal pace again. You seem to be hustling along just fine."

"It's not laced quite so tightly, today," I snapped. "It's still blasted uncomfortable though." And I *did* feel a bit light-headed. Not that I would admit that to him.

"Ridiculous things, corsets," he said.

I blinked, astonished to have my own sentiments echoed back by him. "Would you object very much if I stopped wearing them?" Now that we were engaged, he had the right to make such dispensations about my attire.

"I'd be thrilled if it meant you could move about at a decent pace and stop sounding like a wheezing lapdog."

I couldn't help myself. I giggled despite the pain. I sounded worse than a wheezing lapdog.

"Are you having another attack of the epilepsy?" asked Everett dryly. "Come, have a seat on this bench before it gets *very* dire."

I let him escort me to the bench. He clutched my arm as if concerned I might swoon on him again. Maybe he was starting to believe it hadn't been a ruse.

"What in God's name have you been doing with your arms?" he asked suddenly.

"W-what?" I said.

One of his hands circled my upper arm and squeezed. I tightened my muscles inadvertently.

"You're arms are hard," he said suspiciously. "As if you do labor."

"We—ah—we had to let the servants go," I began, reaching desperately for a likely explanation.

"So what, you've been lifting wet laundry for the past three years?"

"I—ah—" Maman did all the laundry. She wouldn't let me near manual labor with a ten-foot pole. She was already concerned by the muscles I had, and she wouldn't allow me to do anything more labor intensive than making a bed.

Everett's face softened. "Look, I don't hold it against you. I wasn't born into money. I came up the hard way, as I'm sure you might have guessed by my manners. Or lack thereof. Many people look askance at me, including your cousin Helen. Voler doesn't care, but he's a rare bird. You may as well know it; marriage to me will be no cup of tea. Your class slights me as much as they invite me."

I shook my head. "Serenians are snobs," I said, wondering where he had grown up—clearly not Seren. "I don't pay any attention to that sort of thing. You saw how we lived. We've been destitute for years. The only reason we got an invitation to that bruncheon at all was because my mother begged her sister for it. Helen doesn't like me any more than she likes you."

Everett looked out over the rolling green of the park. He placed his hand over mine in my lap. "Look, Emmeline," he murmured. "Can I call you Emmeline?" I nodded. "We'll make the best of this, agreed? Maybe it isn't exactly as we planned, but we'll make the best of it."

"Yes," I said earnestly.

"I want only one promise from you. I am an easy man in most respects, or so I like to think. But I cannot abide dishonesty.

From this point on, we are fresh. You will not lie to me or deceive me, and I will offer the same transparency to you. You may say what you think with me. You need not hide your true feelings. But do not lie to me. Not ever."

His words made me anxious, for what was a lady if she was not artifice? And I had a secret. I had been lying to the world for years, riding racing velos with my brother and never letting anyone else into my secret life. But I lifted my chin and nodded at Cassius Everett, my betrothed.

"Yes," I said. "Agreed."

Everett helped me up off the bench, and we walked back towards my house. He seemed suitably placated; Maman and Gabriel would be pleased with me. I recalled Gabriel's request. As we walked along the path, I asked, "Will you go to the Arena races tomorrow?"

Everett glanced in my direction, eyebrows raised. "Probably. I usually do. Several of my jockeys will be racing."

"Who do you sponsor?"

"Voler and I sponsor four riders together, and then I've two of my own." He wasn't exactly forthcoming.

"Are you looking to sponsor more jockeys?" Six was already more than most men could afford, but perhaps Everett was richer than I imagined.

Everett seemed surprised at my interest. Most women would not have shown such curiosity about the Arena races. "Maybe. I only sponsor the ones that really strike me. But my eyes are always open."

My cheeks colored as he studied me. "My brother—" I began, but I stopped when I caught the look in his eye: annoyance, as if I were a stray cat scratching on his door in the middle of the night. Which was exactly how I felt.

"I won't sponsor your brother, if that's what you're asking," he said curtly.

"But Gabriel's good," I argued. "He takes a little while to get used to new things. But I tell you, he's a strong rider. His time-trial times are some of the very best."

"I don't doubt it. But I won't sponsor him. He's not my type of rider. Everyone would know I only did it because he's your brother."

I opened my mouth to make a retort, but Everett pulled me into his side and tucked me under his arm so that we walked in a most improper fashion.

"Did they put you up to that?" he muttered at me.

"W-what?" I asked.

"Your family? Did they put you up to all of this? Snagging me as a husband, trying to get me to sponsor your brother?"

"N—no. Well, maybe a little. But it's just what anyone would do, isn't it? Every mother tries to get her daughter married well. Every rookie jockey grovels for a sponsor. And they're my family. I have to try for them."

Everett snorted. "Good," he said. "You're learning to be honest. I'll give you a treat tomorrow. We'll go on an outing you might enjoy." He smiled, but the expression had a sharp edge to it, as if he truly thought I might not enjoy the outing at all.

"Where?" I couldn't help but ask.

"It will be a surprise. I'll come for you at nine of the clock."

Proper sociability demanded a later hour. "Very well," I said. "I will be ready at nine."

We approached Escot House. Everett brought me all the way up the stairs, lifted my hand, and placed a perfunctory kiss there. "Remember," he said. "I'm your family now, too."

Maman didn't like to get up early, but for two days running she'd been forced to on my account. Gabriel had left for the Arena to meet up with his coach in preparation for his race. I'd been unable to resist performing my exercises this morning, but I did them in the privacy of my room so Gabriel wouldn't know. I'd only just finished when Maman fluttered in with a large dress bag in her arms, cheeks flushed.

"Mr. Everett sent you something," she trilled in excitement as she thrust an envelope at me. I stood in just my pantalettes and chemise, glad she hadn't caught me at my exertions. I took the envelope and tugged it open. The note was brief and to the point, very much the style I was coming to expect from Everett.

> *Dear Emmeline:*
> *I anticipate that you have little to wear on the occasion of today's outing, so I have taken the liberty of sending along suitable attire. I hope you will not take such an intimate gift amiss. Voler assures me it is entirely inappropriate, but I find I'd rather flout convention than see my fiancée dressed in rags.*
> *Until nine,*
> *Yours,*
> *CE*

"He's sent a gown for me to wear today," I remarked, knowing the gift would scandalize Maman. "He insists I wear it. He is ashamed to be seen with me in my plain old things."

"Then you must wear it," Maman said. "You must do whatever he asks and please him right up until the wedding, Emmeline. You know how important this is."

"He thinks corsets are ridiculous things," I added. "He told me not to wear them anymore." I stretched the truth because I knew leaving off the corset would be hard to put past Maman.

"You spoke of *corsets* with him? Emmeline, how could you! And he doesn't want you to wear one? He can't know what he's saying!"

"He doesn't like it when women swoon, and he likes to walk fast. He doesn't want to have to slow down for me."

Maman shook her head despairingly. "But Emmy, how will you fit into your gowns?" That she called me by my nickname showed just how out of sorts she was. Poor Maman could not understand that my future husband might not be as fixated on the size of my waist as she was. A small piece of me resented her narrow-mindedness.

I leaned over the dress bag and opened it to see what Cassius Everett had sent for me to wear. I couldn't help the small gasp that escaped my lips. *Oh dear.* The dress had been fashioned from a crimson silk so vivid a lightskirt might have hesitated to wear it—that loud, that shocking. I restrained a hysterical urge to giggle; what would Maman make of *this*?

"Well, what is it?" Maman asked, coming to lean over my shoulder to get a good look at the gown my betrothed had sent.

I withdrew the gown from the bag, brushing down the ruched skirt while Maman made sucking air sounds as if she wore her laces too tight.

The dress was beautiful despite the indecent color. The seamstress must have spent untold hours on the complex skirt, shaping the fabric into the train, stitching the gathers painstakingly by hand.

I'd never been that interested in fashion. Dreams of velo racing had occupied my thoughts. But I wanted to wear the dress Everett had sent me, even if my only reason for the desire was to shock Maman into silence. I rather envied Everett, that he had so easily done it.

"No, Emmeline," Maman managed as I pulled the dress off its hanger. "You must not. You cannot wear *that* out. He clearly doesn't have a clue what constitutes decent attire. I suppose you cannot blame him; he is not riesen—" I pulled the dress over my head—"Emmeline!"

"He wants me to wear it, Maman. And I must keep him happy. We aren't married yet, you know." I turned my back to her so she could fasten the pearl buttons running up the back of the gown. She did it. I could imagine her expression as she worked: tight-lipped, narrow-browed, sour-eyed.

I followed Maman downstairs to our dismal parlor to await Everett's arrival. I did not sit lest I crease the delicate silk. The freedom of motion obtained by leaving off the corset reminded me of when I rode a velo disguised as a boy. Even discounting the missing undergarment, my attire was scandalous. A girl my age should not show her arms at all, but this gown was cut with only tiny sleeves that hung from my shoulders and exposed everything from my upper arm down. My muscles flashed as I lifted an arm to adjust my hair. Maman's gaze followed my arm. They widened as I moved, and she turned on her heel and darted from the drawing room.

I heard the knock on the front door and assumed Maman would answer it. Gabriel had gone to the Arena, and Papan had not risen yet. His habit was to sleep late. The knocking sounded again, this time for longer. I hesitated. What would Everett think if I answered the door? As the knocking came again, I shrugged and went to get it. He knew we had no servants.

I pulled open the front door to see my fiancé looking almost dapper. He wore a dark blue frock coat with tails over brown leather breeches. His boots were dark brown and well polished. But black was the color of choice for a gentleman's pants and boots, so brown looked just a little fusty. He quickly removed his hat when he saw I held the door.

"Emmeline," he said, bowing. "Are you ready then?" He assessed me: crimson dress, no corset, arms exposed, without a cloak. He scowled. "What about a hat and gloves?" he demanded. I raised my eyebrows. I had no hat, and my only gloves had been mangled for riding long ago.

I heard Maman's scurrying footsteps behind me. She threw her own black walking coat over my shoulders, and turned towards Everett. "It isn't right," she admonished. "She ought not wear such a dress."

Everett narrowed his eyes at my mother. "She's to be my wife," he said. "I'll dress her however I please."

I turned my face away from both of them and scowled. I hated being discussed as if I had no words to speak for myself, but I knew better than to voice such a thought.

"You shame her," Maman argued. Her feistiness surprised me. "She is at your mercy," Maman went on doggedly. "No one will have her if you break it off. You can't—"

"I have no intention of breaking it off," Everett snapped.

"I need reassurance," Maman demanded.

"What do you mean, reassurance?"

"A date," Maman said, hauling herself to her full height— not very threatening, since she was two full inches shorter than I was, and a good foot shorter than Everett. But I knew enough to be wary when Maman wore that particular expression. "Set a date for the wedding. It needn't be a large affair. The important thing is the signing of the papers. I want her married. The sooner, the better."

Everett frowned. "Fine," he said. "I'll get a license this afternoon. Will tomorrow be soon enough for you?"

Maman managed to make no shocked outbursts. "T—Tomorrow?"

"We'll have a small service," Everett said. "I hope you weren't expecting me to fund a lavish party."

"No, no, a small service will be fine. But then, you will take Emmeline with you, after? Tomorrow, you'll take her to your home?"

"Of course I will. I'm marrying her! What do you expect?" Everett turned from Maman to me. "Emmeline, come, we'll take our leave." He grabbed my bare arm so roughly Maman's walking jacket almost fell off my shoulders. I hunched instinctively to keep it on, flying down the front stairs after Everett. I cast a glance over my shoulder to look at Maman, who stood frozen, biting her lip. I smiled to reassure her.

Everett helped me into his gas carriage. I was shocked when Everett himself walked around to the driver's side and got in, cranking the start shaft to ignite the engine.

"You drive?" It was an unlikely thing for a wealthy man to drive himself, especially in such a new-fangled contraption as a gas carriage.

Everett laughed. "I do indeed. Didn't you know? Before I became Voler's partner, I served as his driver. He hired me after I retired from the Arena, and he helped me invest the money I'd made as a jockey. Voler owned the original gas-carriage—he bought the prototype from Banksy himself. Does it bother you?"

I watched him expertly adjust the shaft and shift his feet to make the carriage go. I leaned forward to study the dash, curious what all the gauges signified. "Does what bother me?" I asked absently. I wondered what Everett would think if I asked him to teach me to drive. After the wedding, of course—I couldn't do anything too shocking until after the wedding slated for *tomorrow*.

"My driving," Everett said. "Most people of your class think it's low."

I ignored his explanation. "How fast does it go?"

Everett chuckled. "This is Banksy's latest model. He's an associate of mine, you know. I haven't pushed it to its top speed. I have to take it out of the city for that. But...no, there's no time today." He turned the carriage at a corner and shifted the shaft again. "But later, would you like to go for a real drive?"

"After the wedding?" I blurted.

Everett laughed again. "Yes. After the wedding."

"Fast?" I said hopefully.

Everett nodded. "As fast as you can handle."

I leaned back in my seat, forgetting all about the harlot's dress I wore. I was even distracted from our mysterious outing, thinking about how it would feel to go fast in the gas carriage. *As good as flying down a hill on a velo?* I doubted it. You couldn't feel the wind inside the carriage. Unless, "Does the top come off?" I'd seen a few gas carriages with open tops out on the streets.

"Yes," Everett replied. "I thought you'd prefer privacy though. People tend to stare when you drive with the top down."

"I like to feel the wind."

"I'll take it down later then."

"Thank you. And thank you for the dress." Mainly I was thankful not to be wearing a corset, but I did not remind him of that, on the off chance that he'd been joking yesterday and might have changed his mind after seeing me without a corset in the gown. I didn't want him to revoke that freedom.

Did I imagine that Everett blushed? "Your mother isn't very happy with me," he remarked.

"She thinks you've dressed me up to look like a...a loose woman," I explained.

"And so I have. But it's for a good reason. Where we're going, you need a disguise. Think of it as a masquerade. You're just wearing a costume. It's not that I think you—" he cut off abruptly.

"Where are we going?"

"Wait and see. I thought you'd wear a hat," he said. "With a veil. To conceal your face. I thought your mother would insist. I don't want people to recognize you. It wasn't my intention to shame you."

"I don't have a hat."

"You don't have a hat?" Everett echoed in disbelief.

"Hats are expensive."

"Yes, I suppose they are. Hang on then." He turned the carriage sharply, all the way around on the empty road. He pushed the pedals harder and our speed increased. Excitement lurched in my belly. I leaned forward to look out the front window.

"The road's empty," I said.

"So?"

"Go faster. Please."

I heard Everett snort before the carriage accelerated and the engine roared. We took off flying down the road.

Eventually Everett slowed and turned down Saville Street. He pulled up to the curb and turned off the carriage. "Wait here," he said as he hopped out of the vehicle.

While he was gone, I studied the dashboard, but try as I might I could not make head nor tail of the devices arrayed there. I counted four buttons in a row. I pushed each of them in turn, but nothing happened. I wanted to see the pedals Everett pushed to make the carriage go, so I got down off the seat and folded myself into the space where his legs went. I discovered three pedals. I prodded at each with my hands, but again, nothing happened. The carriage wasn't like a velo, directly mechanical with all its workings readily apparent. Still sitting in the leg area, I examined the shaft. From watching Everett drive, I suspected the position of the shaft changed the power of the carriage, rather like gears on a velocipede.

"What are you doing down there? Did you lose something?" Everett pulled open the door to the driver's side of the carriage and stared down at me.

I blushed, feeling foolish. I'd thoroughly crumpled the delicate silk of my dress. I wriggled to get myself back into my seat and make room for Everett's legs. As he took his seat, he pushed a hatbox into my lap. "Well?" he asked.

I opened the box to avoid explaining my odd behavior. "Oh!" I gasped. He'd gotten me a hat—a lovely hat, with a wide brim, a black lace veil to fully cover my face, and several black plumes tucked into the band. "Thank you," I said.

"What were you doing down there on the floor of the carriage, Emmeline?" He wasn't going to let me get away with avoiding an explanation.

"I—I thought I dropped something," I muttered.

"What?"

"What?" I said right back, flustered.

"What did you drop?"

"Oh, nothing. I was mistaken."

"What did you *think* you dropped?"

"My—ah—my handkerchief." In truth, I wasn't carrying anything to have dropped.

"Show me your handkerchief." *Oh, why was he pressing so hard?* I flushed bright red and squirmed.

"I forgot that I left it at home," I said.

"Don't lie to me, Emmeline." Everett's voice had gone very dark. "I'm going to give you one more try at this. Let's start from the beginning. What were you doing on the floor?"

I crossed my legs and twisted my hands as I took a deep breath. "I wanted to figure out how the carriage worked," I said in a tiny voice. "I looked at the pedals." I prepared myself for a lecture.

To my surprise, Everett laughed aloud. "That's all? Why were you afraid to tell me that? After you lied I began to think it was something dire!" Everett looked at me from the corner of his eye.

"It's not a ladylike thing to do," I muttered. "I shouldn't want to know about such things."

"It's not considered ladylike to forgo a corset, either," Everett said. "You didn't let that stop you."

I bit my lip.

Everett drove in silence for a while. "I thought we covered this yesterday," he finally said. "We agreed to be honest. So far, I've been keeping my word. You have every reason to trust me. You'll find me a lenient man in most ways, but not about this. Not about lies. I don't mind your curiosity. I won't chastise you for having questions."

"I'm sorry," I said. And I was. I wanted to explain, but still I did not trust him to understand. I had years of history behind this issue, years of lies and deceits, years of Maman's scolding: *Emmeline, come out from the sun. You'll tan and look unladylike. Goodness child, how am I to find you a suitable dress? Only a boy has muscles like these! Is that velo grease on your fingers? Have you been playing with your brother's velo? I'll lock you in your room; you know I will. Don't let me see you such a mess again!*

My heart thumped against my ribcage as the carriage pulled to a stop and I peered through the front window—the one at my side was tinted so dark I could not see well out of it. Everett's was not the only gas carriage in sight, and so many horse carts and rickshaws had gathered that I knew where we must be.

The dress began to make sense, as did Everett's words: *think of it as a disguise... I don't want anyone to see you.* We had pulled into the parking area of the Arena. Everett was already out his door, walking around the carriage to assist me.

He leaned in through the open door. "Put on your hat and draw the veil down," he advised. "You wouldn't want anyone to recognize you."

No indeed. Proper ladies did not attend the velocipede races. What a scandal it would be if I were recognized! I adjusted the ribbons on the hat and tied them securely, arranging the black lace so it covered my face. Everyone would think I was Everett's hired companion, a loose woman who exchanged favors for money.

Not so far off the mark, I thought grimly. For really, how was my marriage so different from what a hired courtesan offered except that I had less freedom once I entered into the arrangement and could not get out of it? I clutched Everett's hand as he helped me rise from the carriage.

The Serenian fog had nearly burned away, leaving a crisp, cool morning. My hands would be cold without gloves, but I didn't care. I could hardly believe Everett had brought me to the Arena. *To see the velocipede races!* My excitement was uncontainable. All my life, I'd wanted to see the races. I'd heard about them enough from Gabriel and Papan, tried to imagine what they were like from words, discussed racing strategy and tactics with my brother late at night when Maman assumed us both sleeping.

I stared at the Arena. It rose up from the flat ground like an ancient monument, a huge structure painted all white, as crisp and clear as the morning. The parking cobblestones ended in lawn, and men in black strode along the path towards the stadium. Some had women on their arms, women dressed like me in bright colors and daring fashions. Everyone had a hat, men and women alike. I was very glad that Everett had thought to stop and fetch one for me. The general ambience along the paths and lawns exuded excitement and anticipation, relaxed in a way that Serenian high society never was. I saw why Papan spent so much of his time here—everywhere I looked people laughed and reveled. I wondered if I might see him. I wondered if he had a courtesan on his arm.

I soaked up the scenery, enthralled. Spectators milled around the lawn. Peddlers wheeled their carts, selling ribbons and souvenirs to the eager crowd. I wanted to savor every moment of my adventure; I wanted to sample everything the Arena had to offer. I tugged on Everett's arm, trying to get him to walk in the direction of the carts. He was being typically fast and efficient, cutting through the crowd as if it were a pudding, making a beeline for the Arena entrance.

"What is it?" he asked, pulling up short.

He'd admonished me to be honest about my curiosity, and yet still I hesitated. I was not accustomed to such openness, and I felt entirely at his mercy. So much hinged on his pleasure with me.

I pointed at the nearest cart, a small, gaily painted affair with a wrinkled old man sitting on a stool behind it. "Can we— can we go look?" I squeezed out, despite my anxiety.

"At the trinket carts?" Everett asked, his brows pulling together. My stomach sank into my feet. He wasn't going to allow it. I bowed my head in resignation. But Everett went on, "Do you really want to? I had thought to get you into my box as soon as possible. I didn't want to alarm you with all the bustle outside the Arena." He glanced at me warily. "I hope you are not offended by this outing, Emmeline. I will not make you stay for long, just to watch your brother's race. Then we can leave, I promise. I'll stay with you the whole time. No one will ever know who you are. My box is private."

He wanted me to see Gabriel race? We'd stay only for the one? Excitement and disappointment clashed in my gut. I wanted to experience all of it. How could I explain without sounding inappropriate?

Everett watched my face carefully. We'd frozen on the path, making no progress forward as we spoke. "Please," I said.

He tilted his head. "Please what? You have to tell me, Emmeline. I can't read your mind."

I opened my mouth and nothing came out of it.

"Don't be afraid to speak freely," Everett murmured. "Tell me."

"I've always wanted to come to the velocipede races. I want to see everything. I want to stay and watch *all* the races." It felt good to admit it, but risky, too.

Everett's face flashed into a smile. "Excellent!" He stepped off the path and led me over to the peddler's cart. I peered at the baubles arrayed on top: silver bangles, colorful crocheted scarves, pins, bells, ribbons, nosegays, and bright metal buttons.

"Have you any gauntlettes?" Everett asked the old man behind the cart.

The little man moved, pulling out a drawer from the back of the cart and resting it atop the vehicle. Everett hunched over the drawer and pushed through it, finally grabbing a fistful of black lace. He and the peddler haggled over the price for a moment, and then Everett pulled me away from the cart and offered me what he had purchased.

They were black lace, rather useless for keeping warm, but pretty all the same. Like racing gauntlets, they had open fingers. "May I?" Everett asked. He put one gauntlette over his arm and held the other. Then he lifted my hand, carefully sliding the gauntlette over my fingers, smoothing it up my forearm, and then buttoning it deftly, with one hand. His actions stirred my senses. My belly lurched as when I went very fast down a steep, curving hill on a velo. He put the other glove on for me. I watched, silent. After he finished, he dropped my hands as if they'd burned him. "Come," he said. "Let's go to my box."

I walked at Everett's side all the way to the grand Arena entrance. The double doors towered overhead—they were held open by two marble sculptures of jockeys mounted on velos. The door guard nodded at Everett, bowing and saying, "Mr. Everett, welcome." He did not ask for tickets. The lobby stretched, wide and open, with a long row of booths running across the back where the spectators gathered to place their bets with the Arena bookies. At the two ends of the lobby, broad staircases soared upwards, leading to the stands and boxes, I presumed.

"Do you want to place a bet?" Everett asked me, nodding at the betting windows.

"P—place a bet?"

"Yes. It makes the races more exciting to watch."

As if I needed more excitement! My heart had been dancing a jig in my chest from the moment we'd arrived. "Do you normally bet?" I asked, suspicious, thinking of Papan. I hoped Everett was not a big gambler.

"Rarely," he said. "I am not interested in gambling. But if you wish to lay a bet, I'll help you."

I stared at the betting windows. "All right," I said. "But just one." Everett took my arm and led me to the nearest window.

He explained the rudiments, pointing at the tote board and giving me the rundown on the morning line. I ignored him and considered what Gabriel had told me last night about his own race.

"Samuels," Gabriel had predicted. "He's the one to beat in my race. But he's a real tough rider, ruthless and aggressive. He's been disqualified for rough behavior more than once, so there's the possibility he won't win because of that. But if he plays nice, he'll win it. Coach Kersey says I should angle to show, not try to win with Samuels in the race. Don't want a tête-à-tête with him. We'll leave that to Martin Scorella. Those two hack it out regularly."

"Who else?" I had asked. "If you avoid Samuels, who will you be up against yourself?" Jockeys were often pitted in dyads in a race. If Gabriel wasn't going to push up against the favorite, it meant he'd have a battle for third place with someone else.

"Probably Horace," Gabriel had said glumly. He didn't like to go up against his friend. "We're the next strongest riders on the field."

I hadn't liked Gabriel's "probably." I'd been thinking about what Everett had said, that Gabriel wasn't his type of rider. I wasn't sure what he meant, but I worried that Everett's lack of interest had to do with Gabriel's lack of confidence. Sisterly loyalty demanded that I put my money on Gabriel, but in my heart I knew he wasn't a good bet. He'd yet to show in a single Arena race. After much deliberation, I placed a quinella bet, naming Samuels and Scorella as my picks to place.

Everett hadn't expected me to place the bet without consulting him, and he was taken aback as I turned to him to ask for the money. "You weren't even listening to me!" he scolded, yet he good-naturedly handed over the coin. Then he snatched my betting slip from my hands to see what I'd predicted. "Not your brother?" he asked. "I would have thought you'd want to root for him. Scorella and Samuels, eh? A quinella?" His eyes narrowed. "You know your jockeys. Does your brother tell you about his races?"

"Yes," I said shortly. "He told me they were likely to take first and second in his race."

"Well, they're the favorites, so if you win, you won't make much. But your prediction is a good one. The odds are heavy on them. They're the two most experienced riders on the field for that race. But you know, if you always pick the safe bet, you can hardly call it gambling."

I couldn't tell if he meant his words as reproof for my caution or as approval for it. Cassius Everett was difficult to read.

Though discretion demanded I keep my mouth shut, I couldn't help my too-knowing retort: "That's why I made a quinella bet, to better my odds."

Everett made no reply, instead sweeping me away from the betting booths in one brisk motion. He led me through the crowd towards a broad flight of stairs. Old betting slips littered the atrium, lost wishes on dark ground. Smoke from cigarillos thickened the air, and I had to suppress the urge to cough. I was thankful yet again that I wore no corset as we mounted the steps. Everett moved at his typical pace, taking the stairs two at a time. I easily kept up with him by gathering my skirt into my right fist. A footman held open the door that led to Everett's box. The man bowed as we passed, but would not meet my eye. He thought I was a woman for hire.

The smoky air of the atrium smelled bad, so Everett's box proved a relief, a perfect tiny chamber of luxury. It contained only a single loveseat, centered in the small room, flanked by two tables. An expensive carpet covered the floor; my slippers squashed into it as I studied my surroundings. The true draw of the room lured me: the window, a floor to ceiling sheet of glass with a spectacular view. Mesmerized, I walked right up to it. I stood so my nose touched the glass.

Inside the box, we hovered above the Arena track. To see it was overwhelming. The stands formed a full circle around it, making a dizzying border that rose up above the view from the window. The track itself was the real wonder. Built from hardwood like a parquet dance floor, its polished surface glinted in the morning sun. The curves banked more steeply than I had imagined, drawing the eye in towards the center. I noticed the inner blue ring, the narrow path of painted wood where the velos were not allowed to ride; to enter it would get a jockey disqualified. Seeing the track brought home the insanity of the velocipede races. To imagine them was one thing, but to see those sharply-banked curves, the slick brightness of the polished wood, the slim parameters for success or failure—the actual track was more intimidating than in my dreams. Yet I wanted to race more than ever; I salivated for it.

A stage had been set up in the center area, and a group of acrobats performed a balancing act before the races began. In spite of the acrobats' amazing physical feats, I couldn't peel my gaze from the wooden track. *How fast one could go on such a frictionless surface!* The old envy came surging through me again, followed by the old dismay: I wanted to race so badly, and Gabriel, who got to live my dreams, only dreaded the Arena. I put my fingers on the glass and leaned even closer, looking down.

Everett had one of the best boxes in the Arena. It hung like an airship above the homestretch of the track, a perfect, centered view of the straightaway that led to the finish line. I could not see our neighboring boxes, though I had the faintest impression that they were there, lurking to either side and extending in a long row away from us. I felt as if I stood on a dark street in a circle of light: I was the center of everything. I suspected that everyone in the stands below and across from the box was staring at me in my bright gown.

Everett came up beside me. "The glass is tinted," he explained. "No one can see in. Go ahead and take off your hat."

I said nothing as I removed my hat, glad to study the track without its interference. I clutched the hat in my hands, too enthralled to turn away from the vista. The acrobats finished their performance. I knew that at this moment Gabriel probably waited in line to have his velo examined for conformation—all the velos were checked before the race. A racing velo had to have several standard features: 32 spokes on its wheels, a diamond frame made only from the approved and patented metal alloy formula, with handlebars dropped a prescribed distance below the seat.

Everett explained, "The race is eight laps. For the first four or so, a pacer regulates the riders' speed up to about 50 kilometers per hour—generally he's another jockey who's not competing—and in every race he cuts off the track at a slightly different moment. After the pacer leaves, that's when the race truly begins."

I know, I know, I thought, staring down at the track with uncontrollable longing.

He went on, "The officiators sit at the corners on the raised platforms." Everett pointed to the four structures at the curves on the oval track. "They raise a white flag if there have been no infractions, or a red one to announce a penalty. A penalty is generally one of two occurrences: riding in the blue zone," he gestured at the inner ring that I'd already examined, "or abnormally rough fighting. That one can be a hard call on the officiator's part. A certain amount of roughness is expected."

I could not tell from Everett's voice whether he approved of necessary roughness. Some velo jockeys abhorred it—Gabriel said it took away the dignity of sportsmanship. But I knew other men, Papan included, who thought the fighting between the jockeys one of the most exciting aspects of a race.

"Is it necessary to win?" I asked. "The fighting?"

Everett pulled away from me, and I felt relieved. I hadn't known what to make of his body, so close to mine that our sides rubbed up against each other. He walked over to the loveseat. On one of the adjoined tables sat a cigarillo case. "Do you mind if I smoke?" he asked.

I shrugged. I didn't like the smell, but the box belonged to him. He lit up and took a long draw before answering my question. "There has to be a balance between safety and risk," he said. "The risk of fighting is falling. But a cautious jockey will never make a winner. A winner needs ruthlessness. He has to make space where there is none, and that is an art. The most graceful jockeys do it with the least amount of violence. But there will always be the hardscrabble riders to contend with—so yes, yes. The violence is necessary. Will it disturb your sensibilities?"

I thought of the races in Vreeland Park. I'd never backed down from the thrown elbows, the tight swings, or the rough play in a final sprint. I'd tried to give as good as I got. "No," I said. "Of course not."

"That's good. It's why your kind doesn't frequent the races, though, isn't it? Too delicate."

"My kind?" I echoed.

"Riesen women." Did I detect just a hint of derision in his tone?

"Most of *my kind* don't have the option to come to the races even if we wished it," I said, trying to sound coolly disinterested and failing.

"Are you upset that I brought you here?" Everett flicked his cigarillo into an ashtray. Again, I couldn't read him: did that lilt in his voice express concern or disdain? Instinct favored the latter interpretation.

"No," I told him. "I want to watch the races." I'd already told him that, but he didn't seem to believe me.

"They won't begin for another quarter hour," Everett said. "Shall I order you a drink?"

"Yes, please."

"What would you like?"

I stared at him, not knowing what to say. A gentleman did not ask a lady her choice; he made it for her. Usually that meant lemonade.

He let out a little huff of breath. "I'm sorry," he said. "I've made another faux pas, haven't I? You must explain it to me. I'm afraid your fiancé is a little…uncouth. Tell me."

"A gentleman should make the selection for me," I explained. "Particularly in a public venue."

Everett's eyebrows drew together. "But that's stupid. I don't even know what you like. How can I pick if I don't know your preference? And why is that considered good manners?"

"I don't know," I said. "It always seemed stupid to me, too. And just a little demeaning, as if I didn't have the mind to make my own choice."

"Just so. Well, what do you like?"

"All I've ever been given is lemonade."

Everett snorted. "This is quite a fix, isn't it? You've never been given a choice, and you've never even been allowed to sample the options! I don't envy you ladies. It seems a raw deal. Do you *like* lemonade?"

"Will you let me have something else?"

"You can have whatever you wish. What's it to me what you drink? What have you always wanted to try?" He flicked his cigarillo again, and though I did not like the smoke, I couldn't help but find the man rather debonair in his motions.

"I want to try a malt whisk." I boldly requested the drink all the men preferred, according to Papan.

"It'll taste like you're drinking smoke," he said. "Still want to try it?"

I nodded. He exited the box. I turned my head to stare out into the Arena again. Workers were deconstructing the stage in the middle of the track. The race officiators took their places on the platforms. They wore all black and carried their colored flags. The jockeys for the first race came out, their coaches pushing their velos in front of them. The coaches would hold the velos while the jockeys balanced at the starting line, much as I'd done for Gabriel during practice races at Vreeland Park.

The jockeys wore a flag of color and their number on their back to distinguish them. Two boys put up a large billboard that listed the numbers and names of the jockeys. The first race would be for the "Spugs," jockeys who had not qualified into the mid-tier group as Gabriel had. The Arena rankings were based on a complex formula that took both the timed kilometer trials and race performance during the trials into account. Gabriel had made the mid-tier because of his excellent time-trials. The Spugs had posted the slowest times for the kilometers—though they were fast by any amateur's measure.

I'd had Gabriel time my kilometer at the Vreeland track several times, just to see where I stood. My best time had been one minute and nineteen seconds, well within the time needed to qualify. I'd been racing another jockey at the time, which always improved my performance. Unlike Gabriel, I liked the competition; it pushed me.

Some of the names posted for the Spug race were familiar—including one famous jockey, Harold Murs, who'd been competing in the Arena for years. In his prime, he'd raced in the elite group. Papan said he'd hung on too long, that he ought to retire rather than ride as a Spug after his days of Arena glory. Gabriel had said the man was an oddball, racing for the love of it with no hope of monetary reward. Spugs past their prime were rarely taken up by sponsors—rumor had it Murs's sponsor had dropped him last season.

I heard the box door open and close behind me. I did not turn away from the window; I was eager to watch the jockeys draw their cards to pick their starting place in the line. I'd root for Harold Murs. He picked the number four slot, so he'd start near the middle of the line.

"Ah, they've picked already," Everett commented, reaching out to remove my hat from my hands and replacing it with a glass tumbler full of amber liquid.

The malt whisk had a woody, warm aroma. I liked the smell far more than that of cigarillo smoke.

"If you don't mind my recommendation," Everett said, "Take a small sip for your first one."

I took his advice. His description of the beverage was perfect: smoke and fire, burning down my throat. I almost burst out coughing, but sheer stubborn pride prevented me. I did not want to appear weak-stomached in front of Everett. My eyes watered.

"Do you like it?" he asked with a grin.

"I love it," I gasped and took another sip.

Together, Everett and I drank in silence, watching the jockeys array themselves across the starting line. All the jockeys gave a ceremonial bow once mounted on the starting line. They would wait for the pacer to make a lap, overtake them, and then a gunshot would herald the beginning of the race. I remained pressed up against the glass, holding my tumbler even after I'd emptied it. The malt whisk lit a furnace in my belly, fierce and satisfying. I floated above the track, longing to be closer. I wanted to be breathing the tense air at the starting line. I wanted to be perched precariously on my own velo, legs atremble, staring down the line with muscles anticipating the shot. My whole body tensed as the pacer pedaled past the line. The shot rang out, clearly audible through Everett's fancy tinted glass.

I trained my attention on the riders as they formed into a single file low on the banked course, exactly in the order of their starting positions. Technically they could battle for position while the pacer was on the field, but etiquette frowned upon such behavior. The velocipede races had a code of honor almost as complex as that of Serenian society. The jockeys followed the pacer, legs churning at a steadily growing speed.

How I wanted Harold Murs to do well—it must be so difficult to try to hold on to a dream in a state of helpless decline. I wanted him to be vindicated for his persistence.

The pacer rode off the track into the center area, and almost immediately two riders accelerated, pulling ahead of the others—Murs was not one of them, but that meant nothing. Four laps remained.

"Many cautious jockeys like to pull into the first wheel position early after the pacer leaves," Everett said. "The leader doesn't crash. It's in the pack where the infighting gets thick."

"But the leader will tire," I murmured. "The air resistance."

"And someone will always draft him and store up the power they save in doing so. As I said, caution rarely wins on the track."

The jockeys were all accelerating into their full speed, legs pumping. The rider currently in second pulled into perfect drafting position behind the leader.

A loud clanging filled the air. "The bell rings throughout the last lap and a half," Everett said. I knew that, but I'd never actually heard the sound of the iron bell. At Vreeland someone just blew a whistle. Struck by a boy, the Arena bell stood in the center of the track. "Now they'll all kick," Everett added.

The jockeys held nothing back. Their velos swayed and veered with the power of their sprint. The rider who'd been drafting passed the leader on the outside. Harold Murs and Number Six came surging up the inside trying to maneuver around jockey Number One, the one-time leader. Number Six went to make a daring pass around Number One, who watched him over his shoulder. Number One anticipated the move and swung right to cut the upstart off—too close! The two velos crashed, and both jockeys went down in a tumbling, spiraling fall. They skidded and rolled, their velos flying off the track and into the center area.

The crash slowed the riders behind, for they had to avoid it, so the jockey who had drafted Number One all through the race was left in a battle with Harold Murs. Murs had a fierce kick, and by the time the two jockeys barreled down the homestretch towards the finish, he'd pulled even with the drafter. But at the last moment, the drafter, Number Two, put on a spurt of speed, leaning forward, and by what looked like will alone, nudged his front tyre a hand's span forward of Murs's to win the race.

Everett let out a held breath that echoed my own. I shifted my weight into my heels, disappointment drooping my shoulders. I had been holding out for Murs.

"Evan Costings," Everett said, naming the winner. "One to watch. He'll be moving into the mid-tier next season, mark my words."

"Do you like him?" I blurted. "Is he the type of jockey you sponsor?"

"I'm watching him. Haven't seen enough to know yet. He rides smart, but he's a little predictable."

The Spugs that were still standing took a final cool-down lap and departed the track. Gabriel's group arrived next. I stepped closer to the glass to see the mid-tier jockeys entering the track. I searched and found jockey Number Six, Gabriel, holding his bright yellow bike. He wore his tight leather breeches, and his arms shone with the racing slick he rubbed on his shaved limbs. My gaze flicked to the tote board to match up the other jersey numbers with names. Samuels was Number Two, Scorella Number Three, and Horace Barre, Five. Despite the bet I'd laid, I rooted for Gabriel. I wanted my brother to show Everett what he was capable of doing—I'd seen Gabriel ride brilliantly on the practice course at Vreeland Park. And a rookie jockey didn't make the mid-tier group if he wasn't good. The Arena standards were insanely high, and a jockey who did not show in his first season could easily get overlooked, which would spell doom for Gabriel's career. He needed sponsorship. We couldn't afford to keep him outfitted season after season. Besides, sponsored riders had access to better tools, better training, and even better food to fuel them. These were advantages Gabriel could not afford to bypass.

"Why don't you come sit on the sofa?" Everett interrupted my spinning thoughts. "You can see just as well from here." He'd moved away from the glass during the interim between races.

I could not have moved to save my life. I barely breathed. The jockeys executed the ceremonial bow. My heart raced as if I were in the lineup myself. The pacer moved down the homestretch. My legs contracted, and I imagined myself inside Gabriel's skin—not for the first time—feeling what he must feel, the giddy, leashed power in his thighs. I almost sensed the narrowing of sight, peering straight ahead through the riding goggles. I pictured what Gabriel saw as he stared down the line: handlebars, front tyre, the gleam of the track. My shoulders pulled down to mimic the stabilizing force of arms on handlebars. I let my ribcage flare with my breath in a drumbeat rhythm.

Bang! My legs jerked with the starting shot, so taut had I been holding them. The race was all there was. I breathed in time with the pedal strokes below. I had forgotten Everett, forgotten I wore the crimson silk dress of a lightskirt, forgotten that I was a woman at all. I was on a velo. I was Gabriel, riding in line behind the pacer. We rode steadily, matching the ever-increasing intensity of the pacer.

The mid-tiers took a conservative fifth lap after the pacer departed. Nobody jostled in the ranks; they would hash it out in the final few laps. At the start of the sixth lap, several riders shifted at once in a smooth choreography. I tracked the changes: Scorella moved into the lead, trailed by Samuels; then Horace Barre in black leather; and in fourth wheel, Gabriel with his yellow velo.

The big kick, when it came, arose from the back of the line. A rider on a red velo wove to the outside and began his attack, moving past both a green velo and Gabriel. I spared half a heartbeat of annoyance that Gabriel did nothing to counter the other jockey's overtaking—no swerve, no burst of speed. The red rider simply flowed by him as easily as water around stone.

Horace did not lay down so easily, bumping up his pace to stay even with the upstart. Meanwhile, in the second and first positions, Samuels and Scorella had been putting on their own heat, pulling even farther ahead of all the other jockeys. Scorella had a good lead, or perhaps Samuels was giving him space, luring the jockey into a delusion of dominance.

The illusion of space shattered as the bell gonged for the final lap. Samuels freed his power and made a textbook overtake of Scorella on the outside, flying into the lead at an astonishing speed. Scorella worked harder to catch up, slipping into Samuels's draft. The red velo hacked it out with Horace, getting in so close they teetered on the edge of disaster.

Samuels rode damned fast. He maintained his lead into the homestretch despite Scorella's drafting advantage. Scorella made a desperate move in the final 100 meters, but it wasn't enough. Samuels's velo crossed the finish line a full tyre-length ahead of Scorella.

I let out my breath in one disappointed sigh. Gabriel had failed to show again. I leaned into the glass and closed my eyes. *Damn it, damn it, damn it. At least,* I thought sadly, *I'm engaged to a rich man.* I knew Gabriel did not love racing. He'd be happy to give it up sooner rather than later. I could make that possible for him if I figured out how best to make use of Everett.

"Are you pleased?" Everett asked from his seat on the sofa.

"No!" I snapped, fully caught up in the let down of the race. As always, I felt the connection to Gabriel. We'd not done as well as I'd wanted, and I had no power to help. *Why hadn't he tried?*

"But you won," Everett said. "Your quinella bet. You won."

"I don't care about the damned bet! I wanted Gabriel to show. He didn't even try. He gave up." *Just like he'd given up on me*, a little voice in my head said.

I remained facing away from Everett, glaring down at the track.

"Come sit with me, Emmeline," Everett said. "This is why I brought you, you know. I wanted you to see your brother in a race. I thought it would explain better why I won't sponsor him. I don't want to make you unhappy. It's just the reality of the situation. Gabriel is not hungry."

"He really doesn't like it," I whispered, still leaning into the glass. "He doesn't want to race."

"That's the impression I get, too." I turned, startled to hear Everett's voice close to my ear. He'd moved so quietly behind me. "Won't you sit?" He put a hand on my shoulder, and I flinched, the tension the race had put in my body uncoiling in a flash. "You're wound as tight as a spring," he said. "Do you want to leave?"

"Leave?" I asked. "But we haven't watched the elite-tier race yet. We can't leave."

"I didn't expect you to know so much about racing, Emmeline."

What could I say to that? I turned back to the glass.

"Do you think you could manage to sit for this race?" Everett said again. "I begin to wonder if the reason riesen ladies are not allowed at the races is because they are too highly strung to endure the excitement."

"It's not the excitement," I snarled. "It's the whores and smoking and drinking. The gentlemen don't want us here because they want to play, and the presence of a riesen woman would prevent them their enjoyment."

"Astute, Emmeline." He pulled me away from the glass and pressed me into the loveseat, jerking his head at the tote board, already changed out to display the names and numbers of the elite jockeys. "Care to make an informal bet on this one?"

"What do you mean?"

"Well, let's say we each pick a jockey to win. If one of us wins, we owe the other...a favor."

I frowned. "What kind of favor?"

He shrugged. "Any kind. The favor of the winner's choice."

"What if neither of us wins?"

"Then neither of us gets a favor."

"What if we both want to pick the same jockey?" I demanded.

"We won't tell each other who we pick," he said. "We'll just write down our selections and wait to see who wins before revealing our choice. If we both pick the same jockey, and he wins, why then, we both get the favor of our choosing."

I couldn't grasp what he aimed to achieve with this little game, but it seemed harmless. "Fine," I said. "Where do we write down our picks?"

He picked up an old betting slip from the table and ripped it in two, handing one half to me. Then he rifled in his pocket. "You first," he said, placing a pen in my hand.

I turned to read the tote board. The final race featured several well-known riders. All the elite riders were sponsored, of course. I tried to recall what Gabriel had said about the elites, but this season he'd been far more concerned about the mid-tier group, since those were the jockeys he'd be facing. "Do you sponsor any of them?" I asked.

"Two on the board," Everett replied.

"Who?"

"I'm not saying. It might give you ideas."

I bit my lip and read over the names. I caught on two that were familiar: Joseph Lanner and Vern Eddings. I knew the names from Papan rather than Gabriel. Two weeks ago Papan had placed an exacta on these two jockeys, and they'd come up big for him. He'd blown most of the money before he'd gotten home, but he'd managed to bring enough to Maman to pay another month's rent on the house. Lanner had won, with Eddings finishing second.

"Eddings was spitting mad," Papan had said the following evening over a rare supper at home. "I expect he'll be itching to make a reversal as soon as possible."

I scratched *Eddings* onto my half of the betting slip and handed Everett the pen. He wasted no time in writing down his choice, then snagged my hat from the table and held it out upside down. "Put your pick in here."

I obeyed. He threw in his paper and tucked the hat away. "Shall we shake on it?" he asked.

I tentatively offered my hand. Everett looked down at it. I still wore the gauntlettes he had bought me outside. His gaze lingered on my hand or the glove, I couldn't tell which. I had a worried moment that he could see through the sheer black lace to the calluses on my palms from clutching velocipede handles. I curled my fingers in. Everett leaned forward and grabbed my hand between both of his.

"Emmeline,'" he said, lifting my hand to his lips and delicately brushing my exposed fingertips with his mouth. "You have never even spoken my name to me, and we are to be married tomorrow."

I blushed. I could feel his stare on me. He expected me to say something. I turned to glance out the window.

"The race is about to start." I leapt up from the sofa to take my position at the window. The pacer pulled even with the riders. My man, Eddings, had drawn Number Three.

Everett grunted behind me, but I paid him no mind. I focused on the happenings on the track. This race played out differently, perhaps because the jockeys had so much more experience. They were smooth and contained as they turned the first few laps, giving each other plenty of space, but never so much that any had a specific advantage or disadvantage. They made it look easy. They even waited for a breath after the pacer departed, as if they could happily amble through the whole race at 50 kilometers per hour. The jockey in the back position, in black, made the first move, darting up the outside of the line with aplomb. He overtook four riders ahead of him, including Eddings. Eddings reacted as soon as the jockey in black passed him; he moved wide, passed, and dropped towards the line to take a strong second wheel position behind the original leader, who was yet to be threatened.

As the black velo drove aggressively behind Eddings, I realized the black blur was Lanner, Eddings's nemesis. Eddings made another wide move to pass the original leader. He lifted up out of the saddle to give a blast of speed, whetting the race to a whole new level. Lanner and the original leader fell in tight behind Eddings. They remained in this formation for almost a full lap, and then Lanner kicked, advancing past Eddings and even gaining nearly half a velo's distance beyond. As the bell clanged, it appeared Lanner would demolish the competition.

But Eddings did not give up. He charged, drew even with Lanner, and raced with him. The velos wobbled treacherously, but Lanner and Eddings were alone in the world. They were so close together I thought they must certainly tangle. Eddings quickened yet again, dropped his head and shoulders, and inched past Lanner on the homestretch. At the finish line, he'd put nearly a foot between himself and his rival. The elite race, concluded, was dramatic, yet not as wild and exciting as the previous two. The jockeys were so controlled. Experience had given them nerves of steel.

"Come away from the window, Emmeline." Everett sounded peeved. His choice must not have won.

I ran from the window to snatch my hat off the table, reaching in to grab the two pieces of betting slip.

"Wait a minute!" said Everett, leaping from the sofa to catch me by the waist. He pulled me against him, and I froze, feeling very odd with his hands on me so intimately. It reminded me of that fateful moment in Aunt Finchley's hedge-maze—mortifying. I squirmed and weaseled my hand into the hat despite Everett's grip, withdrawing the slips. Everett closed his hand over mine.

"I begin to feel jealous of velocipede races," he murmured. "Your interest in them is…intense. I wish I could get even half a second's glance from you, but you reserve all your attention for the track. And for the results of our bet."

"You can't look away from a race," I said. "Everything happens so quickly. And don't you want to know the outcome of our wager?"

"I already know the important outcome." Everett broke into a pleased expression. "I won."

I freed myself from his grasp and opened my hand. When I unfolded the slips I saw that he told the truth: both slips read *Eddings.* "I won, too." I held the papers out to him so he could examine them.

"Did you?" he said in disbelief. "What are the odds of that? Perhaps we should have made more bets today. It seems we're lucky. Now, what favor would you have of me? Spit it out quickly so I can make good on it."

"I'll save my favor for later," I said, thinking, *I'll save it for when I really need it. Something important.*

"But that's no fun." Everett handed me my hat. "You must use it now. I live for your command."

I shook my head. "I don't want anything now. I'm saving it." He'd already given me plenty of pleasure for one day: taking me to the races, buying me a hat, letting me try a malt whisk.

"Well, I don't have such restraint," he said. "I want my favor now."

I clutched my hat against my chest, wondering what he might ask of me. "All right."

He said nothing as he looked at me for a long piercing moment. I had to drop my eyes. I couldn't stand the scrutiny. "Ah God," he murmured. "I should have made it three favors. I can't decide." He stepped closer to me and peeled my hands away from my hat, tossing it onto the sofa. He took my hands in his, stroking his fingers across the lacy gauntlettes. "I want you to kiss me, Emmeline. And I want you to say my name as you do it."

The blush hit me in one devastating wallop. I'd never kissed a man in my life, never even considered it. I'd rarely considered boys as anything but potential competition on a velo, and I'd certainly never been tempted to put *my mouth* on any of them.

"I don't know how!" I gasped, yanking my hands from his.

"I've shocked you," he said, as if to himself. "But shock doesn't get you out of it. A bet's a bet. You owe me the favor of my choice, and this is what I choose."

I put a hand over my mouth. *Stop being a ninny,* I coached myself. *You're going to marry him tomorrow.*

"Right," I said breathlessly behind my hand more in response to my thoughts than his words. I did not know where to start. I put my hands squarely on his shoulders. I could not prevent the creasing across my forehead. Maman would scold me that I'd have wrinkles before my time, if she could see me.

"Everett," I said rather grimly as I leaned my mouth towards his, standing up on my tiptoes to reach. His eyes widened as I approached, lips puckered, and put my mouth on his. I pecked him lightly, as Maman always did when Papan arrived home, even when he smelled of malt whisk or other women. Then I subsided, clasping my hands in front of me and staring at the ground. *That really wasn't so bad*, I congratulated myself.

Everett burst out laughing. "Perhaps I deserved that," he said. "I suppose I have only myself to blame for imagining something different. But for God's sake, Emmeline, call me Cassius."

•   •   •

As we departed the Arena, we paused at the bookie booths so I could collect my winnings. I'd won a total of four marks. Everett handed me the money. "You can use it to get something to wear for our wedding," he said.

I did not reply. I knew I'd just give my winnings straight to Maman. We had so many outstanding debts, and a dress for my wedding was not a priority for the Escot family.

Once in the parking lot, the bright daylight hurt my eyes. I was glad for the shielding brim of my new black hat. I'd never gone in for fashionable things before, but I liked the hat. I liked the way it made me feel—like an adult, but also anonymous behind the veil. To have no identity freed me from the normal constraints of my riesen status.

Everett—to think of him as Cassius was too intimate—paused at his gas carriage and messed about with it for a moment. I clapped my hands as I saw that he unfurled the top so that we might drive home with it open, just as he'd promised. I bounded into the passenger seat without waiting for him to open the door for me.

"Oh, it's lovely," I said as Everett pulled out of the Arena lot. I threw my head back over the seat and stared up at the sky, dotted with high white clouds. "It's been a perfect day!' I crowed. The sky and treetops whizzed by. "How fast are we going?" I asked.

"Forty kilometers per hour," Everett answered.

"I can go faster than that on a velo," I scoffed, unthinking. I'd begun to feel comfortable with him. I spoke to him as if I were speaking to Gabriel.

"Riding a velo at that speed is much harder than the jockeys make it look," Everett said. "You've only ridden touring velocipedes through the park, if you've ridden anything at all. Their top speed is barely ten kilometers per hour."

I bit my tongue, hard. Then I said, "Well, can't we go faster anyway?"

Everett laughed and pressed his foot on the mysterious pedals concealed by the dash.

On the morning of my wedding I did not perform my usual exercises. I'd planned to do them, but Maman came bustling into my room before dawn.

"Get up, Emmeline, we've a thousand things to do before ten of the clock."

I couldn't imagine what we had to do, but I scurried out of bed.

"We must pack your trunk and decide what you'll wear to the wedding," Maman said, surveying my wardrobe with an anxious frown. I'd hung the crimson gown up after I'd come home from the velocipede races. Against my drab clothing it glowed in my armoire like a gaslight.

A few minutes later Gabriel shuffled into my room dragging a battered trunk—the only one remaining of those that had moved us from the townhouse in the East End to our current dwelling. Maman yanked my sorry blue dress from the closet, threw it across the bed, and then gathered up the remaining dresses in one sweep to toss them into the open trunk. She packed up my other items: chemises, boots, corsets. I couldn't help but notice she left the Whittler out on the bed.

Gabriel leaned over and whispered in my ear, "So, did you ask him?"

"Ask who what?"

Gabriel rolled his eyes. "Your fiancé. Cassius Everett. About sponsoring me, of course."

I winced. "He said he'd consider it if you started to show." I weighed the fact that Everett owed me a favor. I just might use it to help Gabriel, *if* he'd stop being such a groveler.

Gabriel looked as if I'd slapped him. "But—but—" he spluttered.

"Emmeline," Maman called from the depths of the wardrobe. "I can't believe you lost your only white gloves. Bad enough you attended a bruncheon without them, but how can you be married in bare hands?" She shuddered.

"Mr. Everett bought me gauntlettes yesterday." Maman would never consider black lace a suitable choice for a wedding.

"Let me see them." She did not trust the taste of my husband-to-be after the fiasco with the crimson dress.

"He got me a hat, too," I told her, pulling the wide-brimmed, veiled thing down from the shelf to show her. "Isn't it pretty?" I turned back to the wardrobe to find the new gauntlettes.

"Pity it's black," Maman said. "But I suppose any hat's better than no hat." She took the hat from my hands and laid it on the bed. I offered the lace gauntlettes, which she pinched between her first and second fingers as if they were soiled. "Oh Emmeline, you cannot possibly wear such things inside the Worship Hall! They're scandalous. Why, they haven't any fingers!"

"Like racing gauntlets," I murmured. That was the reason I had been so pleased by them.

Maman threw the black lace gauntlettes into the trunk, sniffing. "Bare hands are better than those." She turned to my brother. "Gabriel, bring this trunk down to the front door. Mr. Everett said he'd send a carriage for it."

It dawned on me that the trunk contained the few possessions I'd be taking with me to Everett House. I'd be moving into a strange home, a place I'd never seen. I gulped nervously.

"What are you waiting for?" asked Maman. "Get your clothes on!"

A battle ensued between Maman and me over the Whittler—she won, leaving me sullen and breathless. My dress looked even shabbier against the finery of my hat, but I did not care.

I tried to eat a little porridge for breakfast, but my appetite flagged. Maman sat me down in the drawing room and attempted an awkward conversation wherein she made ominous noises about "keeping a man satisfied by gladly submitting to your wifely duties." I stared at her like she'd lost her mind, but could find no voice to mouth my many questions.

Maman took one look at my troubled expression and fled. "You must please him, Emmy," she said desperately over her shoulder before departing the room as if she had a pot about to boil over in the kitchen. I did not know exactly how I might please Cassius Everett; the man seemed highly capable of pleasing himself. Whatever Maman spoke of—I knew it had to do with the activities of the marriage bed—it must be bad, because it made her blush.

Reality began to set in. I was moving away from Escot House, moving away from Gabriel, and thus moving away from any opportunity to ride. The loss of riding distressed me most. Once married, I'd have no way to train. I'd shunted aside such thoughts over the past day, but now my predicament loomed inescapably before me.

Maman returned to the parlor where I sat consumed by my dismay. "Are you conscious of your duty?" she snapped, as if, in the interval of her absence, the good fairy had come down to explain to me the mysteries of marriage. "Do you understand what you must do?"

"Yes, Maman," I answered, just to end the whole embarrassing ordeal. I didn't have any idea about such things, but it couldn't be any more difficult than the kiss I'd been asked to produce for Everett yesterday.

She looked relieved. "You're a good girl, Emmeline." In a move utterly out of character, Maman sat beside me on the sofa and laid an arm over my shoulders. "I know you are too young to take on such burdens," she said. "I would have waited if it were possible. But you must make the best of it. Mr. Everett lacks manners, but he has money. It's an advantage you've never had. Make the most of it. Not just for us; for yourself, too. You can have a good life with him."

I nodded, but my mind raced frantically, scrambling against the notion that my days of velo riding were over—*over*! I'd never ride anything but a touring bike in Vreeland Park, and that only if I was lucky. I felt lost.

The rest of the morning passed in a daze. Maman presented me with an heirloom piece of porcelain that had been handed down in her family for generations, mother to daughter, on wedding days. She'd saved it for me all these years. The figurine showed an ideal woman in an old-fashioned green dress, all the details carefully painted by skilled hands: delicate blue eyes, rosebud lips, pretty green sash, and ivory skin. I clutched the dainty thing as Everett arrived. He wore a dark grey suit that probably cost more than Maman's monthly household allowance. A sudden crack jolted through my hands. I stared down. I'd squeezed the figurine so hard I'd broken its slender neck. My fingers curled around the broken porcelain, and I searched the room to see if Maman had noticed what I'd done. She'd be horrified.

But Maman had gone to Everett's side to welcome him. I hastily tucked the two pieces of the broken figurine into my shabby reticule and tightened the drawstrings while Maman and Everett spoke.

He offered to drive us all to the Hall, and Maman readily accepted. We followed him out to the street. Papan took the front seat in the gas carriage, chortling, "What a fine vehicle!" Papan had a way about him; he never seemed envious of others' wealth, never perturbed to see an example of good living that his own family could not attain. He really did not understand where all his money went. He was a creature of the moment.

Maman, Gabriel, and I were squashed into the back seat.
I exhaled in relief as Everett helped Maman and me to exit. He
kept holding my arm as he walked me up the stairs to the Hall.

"Have you no family to see you wed?" Maman asked Everett
tentatively.

He shook his head. "I have asked my business partner to
stand with me. He should arrive shortly."

Inside the Hall, the bishop awaited us, dressed in ceremonial
finery. He ushered my parents and Gabriel to seats on the front
bench and then directed me to stand before the altar. The
only light in the Hall came through the colored glass windows,
four long panels that faced the altar. The darkness made for a
somber mood, more akin to a funeral service than a wedding.
Normally a bride's family would pay for gaslights or candles for
the celebration. Obviously my family had not.

I needed the bishop's directions on where to stand, for I
could find no will of my own to move my feet. My black hat
and veil, despite the unfashionable color, gave me the comfort of
knowing that my family could not see my face clearly enough to
read the anxiety there. I took short, stumbling breaths and waited.
Everett would not come to the front until the bishop called him,
and he had to wait until his friend arrived. Every groom required
a second in the Serenian marriage rite. A woman could neither
hold property nor represent herself, so a man had to formally
designate a second to take responsibility for his bride should he
die or become incapacitated. Legally, a daughter transferred from
her father's care when she married, and I couldn't help but feel
that I was a burden my family was glad to be shifting.

Everett and his second walked up the passage. My fiancé
arrived beside me. I peeked and saw that Adon Voler stood with
him, as flashily dressed as ever. Maman would be happy that
my husband's second was such a well-to-do man. I prayed that
nothing would ever happen to Everett. Helen would be furious if
I ever became her husband's responsibility.

The bishop spoke the traditional words at Everett and me, but they would not stick in my head. I found myself staring down at my shabby dress, counting the threads on the frayed edges.

"Do you accept this man as your husband?" the bishop asked me the only question I had to answer in the vows. Everett had already made a series of oaths to assure my family of my good care.

"I do," I said, trying to keep my voice steady.

"Hold out your hand," the bishop told Everett. Everett held out his right hand, palm up. "Place your hand in his." I laid my left hand atop Everett's. The bishop tied our wrists together with a length of golden ribbon.

"By the grace of God," the bishop intoned, "you are wed."

Tradition dictated that Everett and I walk with our hands bound together out of the Hall and back into our conveyance. Voler would drive us, since Everett could not do so while tied to my wrist. Untying the wrist bond before we crossed the threshold of our shared home signified an unlucky marriage.

Maman cried as I passed her, dabbing at her tears with a handkerchief. Papan looked bemused, as if he hadn't quite expected it to happen so fast. Gabriel offered me a halfhearted smile. Mr. Voler held open the gas carriage doors, and Everett and I wriggled awkwardly into the back seat.

Everett and I did not speak as we drove away from the Hall. His hand lay beneath mine, warm and relaxed. We'd been tied so tightly together that I had no choice but to let my palm sit in his. I worried that mine was clammy. The ride to Everett's townhouse was interminable; the carriage filled with ominous silence.

Mr. Voler held the door open for us again, chuckling. I scrambled out first. I stared up at my new home. Everett had not told me he lived in one of the townhouses across from the entrance to Vreeland Park on Green Street. These were the finest residences in the city. I looked up the flight of stairs to the double-doored entry, where four servants awaited us.

The nerves hit me hard. I was not prepared for this.

"Mrs. Everett," Mr. Voler bowed over my free hand and kissed my fingertips like a dandy. "Congratulations. I wish you every happiness." Then he turned to Everett. "Cassius, my friend. A riesen for a wife. You've almost made it now." With that, he lifted his hat, smirked, and departed down the street. Everett ignored his friend's rather rude remark.

"Where is he going?" I wondered aloud.

"He lives just a block down," Everett said. "He's going back to his house."

"I see." I glanced up at Everett's home, our home.

"What do you think?" he asked. "Will it suffice?" He interlaced his fingers through mine and clasped my hand fully.

"Suffice?" I murmured. "It's one of the finest houses in Seren!"

"Come, let me show you." He led me up the stairs where he introduced the four servants: Orson, the butler; Ben, the footman; Mrs. Hoving, the housekeeper; and Letty, a maid of all work.

Orson led us into the grand foyer, and there the servants faded back into the house to leave Everett and me alone. I expected Everett to cut the gold ribbon connecting us then, but he did not. "We'll get you a personal maid as soon as you are settled. I thought you would want to pick her yourself."

"That is not necessary," I said. "I've never had a maid, and I do not need one."

"We'll discuss it later."

I got the feeling Everett did not much care for my contradicting his decree. Well, we were married now, and I had less cause to be meek with him. He could not get rid of me, though he *could* make my life miserable. I wriggled my left hand. "Shall we cut this?"

Everett looked down. "They say it is good luck the longer you wear it."

"A silly tradition," I said.

"We don't know each other very well," Everett said. "Let's keep it, at least for an hour or two. We'll walk the house and get to know each other. Silly or not, it cannot hurt."

Well. Everett was as superstitious as any velo jockey, and already I could sense that he liked to get his own way, even in the smallest matters. I liked to get my own way, too, and I was accustomed to bending Gabriel to my will. Everett seemed less likely to accede so easily.

Everett gave me a tour of the house that ended in my room. My chamber's best features were the picture windows that overlooked Vreeland Park. Everett brought me over to admire the scene. The wrist ribbon that still tied us together chafed and annoyed me.

"You can see the track," I said, pleased about my view—not of the park, but of the practice course. It made me feel closer to myself, as if by seeing the track, I could recapture what the marriage forced me to sacrifice.

Jockeys practiced on the course, four of them, racing. I could not identify them from this distance. I did not move from the window despite Everett's tugging. I wanted to see the outcome of the race.

Everett went still as he watched me gazing at the distant track. "Again," he murmured. "I think, Emmeline, you have the makings of a track swaddy."

I did not turn to answer him until I'd seen the jockey who had been trailing the other three make his move and soundly overtake them. Everett's comment bordered on insult: A track swaddy was someone like my father, who spent all his time and money betting at the races.

"I don't care about betting," I snapped.

"But you like the races," Everett said. "You like the races very much."

"They excite me." I saw no reason to lie.

Something flashed in my new husband's eyes—interest? Annoyance? I could not say. He pulled on our wrist bond and hauled me away from the window. "I am glad I gave you this room then," he said. "If it will give you pleasure."

The rest of the room was quite nice, too. I had a large bed with a yellow silk covering, fluffy down pillows unlike any I'd ever slept upon, and a white brocade fainting couch pushed up against the base of the bed. A whole separate dressing room attached to the bedchamber. Everett led me over to examine it. My four dresses, the crimson silk Everett had sent me included, looked forlorn in the too-large space.

"I'll set up an allowance," Everett said. "You can order new things."

I had to remind myself, as I began fantasizing about a leather racing costume and helmet, that he meant *dresses*. "Do you expect me to socialize much?" I blurted. I hoped he did not. I was not accustomed to taking part in society.

"You mean attend parties and events?"

I nodded.

"I expect you to set your schedule as you please," Everett said. "I will make few demands upon your time. You should know I am a very busy man. Marriage had not been in my sights until I—" He broke off, looking almost embarrassed.

"You aren't busy today," I mused.

"It's my wedding day. A man can arrange a day off for that."

I shrugged. "You needn't have."

"It pleased me to clear my schedule to welcome you."

"Oh."

"My rooms connect to yours through this door." Everett gestured to a door beside the bed. "Would you like to see them?"

"Do you have a view of the park, too?"

"Yes." *Did I imagine it, or was Everett's reply slightly irritated?* He led me through the passage to his domain, a typically masculine place—dark colors, the furnishings done in black grenadilla. The bedroom set alone must have cost a fortune, for grenadilla came very dear. Two paintings hung on opposing walls, both portraits of the same subject. In the first, the woman stood looking out an open archway, turned in profile—a very fine profile—and she had a somber cast to her expression. The second painting showed the same woman in a more classic portrait. She wore a black lace gown of unfamiliar style—the bodice draped like a tent to hide her figure—and she reclined in a languorous pose on a settee.

Everett saw me looking at his paintings, but he made no comment about them. Nor did I, though I found it odd that my husband had two pictures of an unidentified woman in his bedroom. But could I really expect Everett to favor me? We'd known each other a total of three days. So far, he'd been better to me than I deserved.

"Your rooms are luxurious," I commented. The giant bed piled with velvet pillows could claim no austerity. The deep carpet in burgundy wool must have cost a small fortune.

"I did not grow up with money," Everett explained. "I enjoy what I have now. I know what it is like to have less."

"I see," I said. And I did—in my head, I maintained a list of all the things I wanted, ranked and ordered, so that if or when I finally came by wealth, I knew exactly how I would enjoy it. Of course my wishes all revolved around velos. Everett's had apparently been for other luxuries.

Everett stood for a moment, eyeing the portrait of the woman. I felt the contraction of his mind; he grew immediately more distant—a situation which caused me both distress and relief. Being in his bedchamber made me nervous as it forced me to imagine what would be expected of me here. Not that I could—Maman had alluded to the cryptic marital duty, but I had no notion of it, except that it involved the body, and Maman had said I must endeavor to please Everett.

I nurtured curiosity on that front. I had always enjoyed activities that allowed me to use my body. Perhaps if I had been more welcomed by society I would have had a better idea of what the marital duty was—but I had never spent much time with girls of my own age. I'd had only Gabriel for company, and he'd flat-out refused to tell me anything. Ladies were protected from such information. To know what went on in such a seedy place was considered ruinous—just as tainting as the situation I'd been caught in with Everett. Gabriel had protected my innocence as a matter of family pride. But even so, I couldn't help but understand that the world applauded a man for pursuing his pleasure. A young man was encouraged to toss off his innocence at the first chance. Most of them, I'd gathered, went to the brothels on Rouge Street to take care of the matter.

My brother knew things about what happened between men and women that I did not. It had annoyed me. I'd begged him to tell me about the activities that went on in the Rouge Street brothels. He'd described kissing, but beyond that Gabriel had drawn the line. *It is not done,* he'd said. *Your husband would expect you to come to him ignorant of such matters.*

Everett lifted our bound hands and touched my cheek. Was he beginning the mysterious thing that was the point of our marriage? He caressed my face softly, and I closed my eyes, trying to quell the equal swells of fear and anticipation in my belly.

His other hand moved up to hold the back of my neck. My eyes opened to find his face close to mine. He looked so dark and intense. I had not looked so directly into his eyes before.

"There you are," he whispered. "You have been hiding from me. Come out." I didn't know what he meant. I tried to look away, but he squashed our bound hands into my cheek.

I steeled my nerves and sought to please him as Maman had instructed. We stared at each other for several of my shallow breaths, my gasps the only sound between us.

He laid his mouth over mine. My head jerked in surprise, but he steadied it with his hand. My bound hand quivered awkwardly against my face. He moved his lips, and I thought blearily that I must be expected to respond. I did, but frustration rose inside me as I considered that someone—Gabriel or Maman, since I had no trusted friends—could have mentioned what I ought to do in response to this! Kissing reminded me of riding a velo for the first time, wobbly and precarious. A little advice would have gone a long way towards calming me.

What a strange business, I thought. Everett tasted like malt whisk. Had he been drinking so early in the day? What did that signify—was he anxious about our wedding, or did he often drink in the morning? Was he like Papan, the kind of man who could not function without his drink?

Perhaps to think such things during my first real kiss displayed my unromantic nature. The mythology said I ought to have been swept away, unable to think but for my desire. But I had no inkling of the existence of an intimate desire that could sprout from within me. I might have felt the physical hallmarks of it: the tightening of my belly, the rush of circulation to my face and other parts, the loosening of my muscles, the melting of my body into a more pliable and supple mien. But I had no reference point for these sensations.

It could not have been *my* desire I was supposed to feel. I was meant to understand that he wanted me, and, in his wanting, I was to feel whole. Being a wife ought to have completed me. I was to please my husband, and only in his pleasure was I to understand my own. *You must please him, Emmy,* Maman had said. Forget about pleasing myself; Serenian life held no script for such a thing.

Everett drew away and let our hands fall. He used his free left hand to rummage in his coat pocket, pulling out a folding knife, the kind a gentleman carried for opening letters or bottles. He fumbled with it unsuccessfully, trying to open it using only his left hand. He grunted in annoyance and brought our bound hands up to help. He finally opened the knife, and he cut away the gold ribbon holding us together.

I shook out my wrist, for my hand had been tingling since the knot had been tied.

Everett smiled wryly. "Well," he said. "It is done. We are married." He looked searchingly at me. "I hope you are not too unhappy."

I shook my head. "No. Of course not. You have been... very good to me. I am not unhappy." I could not explain what I was losing. It would make him angry to know his wife practiced a manly and unacceptable pastime. Besides, an odd, fluttering feeling had been born inside my chest the moment I'd heard I was to have an allowance. *Possibility. A chance.* He'd said he was a very busy man. I would have hours and hours of free time. Everett was no gentleman with days of leisure on his hands—he might not even expect me to observe all the rules of propriety that a typical riesen must follow. Perhaps he would not think anything of it if I went out without an escort. And with an allowance, I could buy a velo and hide it. I could sneak off to the park to ride on my own, a pleasure I'd never considered. My velo riding had always been entirely dependent on Gabriel's good graces, but if Everett meant to give me money, I could outfit myself and ride whenever I pleased. It might not be like getting to race in the Arena, but it gave me something. It might even be enough.

"Not exactly a resounding declaration of your passionate affection, but I'll take it," Everett said.

I blinked back to the present, having little sense of our conversation. "What?" I asked distractedly.

He sighed. "You are so young. We'll go very slowly, Emmeline. You don't have to—you don't have to do anything you do not wish to do." He gestured towards the door. "Make yourself at home here."

Days passed as I settled into the routine of my new life. Cassius Everett had lived as a bachelor for many years, and his household nearly ran itself. I was not needed, and idleness colored my days. At home Maman had always made a daily list of household chores and activities for me to complete. She never let me do any labor that had a chance of building up my muscles or further ruining my physique—no laundry or dishwashing or churning or carrying water for me—but I often folded the clean dry linens, made the beds, cut the potatoes, or sewed. I had filled my days with these little household chores. Daily I had been permitted to go out with Gabriel under the guise of going for a walk, when really we'd ridden like mad things.

Everett House bored me. The servants took care of everything, even turning down and warming my bed in the evening. Everett had a library, and I spent my first two days in there, looking through his collection and reading a few novels. I saw very little of Everett—his business took him away for the entire day, and, like my father, he did not return for supper. Which made me wonder what he did—was he at the Arena for the evening races? The season was in full swing, of course. On nights without velocipede races, the Arena hosted various events: concerts, performances by acrobats, burlesques, and circus features. A man with his own private box likely attended all the shows.

After his first mention of it, Everett said nothing more of my allowance, so for the time being I was utterly hemmed. I did not have a single mark to spend. I wore my old frayed gowns and stayed home for lack of an escort. Often I pulled a chair up to the window in my bedchamber and watched the jockeys practice on the Vreeland Park track. Sometimes I would see Gabriel's bright yellow velo out there, and I would think longingly of the hours he and I had spent on the track together, me riding his old grey velo and still managing to keep up with him. I both hated to watch the track practice and loved it: seeing those riders connected me again to my dream, but I could not live just by watching. I needed to ride.

I finally saw Everett again over the weekend. Worship Day morning dawned bright and clear, and I hoped Everett was not a religious man. My family had not frequented Worship Hall, as Maman felt shamed by our circumstances and did not like to face friends from the past. I crept down into the breakfast room early. Days ago I had resumed my morning routine of floor exercises and stretches, but even so I was restless as a caged animal. The exercises only partly dispelled my excess energy. I'd learned that Mrs. Hoving had breakfast ready by eight of the clock, so after I finished my exercises, I waited in my room until exactly the hour and then went to eat.

This morning, no breakfast waited spread upon the sideboard. The room stood empty and quiet like the entire house. I could find no one about, and I even went all the way to the kitchen, though I knew my presence might be construed as an insult to the servants. I found even the kitchen empty, so I crept in and made myself a cup of hot water as I used to do at home. As Maman had predicted, I was now served coffee in the morning, but I did not know how to prepare the drink, though I liked it very much.

I sat at the kitchen table with my hands around the stoneware mug, warming them.

"Emmeline!"

I lifted my head, startled to find Everett standing in the kitchen doorway. He must have just risen from bed, for his dark hair was mussed and he looked tired.

"Good morning," I said politely.

"Good morning, *Cassius*," he snapped. "Would it kill you to say my name?"

His annoyance surprised me. I cleared my throat and tried again. "Good morning, Cassius." His name felt odd on my tongue, foreign and illicit.

He walked over to the kettle. "Did you make coffee?" he asked, looking around for the carafe.

I shook my head. "I'm having hot water."

"Why?" he barked. Obviously *Cassius* was not a morning person.

"I don't know how to make coffee. I'd never had it until I came here."

"Well, come over here, and I'll teach you how. You're going to want to know, or on the servants' days off you'll have a terrible headache."

He showed me how to put the dark brown beans into the grinder and crank them into a fine powder. He let me do the grinding, and I enjoyed using my arm muscles to turn the crank. Maman would never have let me do such a thing. Everett produced a special kettle that made the coffee, with several metal parts. We stood in silence as we waited for the beverage to brew. Everett—Cassius—looked grim and forbidding.

"Did you—ah—have a good week?" I asked. I almost asked if it had been a bad week, but I thought it too negative. *A lady must bring cheer to her husband*, Maman's voice said in my head.

"What?" he said as he snatched the coffee kettle on the stove and poured two cups. "Do you mind not having servants two days a week? I always give them the entire weekend off, so they can see their families."

"I'm used to doing for myself." I felt ridiculously hurt that he had not answered my question.

He gestured at the kitchen table. "Shall we sit?"

I took a place across from him and sipped at my coffee. He had brewed it strong, but I had already grown to love the beverage. It tasted like privilege.

"What have you been up to?" he asked. After just one sip of his coffee, he relaxed.

"I read a few books," I said. "You have a large library."

He stared at me. "That's it? You read? I've been away five days, and all you've done is read?"

"I—the servants manage the house so well," I stammered. "There wasn't much for me to do."

"I told you to get yourself some clothes," he said. "I thought you'd send for a dressmaker to get what you needed."

I stared at him. "You did?" He'd mentioned an allowance for shopping, but he'd not made any direct commands to actually do the deed. "But I haven't any money," I added. "I can't place orders without money."

"Just give the dressmaker my name," he said. "I buy on credit."

Only a very rich man could buy on credit. Papan hadn't been allowed such leniency in ages, as everyone knew the Escots could not pay their debts. I frowned. Buying on credit was a luxury I did not want—if I used credit, Everett would know exactly what I purchased. Maybe that was the point. I did not like it.

"I don't feel comfortable purchasing on credit," I said, trying to sound haughty.

"Why not?" Everett demanded.

"Debt has a way of growing," I said primly.

He rolled his eyes and finished his coffee in a gulp. "Fine, Miss Frugal. I'll leave you some cold coin. You can bring me your receipts, and I'll keep track of them."

Ha! I thought. He *was* going to keep tabs on what I bought! "Thank you," I bit out. I gulped my coffee in a perfect imitation of Everett.

"Would you like to go somewhere this afternoon?" he asked out of the blue just as he departed the kitchen.

"Where?"

"To Vreeland. It's going to be a lovely day."

I'd been cooped up in the house all week, and an outing sounded like good medicine. "Yes, please. I'd love to go."

"I'll meet you here at three of the clock," my husband said.

•　　　•　　　•

Three of the clock came and went. I sat in the fine drawing room, dressed in the blue dress I'd worn to be married. Free to dress myself, I hadn't worn a corset since the wedding. I'd shoved the Whittler deep into the back of the dressing room, and I was gathering the courage to throw it in the refuse bin. Everett was right—I had trouble doing things that weren't frugal. Penny-pinching had been ingrained by my upbringing. I thought perhaps I should offer the Whittler to Letty the maid—but could I condone any other girl wearing it when I knew how awful it was? Part of me thrilled to the idea of slashing it to shreds or even burning it.

Where was Everett? Had he forgotten me? I'd been looking forward to the fresh air and a brisk walk in Vreeland Park. My body screamed for exercise. I bided the time waiting for Everett by fantasizing about sneaking off to the track at Vreeland once I had a velo to ride. I'd decided to go whole hog and get a custom racing velo, built to my size perfectly. The problem of placing the order vexed me. I couldn't just walk into a velo shop and have them measure me for one, and how could I disguise the order when Everett planned to track my spending?

"Sorry I'm late," Everett said, stepping into the room. I blinked up out of my reverie. He offered his arm, and off we went, moving at Everett speed. For the first time since I'd known him, I felt comfortable matching his pace. I wore no corset to hamper me; I had no fear he'd find my stride unladylike and turn from me in disgust. It didn't matter now. He'd married me, and he could not get rid of me even if he did find me or my gait unsatisfactory.

How a man who moved like Everett could have cause to complain about how I walked I did not know, for I found that as I matched his steps, he only moved faster. Though we did not run to the entrance of Vreeland Park, we moved so efficiently we might as well have. Neither of us was breathless as we arrived at the beginning of the network of paths that led through the park.

I darted towards the path that I knew led to the racing track. Everett pulled me in the opposite direction. "This way," he said. "I've a destination in mind."

I swallowed my disappointment and told myself I'd be at the track soon enough once I'd ordered my *very own velo*. Watching only tortured me, anyway.

We arrived at Everett's destination. It was a mark of how truly restless I was that it did not annoy me: he'd brought me to the touring velo rental station.

"I though you might like to try riding," Everett said, gesturing to the rack of velos, their fat tyres stuck backwards into the slots. He looked pleased with himself.

He tried to do me a kindness. He'd seen my interest in the races; he wanted to give me pleasure. He couldn't know how little satisfaction a touring velo gave me. Comparing a touring velo to a racing one was like comparing pudding to meat. The first was fluff; the second could feed a person.

He took my hesitation as rejection of his idea. "We needn't do it if you don't wish it," he said hastily. "I know most ladies frown on such active pursuits."

I glared at him. "No," I said. "Let's rent some. Gabriel took me riding here."

"You've been on them before?"

"Yes," I said, following Everett as he walked towards the racks. I looked through the rentals with Everett. He avoided the racked velos, instead examining the trikes and quads considered appropriate for women. I turned to the racks where the two-wheelers stood. The Renn-Bicy, a velo with a front crank, a huge front tyre, and a tiny rear one for stability, tempted me. The Renn was notoriously difficult to balance, a vehicle for a lone dandy in the park. The young men rode them to garner attention. I lingered beside the Renn for a long while, even though I knew I could not possibly ride it in my dress. I sighed.

Beside the Renn-Bicy stood a monowheel, a single wheel topped by a seat. But again, such a vehicle would be impossible to ride in a skirt. That left the standard fat-tyre touring velo, often called the Rover. Designed along the same lines as a racing velo with two tyres, a rear-wheel crank, and a diamond frame, the Rover mimicked what I usually rode. But the Rover had ungainly rubber tyres and a seat that reclined at an angle and prevented the correct body position to achieve any sort of speed. If I tucked my skirts up a bit, I could ride it without hazard. I so longed to ride that I was willing to settle.

I pulled a small Rover from the rack and wheeled it to the rental both. Everett emerged from behind the booth, beaming, pushing a lumbering beast of a tandem-quad. I couldn't believe that he proposed we should ride the wretched apparatus. First of all, with four wheels and two broad seats side by side, the thing might as well have been a foot-powered carriage. Its top speed could be no faster than walking.

"You can't mean for us to ride that?" I snapped. I couldn't help it. The fact that he'd picked the tandem-quad meant he expected me to be a terrible rider. It was a velo for a truly unskilled person—he'd pedal for me, as if I couldn't!

He looked down at the Rover I held. "But you can't ride that one," he replied. "Your dress will get in the way." He gestured at the foot pedals on the tandem-quad. "This one is possible to pedal while wearing skirts. You needn't be afraid. We can ride it together."

"I won't ride that," I protested. "I'd rather walk."

Everett turned towards the velo he'd picked, looking bemused. "What's wrong with it?" he asked. "I thought—"

"It's slow," I cut him off. "It's boring." I knew that I behaved like a spoiled child. But I was strung out—I needed to ride, and I needed to ride as fast as I possibly could.

"Slow," Everett muttered, looking at the tandem-quad. "God forbid we go too *slow.*" I heard the sarcasm in his voice. He shoved the tandem-quad backwards and marched over to the racks, pulling free another Rover, one that suited his size. "Rovers it shall be, my lady," he said. "How many times have you done this, anyway?"

"Often," I lied as we walked to the booth where Everett paid for an hour's rental. Gabriel and I had rarely had the money to rent velocipedes.

"So you know how to ride," my husband concluded. Did he sound disappointed? I could not tell.

"Yes," I said. "I definitely know how to ride."

Everett raised his eyebrows. I pulled up my skirt and petticoat and knotted them at about knee height. It wasn't proper to do such a thing; it would have horrified my mother. But I was a married woman now, and ready to push the boundaries. Everett stared at me, his gaze lingering on my exposed ankles. Not that they were truly exposed—I wore full lace-up boots, and my bloomers came down well over the tops of my boots. What was there to see?

I held my breath, wondering if he would reprimand me. He said nothing, only watching as I mounted the Rover. The velo forced the rider to slouch into the seated position. The body position did nothing for speed, and I felt like an idiot, riding such a slug. I couldn't use the muscles of my torso at all, and my back felt squashed. Though the velo did not play to my strength, I knew how to get the most out of the damned Rover. The secret was the legs. You had to really haul yourself along with your legs.

I took off without a word. Despite the Rover's fat tyres, despite the awkward body position, it was heaven to ride. I hadn't realized how much I'd missed it. I found a freedom in riding that only a wayward woman would understand. When I rode, none of the rules could touch me. I could go anywhere, as fast as my body would allow. I could outride everyone—it was a fantasy of escape. I broke away from the tight lacing of my place in the world. I became body, movement, and breath—nothing more, nothing less.

I angled the Rover down the path that led towards the practice track.

"Emmeline!" I heard Everett calling behind me. I pedaled harder, squeezing my buttocks in the way the Rover demanded. The practice track loomed ahead of me. Three velos clipped along on it, none of them yellow. I'd hoped Gabriel would be there, for his own sake as much as mine. If he wanted to win, he needed to practice.

I pulled up at the low wall that separated the practice track from the park, leaned forward off the Rover's seat, and brought both feet down from the pedals so I stood, straddling the velo as I watched the race at hand. I studied the jockeys, trying to identify them. They flew down the track, very fast, very skilled—clearly Arena riders. I liked to watch such expert riding from a close vantage. They rode hard, heads down. One person stood at the finish line, holding a timepiece and whistling out the final lap.

As the jockeys kicked, they subtly changed their body positions, dropping heads and shoulders even lower to propel their weight and momentum forward, exactly what you could not do on a Rover. One rider, obviously the strongest, bolted ahead of the other two by a velo length on the homestretch. Crossing the finish line, he was a full ten yards in front of them.

"Eddings," I heard Everett say behind me. I hadn't noticed him arrive. I looked over my shoulder. Everett stood beside his Rover, shaking the hand of a jockey. The jockey held a racing velo in front of him in just the manner that Everett held his touring slug.

"Did you come to watch us practice?" said the jockey, who was apparently Eddings, the winner of the elite race on which Everett and I had bet.

"No," Everett said. "My wife led me here quite unexpectedly." He gestured in my direction, and Eddings turned to look at me.

I got quite a shock when I met the jockey's eyes—I knew him! Not by name, of course, but I'd raced against him more than once here at the track. He had distinctive eyes, very pale bluish silver, very cold. One didn't soon forget them. He was a ruthless jockey, the kind who'd knock you over in a practice race just because he could. I hadn't realized Eddings was this man. I'd never come close to beating him, and now I understood why.

Eddings walked up to me, bowing. "Mrs. Everett," he said. "I am ashamed to say I did not even know a Mrs. Everett existed." It took me a moment to realize he spoke to me. "You are very familiar," he mused. "Have I met you before?"

Eddings stared at me as Everett leaned his Rover against the track wall and shifted closer to me. "You know each other?" Everett asked.

"You must be mistaken," I said to Eddings. "I am sure I do not know you."

"Your eyes—" he began.

"I know!" I almost shrieked. "My brother! I have a twin brother who is a jockey. Likely you have raced against him here at the practice track. We look alike."

Eddings frowned. "I hardly think it likely I would confuse a man and a woman." He seemed baffled, for which I was grateful.

"Gabriel and I are of a size," I said. "We have the same coloring, the same eyes."

"Ah," Eddings said. "Your brother is Gabriel Escot. I do know him."

"Yes," I said too brightly. "You see? He frequents the track."

"Yes, yes, of course. I've raced against him several times here."

I breathed a sigh of relief and turned back to the track. Eddings and Everett continued their conversation. "I never thought I'd see you on a *touring* velo, Mr. Everett. Slumming it?" Eddings joked.

"I am merely indulging my wife. She likes to ride."

"Ah, of course. Well, I must head to the track now. Good day, sir. It was a pleasure to meet you, Mrs. Everett." Eddings bowed at me and gave me rather too long a look as he did.

Everett and I stood side by side in silence, watching a practice race. My husband emanated annoyance, but he did not say anything until the conclusion of the race. Then he turned to me, putting a heavy hand on my forearm. "*Have* you met Eddings before?" he asked.

"No," I replied, possibly too quickly.

"That isn't why you picked him at the race the other day? Because you knew him? Because you…favor him?"

"I picked him because of something my father said," I explained. "About the rivalry between him and another rider, Lanner. Papan said Eddings wanted retaliation after being beaten."

My husband scowled as if he did not believe me. "He seemed quite startled by you. Quite enthralled, too."

"The resemblance between Gabriel and me is striking." I argued, feeling slightly panicked. "Especially our eyes. If he has only seen Gabriel on the track, he would have seen little of his face, but if he saw Gabriel without his goggles, he would naturally have seen his eyes. We have the same eyes, and many people say they are quite unusual." I stopped, realizing I babbled.

"Quite," Everett said, glaring at me. "Shall we ride?" He gestured up the path.

I lifted myself back up onto my Rover's seat and generated immediate leg power. Once again, I had a much better start than Everett, and after his nasty little interrogation, I did not feel bad riding so hard that conversation was prevented as we went flying through the familiar paths of Vreeland Park.

· · ·

By Moonday morning I regretted how I'd treated Everett at the park. He'd been cross when we finally arrived at the velo rental booth, jerking me down from the velo and hauling me out of the park at a pace that was almost a run. Tight-lipped and silent, he hadn't said a word to me since. I'd known he'd been in the house all day Sonneday; I'd heard him rattling around in his office and the library. He'd not come down for supper, so I'd sat at the dining table alone—again—and picked at my food, worrying at just what, exactly, he suspected. Had he only been angered by the fact that I'd ignored him while we rode the Rovers? Did he suspect me of a *dalliance* with Eddings? He'd rather implied it in his questioning. Or was he upset because I was so fast on a velo? Had he guessed my true secret?

Everett was nowhere to be found Moonday morning, so I assumed he'd already left. I crept into his office, but heard footsteps behind me, and the butler, Orson, gave a small bow and held out a tray to me.

"A message for you left by the master, ma'am," he said. I took the tray from Orson and brought it over to the sofa. To my pleasant surprise, a pile of marks rested on the tray beneath the paper.

Emmeline:

Please use these funds to buy yourself some decent everyday clothing. We will discuss the finances required for a more elaborate wardrobe at a later time. Please retain the receipts for your orders for me.

Yours, Cassius

The tone of the note worried me. I suspected Everett was mistrustful of me, but I put it out of my mind and instead turned to the pile of notes, counting out how much he had given me: 25 marks, enough to get a leather riding suit, but not near enough for a velo. My custom velo would have to wait until the plans were made for that more elaborate wardrobe. I tucked the marks into my dress pocket, went upstairs to my room to get my hat and gauntlettes, and then arrived face to face with Orson at the front door.

"I'm going shopping," I told him. I wondered how he would react to such a statement. I intended to go out alone—to test the limits of my new lifestyle. Maman would never have permitted it— *a lady must never leave the house without a man for an escort,* she would have said. But Everett and his household were not so concerned with the riesen rules.

"Very good, my lady," Orson said. "Shall I send for the carriage?"

I had not anticipated this reaction. The shops on Saville Street were only four blocks away. It would take longer to negotiate the traffic in a carriage than it would if I went on foot. "I'd rather walk," I said. "I'll enjoy the exercise."

"Let me send for Letty and Ben, then," the man said. I scowled. I had not wanted to take the escorts, since I meant to go to a shop where I could get a riding suit made, and the servants would report where I went to Everett. But Orson was too quick, already halfway up the stairs to fetch them.

I paced in the foyer. I didn't have a good plan. Everett would be suspicious if I had no new clothes despite spending all his money. My best approach would be to go to a dressmaker first, see if I could convince her to make me a couple of plain dresses for a very good price to keep up appearances, and then try for the riding suit at the leatherworker's. In the meantime, I'd try to figure out what to do about the receipts. *Could I convince the dressmaker to write them out for more than I'd actually paid?* That seemed an unlikely thing for a shopkeeper to do.

Letty and Ben arrived, and we set out walking. Letty managed to stay caught up with me though I walked quickly. Ben followed at a more respectful distance.

"Where will you be going, ma'am?" Letty asked me as we turned down Saville Street.

I'd never had the occasion to shop on posh Saville Street. Maman had procured my gowns from secondhand consignment shops or as hand-me-downs from my cousin Helen. Letty seemed to understand my hesitation. "You should start at Delaney's," she advised.

I was surprised that the housemaid would know about fine dressmakers on Saville Street. "How do you know?" I blurted.

Letty blushed a full, deep crimson and said nothing.

I paused on the sidewalk and grabbed Letty by the arm. "Tell me!" I couldn't fathom what the girl knew of Saville Street shops.

Letty winced and looked away from me, over her shoulder at Ben, as if to check that he could not hear us. "I shouldn't a' said anything," she murmured. "I'm sure you know where you like. Don' mind me, missus. Mam says I speak out a' turn."

I frowned. "I don't mind, Letty. I appreciate your knowledge of the shops, for I have none. But I would like to know how you came by it." The poor maid looked terrified. "I won't be angry," I added soothingly.

Letty glanced nervously at Ben again. He had that knowing quality of footmen, however, sensing when privacy was required. "Well," she said. "You won't tell the master what I done, telling you?" she asked. "He wouldn't like it."

"Everett?" I asked with surprise. "No, why should I tell him? It cannot be any of his concern if you know the shops or not."

Letty looked doubtful, but she leaned in close and whispered, "*She* used ta come 'ere. She brought me as she didn't 'ave 'er own maid. She always preferred Delaney's for dresses."

She? "Who was she?" I asked.

Letty looked truly miserable. "The lady who was the lady 'fore you," she mumbled.

I cocked my head. Surprise trickled through my limbs. I had not had the faintest notion that Everett had been married before me. He'd not told me. For someone who prized honesty above all else, it seemed a large omission. *Had she died?* "Everett's first wife?"

Letty squirmed. "Well, no. They wasn't married, you see."

"His mistress?" The words came out inadvertently. This wasn't a topic a Serenian wife should discuss, especially not with a housemaid.

Letty nodded. "She lived up at the house until recently. When 'e sent 'er away there was a ruckus you wouldn't believe." Letty leaned in close. "She punctured the tyres on 'is favorite velo. Then 'e cut up a bunch of the paintings 'e'd had done of 'er, slashed 'em, like, with a knife. They screamed and screamed at each other for days, it seemed like."

"Who was she?" I couldn't help but ask. It shocked me that my husband had been so improper as to have his mistress live in his main house, the one, I, his wife, now occupied. *Did he love her?*

"She was a foreigner," Letty explained. "The master called her Lena, but we were simply to address her as *my lady*."

It rather felt as though the ground had fallen from beneath my feet. I didn't know what to make of the fact that my husband had another woman who was addressed as *my lady*—not even I was *my lady*, because Everett had no riesen title. Ladies were brought up never to show jealousy; a man would indulge in dalliances, but wives never acknowledged such things. I had not thought about what it would feel like to know my husband went elsewhere for affection. His days and evenings away from home began to make more sense. A warm wave of rage burned up from my belly. I'd ever been a competitive person. I did not like to come in second; I'd just never thought about competing in any domain besides a velocipede race.

"She liked Delaney's, did she?" I demanded. Letty nodded. "Then let's go somewhere else." I scowled and marched up Saville Street.

Letty, Ben, and I passed Delaney's. Two doors up I found *Jacquelenne's: dressmaker, glover, and milliner*. I pushed the door open. A girl looked up from a table where she had been applying a ribbon to a straw bonnet.

"May I help you?" she asked. I liked her immediately, for I could see she wore no corset. Her dress was most unusual, too.

"I've come to order a dress or two," I announced, trying to sound as imperious as Maman.

The girl looked me up and down, clearly unimpressed by my out-of-mode and threadbare dress.

Letty stepped forward in my defense. "This is Mrs. Cassius Everett," she told the shopgirl.

My husband's name appeased. "Very good," the shopgirl said. "Miss Jackie doesn't arrive until twelve of the clock, generally. But I can show you some patterns and fabrics and take your measurements."

Letty had already gone off to the row of fabric bolts on the far wall. Ben waited at the door outside the shop. The shopgirl sat me down at her table and shoved a stack of patterns in my direction. "These are the traditional styles," she said.

I looked through the patterns, but I did not find anything to my liking. All the dresses depicted required heavy corsetry. I recalled the examples of rational dress I'd seen in Lavinia Beau's pamphlet—she'd included several patterns for skirts and blouses. Then I eyed the unusual dress the shopgirl wore. It looked decidedly more comfortable than anything in the patterns she'd offered. The bodice dropped in the waist, cut to skim the body rather than fit it tightly. I could see a good foot of her petticoats beneath the skirt. The dress moved with the girl, and I thought she looked very jaunty and modern. Maman would have told me my taste was "in the gutter."

"I want a dress like yours!" I blurted.

"Really?" the shopgirl asked. "I designed it myself. Miss Jackie doesn't like it. She says it makes me look like a hoyden."

I pushed the patterns away. "I like it," I said. "It looks much more comfortable than these. Is it what you would call 'rational dress'?"

The girl beamed. "It is! Why, have you read Lavinia Beau's chapbooks?"

I nodded eagerly.

She leaned forward to whisper, "When I'm at home, I don't even wear petticoats. It's amazing how free the legs feel without long heavy skirts."

"It would be perfect for riding a velo," I mused.

The shopgirl's eye sparkled. "I like how you think."

"Listen," I said. "Can you make me two of that kind of dress for less than ten pounds?"

The girl pulled up a sheet of paper and a pencil, briefly jotting down a few calculations. She frowned and studied her math. "I could, but you'd have to pick an inexpensive fabric. A cotton, I think." She got up and pulled down a few bolts from the shelves in plain colors.

I wasn't concerned with the colors of the dresses, so I said, "Just pick the two cheapest cottons."

"All right," the girl chirped. "I must admit I'm excited. I've not had an order for one of my mod-gowns. Let me take your measurements. I can start your dresses today. They don't take long; they're so much less fussy than the old styles. You'll have them before the end of the week." She gestured towards a curtain at the back of the shop. "You go back in the dressing room and unclothe. I'll be just a minute." She hesitated. "You do understand that this kind of dress is typically worn without a corset?"

I nodded. "That's a large part of the appeal."

"Very good, Mrs. Everett."

In the dressing room, I removed my dress, petticoats, and, after a moment, my chemise. The voluminous garment would not fit under the body skimming shape of the mod-dress.

"Are you ready?" called the shopgirl.

"Yes."

She came bustling in, carrying a handful of what looked like gloves. She held a pair out to me. "I designed these to go with the mod-dress," she said. "Look, they're long, to cover the arms, since the mod-dress has no sleeves."

I took the proffered gloves and studied them. A devious thought formed in my mind. The gloves were made of fine white goatskin. The stitching on them was very good—someone who knew how to work with leather made them.

"Did you make these yourself?" I asked the girl.

She smiled proudly. "I did. It took me a few attempts to get used to the leather—usually we make the gloves from moleskin— but the leather is so much more durable. And you know," she mused, "I like leather. There's something flash about it." She lifted her measuring tape. "Turn around. I'll just do all the standard measurements so we have them on file, then you won't have to be measured if you come back for anything else."

She went through her routine, moving the tape all over my body, around my waist, hips, ribs, neck, arms, along my back, and across my shoulders and down my arms. She was a professional; she made no commentary about my shape. She studied me, however. I looked a far cry from a standard lady beneath my clothes. My years of training with Gabriel had given me a rangy, mannish body—or so Maman had always said. Luckily my bloomers still disguised my upper legs, for those were by far the most distorted part of my anatomy—there was no help for it. Riding a velo as much as I did built up the thigh muscles.

"There," she said. "I've got what I need." She wrapped her measuring tape into a coil.

It's now or never, I thought. I instinctively trusted the shopgirl, and it wasn't just because she'd also been inspired by Lavinia Beau's pamphlets. I recognized in her a kindred fire, a rebellious nature, and a desire to be something more than what we were allowed. She seemed joyous in her rebellion, while I was only frustrated. I wanted to be like her.

"I have another request," I said in a whisper, leaning towards her in the confines of the dressing room.

She lifted her gaze. "Yes? What is it? Are you all right?" She seemed unnerved by my intensity.

I put a hand on her forearm, pulling her close so I could whisper, "It must be a secret," I said. "You won't tell anyone?"

"About the dresses?" she asked. "But if I use fabric from the store's stocks, I must note it for Miss Jackie's records."

"It's not about the dresses," I said. "I have something else I want you to make…something different. Could I—could I hire you to make me a custom item? Just you, alone, not through the store?"

"I suppose. But what is it? I'm dying of curiosity!"

"You swear you won't tell?" I demanded.

"Of course. I can keep a secret."

I took a deep breath. "I want a riding suit. The kind the jockeys wear for the velocipede races."

She stared at me for a few moments. "You ride!" she finally crowed.

I put a finger to my lips, gesturing towards the curtain that separated us from Letty.

She giggled. "This is so exciting! I'll need to do some research. Maybe it would better if I came to your house later this week to do the fittings for the dresses. I'll tell Miss Jackie that's what you prefer." She winked at me. "Shall we meet Mercenday, early? I have to be here at the shop by nine of the clock."

"I'll meet you at Everett House at eight then," I said.

I wrote down Everett's address for her after I'd dressed. The prospect of my secret project quite thrilled her. As I was leaving, she happily called, "My name's Maimie, ma'am. I'll see you Mercenday."

I'd forgotten to get receipts for the dresses. I hoped Everett would remain scarce until Mercenday, when I could ask Maimie to write doctored ones for me. Just as I'd hoped, he did not arrive for supper Moonday evening. I couldn't help but wonder if he was visiting his Lena, wherever he might have her tucked away now that I occupied the house.

•   •   •

The next morning I was so restless that I woke by five of the clock and performed my usual exercise routine on the carpet in my bedchamber. I missed riding. I decided to visit Gabriel at home. If I hurried I'd likely catch him before he took his velo to the practice track. I threw on a dress and scurried downstairs, sneaking out the back door to avoid Orson, and, by extension, being accompanied by Ben or the driver.

I felt delightfully illicit as I walked through Vreeland Park *alone*. My walk took me past the practice track. Already riders were racing, but I didn't have time to stop and watch. I jogged along as quickly as I dared, my heavy skirts obstructing each step. I thought longingly of mod-dresses and riding suits.

Finally I arrived at Escot House. To avoid Maman, who would be horrified by my arrival at the house unaccompanied, I snuck into the back courtyard. She hated that yard and avoided it at all costs. I pushed through the bushes and peered up at Gabriel's window. At this hour he'd be working on his trainer. I picked up a handful of pebbles and tossed one at the window, hitting it with a smart rap. I did it a few more times, in rapid succession, until Gabriel threw open the casement and leaned out, scowling.

"Emmy!" he snapped, looking down at me in the yard. "What are you doing here?"

I looked up pleadingly at my brother. He would know what I was asking with the look.

He rolled his eyes as he turned away from the window. "I'm coming," he hissed as he closed the window.

My brother knew me well. He came out the back door of the house loaded down with an armful of leather and the old grey velo that usually sat in the trainer in his bedroom. He set the velo down and shoved the riding clothes at me. "I know better than to argue with you," he said. "But you know this is very ill-advised. What if Mr. Everett catches you at it?"

I shrugged. "He won't, Gabriel. He's never around."

"I'll meet you out front in a few minutes," Gabriel said, stomping back into the house. *Maman must be out*, I thought, *or not up yet*. Gabriel had left me so I could change my clothes. I yanked up the old leather breeches—they were just a hair tight. They had been Gabriel's two years ago, when he was sixteen and very narrow-hipped, but it didn't matter—they were supposed to fit tight. I rolled the cuffs with practiced ease. I'd worn Gabriel's old practice clothes many times before, but I couldn't wait to have ones that fit me perfectly. I had bound up my breasts in tight linen as I'd dressed earlier, and now I pulled the leather jerkin over my rigging.

The shoes were too big, but I'd brought two extra handkerchiefs to wad in the toes so they wouldn't slip, and I'd worn my thickest pair of wool socks. I carefully folded up my dress, bloomers, and chemise to stow them behind one of the rotting planters in the yard.

As I wheeled Gabriel's old velo out front to meet him, he held out his old helmet, my altered gloves, and the ancient goggles I'd cracked in a fall I'd taken a few months ago when I'd hit a patch of wet leaves at the bottom of a hill.

Once we were strapped into our helmets with goggles drawn tight, we set out. We didn't need to talk about where to go—we'd done this so many times before. Our routine was to ride for a few miles along the outskirts of the city to warm up our legs at a relaxed pace, then kick up the heat as we returned to Vreeland Park just in time for the practice race that began at nine of the clock. We made a point of arriving just in the nick of time so that there would be no need for socializing with other jockeys before the race started. I always took the first race, with Gabriel acting as if he were my coach, holding my seat at the starting line. He'd have the second race, and so on, until we'd both done four races each.

It felt like heaven to ride; it had been too long! Gabriel and I fell into our natural rhythm; he took the lead on the way out of the city, and I rode in front on the way back in. Sometimes it felt as if Gabriel and I shared one body and one mind when we rode together. I listened to the sounds of his velo and breath as I matched him pedal for pedal. We were a perfect unit.

I was smiling as we pulled up to the Vreeland practice track. Several other jockeys milled around the starting line—four of them. The practice races were first come, first served. I slipped into the fifth starting spot as Gabriel stowed his bike in the track racks. Then he came to hold my seat as I assumed the starting position.

All our motions were smooth and practiced as we prepared. Just before the race began, a sixth rider pulled in beside me. I couldn't resist a sideways glance at my new neighbor.

I caught my breath and snapped my eyes straight ahead again, thankful for my goggles even if they were cracked. Vern Eddings hovered at my side, brushing his thick hair back before he put on his helmet.

"Escot," I heard him say to Gabriel behind me. I stared straight ahead, trying to focus on the track and the race ahead. "How are you?"

Gabriel mumbled a reply I couldn't hear. I felt rather than saw Eddings pull down his goggles and drop into his handles. Damn, I hadn't raced in too long, and to have an elite rider at my side unnerved me.

"Ready!" The caller cried. "Set!" The gunshot fired.

The designated pacer rode ahead, wearing the black flag on his back. The rest of us fell into line behind him in descending order from our starting positions. I was abnormally aware of Eddings behind me. I knew once the whistle blew he'd be a force to be reckoned with—most jockeys of any experience liked to position themselves in the pacing line either at the front or the back—both positions offered a little protection from the jostling and fighting that occurred in the thick of the pack. Even at the practice races, things could get pretty hot since the jockeys needed to practice fighting just as they needed to practice anything else. I had to be exceedingly careful about getting involved in fights.

Having Eddings behind me made me intensely anxious. He was known for cutthroat maneuvers, and I could tell that Gabriel and I had pricked his curiosity. Gabriel, a professional, first-year Arena jockey, would not normally be acting as coach rather than riding.

We completed our third lap. The pacer increased our speed, preparing for the fourth lap when he would depart the field. Then the race would truly begin.

I intensified my breathing: in through the nose, out through the mouth, making it rhythmic. As the lap line approached, the pacer faded off into the center of the track. The whistle blew to signal the end of the fourth lap.

I drove into my pedals as I felt the collective speed increase. Eddings made his move early, overtaking me on the second corner after the whistle. I pedaled furiously and dipped into his draft, moving with him up the outside of the line. We passed the two men in front of us, and then Eddings pressed on me, trying to get into a tighter position beside Number Three ahead of us. I let him in, not wanting to make contact. I shifted to his outside as he jostled the man he tailed. Number Three careened into chaos, luckily crashing inwards and away from me. Eddings closed in on Number Two, and we had two laps to go.

Eddings and his next mark bulleted ahead of the original leader, and I found myself neck and neck with Number One. Number One and I were well matched for sprint speed, or so it seemed. I gave up on Eddings and Number Two and concentrated on my battle with Number One. At the start of the final lap I kicked. So did my partner. He managed to pull ahead of me. I tried to pass him on the outside on the corner, but had to fall back as he moved to block me. I couldn't afford a contact. He swayed a little out of control, so I took advantage and swerved to his inside, where I had plenty of room to pass, since we'd gone up high on the track. Now I had the advantage, dropping to the line and holding tight to the edge of the blue. I pedaled. My legs and lungs burned. I loved it.

I crossed the line ahead of my rival, coming in third in my race.

Gabriel slapped me on the back after I took my post lap, helping me brake. As I clambered off the velo, he hissed, "Emmy, I think we should go."

"Why?" I demanded. I wanted my other three races. I followed Gabriel over to the racks where he pulled his velo free.

"I think Eddings suspects us. He's staring, and I'm—"

He cut off as Eddings strode over to us, removing his helmet and goggles. "Good ride," he said to me, though he couldn't possibly have seen much of it. "You have good control."

I took his hand because I could not imagine what else to do. I pumped it vigorously, hoping for a manly effect.

Gabriel looked panicked. "Do you have the time?" he asked Eddings for distraction.

The professional jockey waved his coach over. "Stoppard, what's the hour?"

The coach pulled out his timepiece. "Ten after,"

"Already?" Gabriel said. "Good lord, we have to meet someone in ten minutes! C'mon, we'd better go! Excuse us," he said to Eddings. "We're in quite a hurry."

I didn't need to be told twice. I was already in the saddle, pedaling. Gabriel and I spurred out the gate of the practice track and onto the path. Gabriel took the route through the park that led to the west gate. Just as we crossed through the gate, I heard the crunch of tyres on gravel behind me. I threw a glance over my shoulder.

I broke position and pedaled up beside Gabriel. "Eddings is following us," I hissed.

"Damnation," Gabriel said. "What should we do?"

I couldn't help it; I laughed. "Outride him, of course!"

very jockey has a different talent, and not every talent is equal. The Arena ran only one kind of velocipede race— the eight-lap, paced set called the keir. Some jockeys were perfectly suited to the keir, but others thrived with an endurance task or a time-trial. Some riders shone in a short, no-holds-barred sprint. The keir required speed, control, cunning, and recklessness, though not necessarily in that order.

A jockey's talents depend on many factors: training, body type, even personality. I'd always privately reflected that Gabriel's best skill, had it been cultivated, would have been an endurance race. He most loved the road-riding that we did, and he could ride at a good pace forever. Both of us had a body type suited to endurance; we were smaller, lighter, and less bulky in our musculatures than a pure sprinter. We also did more distance training than most Arena jockeys because riding out through the empty hills offered a more discreet alternative for me than the Vreeland practice track. We were both superb hill climbers.

With Eddings tailing us, Gabriel and I naturally fell into a pace that we used for our long ventures, riding tight together as we were accustomed. Eddings caught us quickly; he still rode at a sprint pace. He dropped in behind Gabriel and called, "A meeting, is it?"

Gabriel made no reply. We did not pick up our pace, though I could imagine Eddings chomping at the bit behind us. Our unspoken plan was to wear the sprint jockey down. He was much bulkier than we were; if we took him into the steep western hills, he'd fatigue.

We rode for about three kilometers on the flat valley road that cut through the western hills. Eddings, annoyed by our careful pace, took the lead, making us go faster. We let him. Eventually I overtook Eddings and turned a sharp right onto a little used road that climbed north towards the city of Basile. The hill started gradually, but would continue for several kilometers. Gabriel and I had ridden it many times. As we paced for the climb, Eddings again urged us to more speed by racing ahead. He wouldn't last long going that fast.

Racing velos have few gears—they are designed to be ridden on the unchanging track. The two or three gears on most velos offer enough different options for different races and tactics, but Gabriel's velos had two extra gears to accommodate hill climbing.

We burned by him even as the hill intensified. Eddings couldn't adjust for the ever-steepening climb.

"You runty little shits!" he hollered as we passed. "I'll catch you on the downhill."

I breathed too hard to laugh. We came to an intersection where we could turn right to descend on a different road back toward Seren, go straight and continue a longer climb, or head left into a more gradual ascent. I didn't even have to ask Gabriel—we continued on the steep route. With any luck, when Eddings arrived at the intersection he'd opt to go downhill back to Seren.

Gabriel and I finished the climb, despite the fact that it took us more than an hour. We made a brief rest at the top of the hill. Gabriel stepped down from his pedals and looked at the vista, smiling. He liked this kind of riding so much better than Arena races. "That felt good," he said. "Dusting the cocky bastard like that. I wish we had water."

"Why do you think he was so intent on chasing us? Do you think he suspects?" I couldn't help but be anxious after my encounter with Eddings and Everett at the track. "Everett sponsors him, you know."

Gabriel remounted his velo, and I followed suit. "You shouldn't come to the practice track anymore, Emmy. It's too risky. When you finish third in your race with finesse like that, people want to know who you are. You should have backed off." He got back into his saddle and took off down the hill.

The sun had passed its apex by the time we returned to Escot House. Gabriel went through the front door while I snuck around the back. I waited by the fence until Gabriel leaned out his bedroom window and gestured for me to go deeper into the courtyard. I changed in a hurry, leaving Gabriel's practice clothes in a folded pile atop the wooden bench near the back door. Gabriel would come fetch them and the practice velo that I'd leaned against the garden wall.

I needed to get back to Everett House. Orson was probably frantic at my long absence. I could only hope he would not say anything about it to my husband.

I jogged through Vreeland Park, but my legs were too tired and rubbery to move very fast. I would be wickedly sore tomorrow. I glanced up at the overhead sun—it must be nearly two of the clock. I winced. How would I explain where I'd been— *unescorted*—to Everett's staff?

I paused on the street before Everett House, looking up the front steps. Would it be better to brazen it out by going through the front door, or should I try to sneak in through the back? I hated to lie after what I'd promised Everett, yet I had no other choice. I decided to act as though I'd done nothing wrong. After all, they weren't used to the rules of conduct for a riesen. I marched up the front steps and turned the handle on the front door unsuccessfully. Feeling wretched, I rapped the knocker.

It took a few moments before Orson hauled open the door. "Mrs. Everett!" he cried. "We've been so anxious—"

"Is it Emmeline?" My husband's voice echoed through the foyer, cutting off the butler.

Everett tore down the grand staircase at full speed. "Where in the name of God have you been?"

I flinched away from him, but he managed to grab me by the upper arm. Dehydration and fatigue overset me. I fell forward, and Everett had to catch me.

"What's wrong with you? Are you ill? Has something awful happened? Are you wearing a corset?" He prodded at my torso to feel for boning.

I attempted to stand up, but again I was too dizzy. I leaned into Everett to hold myself up. "I could use a pitcher of water," I said, attempting to maintain my dignity.

Orson scurried away, I dearly hoped to bring me water. Everett swept my legs out from under me and carried me into the front parlor. He dumped me—none too gently—onto the aptly-named fainting couch. I reclined.

"Explain yourself," my husband barked.

"I didn't have breakfast, and I neglected to drink any water today," I muttered. It *had* been stupid, doing such a long ride without food or water.

Orson returned with an ewer of water and a glass. He poured for me, and I snatched the glass, gulping the contents without once setting it down. He poured again; I drained it again.

"Out," Everett snapped at Orson, who departed forthwith.

"Now," Everett said. "I want to know what happened. How did you get ill? Where have you been? When Orson told me you had disappeared I was worried sick!"

I sat up. "I—I felt lonely, so I visited Gabriel. We went to Vreeland Park for a while. Then he had to go, but I stayed at the park, as I wanted to walk. I was restless. I lost track of time." *Not entirely a lie*, I convinced myself.

My excuse of wandering unescorted through Vreeland Park for hours would have caused my mother an apoplexy of dismay. Everett only paced before the mantle. "You took no one with you when you went to Escot House? You told no one where you were going?"

I shrugged. "I went to see Gabriel," I explained, though of course Everett could not condone such behavior.

"I'm tempted to send for your brother and give him a piece of my mind! Leaving you alone at the park!"

"It's not Gabriel's fault. I wanted to be alone."

Everett grimaced. "But it isn't done! Ladies don't walk in the park alone—even I know that! And you went all the way to Escot House alone and back? That's far too great a distance to walk unchaperoned!"

I rolled my eyes. "Nothing happened. I just forgot to drink enough water."

"You look flushed," Everett complained. "You almost fainted again!"

"I walked briskly to get home," I said.

"Emmeline! Imagine my worry when Orson came to my business offices to tell me you were missing! I thought you'd left me." He slammed a hand on the mantle.

"I'm sorry," I murmured.

Everett shifted into a more business-like demeanor. "Why haven't you bought new dresses?" he demanded.

The sudden change of subject whiplashed me, and I couldn't answer for a moment. I had anticipated more scolding for my unescorted outing. Possibly even a punishment. "Oh!" I pulled myself together. "I ordered some yesterday, but they won't be ready until the end of the week. The shopgirl is coming here tomorrow to do a fitting."

"Have you the receipts?"

I shook my head. "She'll make them for me tomorrow."

"Very good. Are you satisfied? Have you need of anything else for the moment?"

Was he offering more money? I couldn't pass up the opportunity. "Well…the dresses were rather costly," I said. "I could not buy any shoes, or gloves, or hats or—or underthings."

"Why not put it on credit?" Everett said.

"I told you how I feel about that."

"And yet you must have these things, no?"

I scowled. "I can put them on credit if you insist. I don't understand why I cannot buy them in cash, though."

"Why are you so eager for my cash?" Everett said accusingly. I felt like he'd slapped me. Did he begrudge me the money? I had not thought such a wealthy man would be miserly.

"You are the one insisting I buy new clothes," I argued. "I can wear what I have, if it is such a burden to you. I have never had nice things, and I do not expect them. I understand you were forced into this. I don't expect you to squander your money on me."

"You want cash so you can give it to your scheming mother and support your brother. I do believe he's the only person you love."

Everett's outburst quite astonished me. I opened and closed my mouth as I attempted to organize my thoughts. "Is it so wrong to love my own brother? Gabriel understands me, and I understand him. We are like two halves that make a whole. I wish to make his life better. He hates it, you know, being a jockey. It doesn't suit him. I wish he didn't have to race. He doesn't want to, but he hasn't a choice in the matter."

"Poor Gabriel," Everett said dryly.

I stood up. "I think I would like to take a rest." I moved towards the door to escape.

"Sit down," said Everett. "We aren't finished. How much do you need?"

"How much?" A cascade of calculations tumbled through my head. A custom velo ran upwards of 50 marks, but I'd need more in order to get actual clothes so Everett wouldn't be suspicious,

and of course I *would* like to give a little money to Gabriel…
"Seventy-five marks," I said boldly, hoping he did not know the
usual cost of women's clothing.

"Seventy-five?" Everett exclaimed. "That's robbery, and you
know it." So he *did* know the cost of women's clothing. I shoved
the thought of his Lena out of my mind. "I'll give you 25."

"Thirty," I said, hoping to push him. I couldn't get a velo
with it, but I could begin to save for one.

"Very well," he capitulated. "I'll see that you have your thirty
marks by tomorrow morning. And in the future, please inform
us of your intentions of spending the day away from the house.
At least take Ben with you when you go out to walk. I know you
don't like it, but what will people think if they see you out alone?"

Feeling rather justly chastised, I retired to my room.

I t rained on Mercenday morning. I did my exercises in my bedroom and hurried down to have a cup of coffee before Maimie arrived for my fitting. Orson had not appeared yet, so I waited by the door to welcome the shopgirl, shifting my weight into my toes, glad no one could scold me for walking through the house barefoot.

Maimie arrived on time. I offered her coffee. "Oh, really?" she said, eyes wide. "I've never had it, but I've always wanted to try it."

I led her to the breakfast room and served her a cup, all the while eyeing the large satchel she'd brought. "Are my things in there?" I asked.

"Oh, yes," she said, grinning. "I think you'll like 'em."

"Bring your coffee," I said. "Let's go up to my room." I led the way.

First Maimie fitted my new dresses. Very gingerly she pressed a single finger into my bare upper arm. "You've got muscles," she said. "I wondered, when I measured you. It's from the riding, isn't it? The velocipede?"

"Yes," I replied.

"The strength suits you, and I think it looks mighty fine with the mod-dress. You look like a *modern* woman. Fresh. Different."

"Thank you." Her compliments startled me. I'd never known another woman to like muscles before. "The mod-dresses feel wonderful," I added as she pinned me into the second dress. "I can't wait to wear them. I think I'll order one more, in silk, for evenings. Can you do that?"

"Of course, ma'am. What color are you thinking?"

"You can call me Emmeline. And I'll take whatever color is cheapest. I'm on a budget."

Maimie glanced around my very fine bedchamber, a look of doubt on her face. "Your man keeps you on a budget yet he owns a place like this?" she said.

I frowned. "The amount he gives me would be generous if all I wanted to buy was dresses. But there's the other, and I must do *that* in secret." I lowered my voice. "I'm saving up to get a racing velo."

Maimie's eyes danced. "Oh, yes? And what will you do with that?"

I wriggled out of the pinned mod-dress. "I mean to race it in the Arena," I announced, as much to myself as Maimie.

She stared at me. "How?"

"I really don't know yet, Maimie. I just know I've got to try."

Maimie leaned over the satchel and pulled out the items I'd been longing to see. "I know what you mean," she mused. "I get like that about my clothes. I see what I want to make real clear in my head. I know it's too daring, too risky, too unrestrained. But I just have to make it. And then, once I've made it, I have to wear it, propriety be damned."

She held up a half-sewn pair of white leather breeches. "Now these, these are going to be something else. Breeches on a lady! I bet you it's all that we'll wear someday. Why, I've seen working girls who've split their dresses right up the middle and stitched 'em up to be like trousers. Then they can ride Rovers to work, see, and it saves them time so they can do other things. They can write or learn to draw, or take a course to be a typist, or even do something just for fun, to amuse themselves. The touring velos, they're changing the lives of girls like me, you know. I want to get one, but I haven't got the money just yet. But I have all kinds of ideas for ladies' riding clothes. You mark my words,

Mrs. Emmeline, we gals are coming up in the world, and we'll be riding velos when we do. Try them."

She tossed the breeches at me. I put them on and she came with her pins to fit them. "You want 'em real tight, I expect?"

"Yes." I wondered how she knew the jockeys wore their breeches tight to decrease air resistance. "Have you seen the velocipede races?" She occupied a class where she might have done—a working girl had more freedom to move in the world than a riesen.

She shrugged. "My sweetheart likes to go to the Arena. He takes me when he can get us a good seat. Only been twice, 'cause usually he hasn't got enough blunt to get *any* seat, only in the standing area, and he says I can't go in the standing area, as it's too rough for a woman. There now, how do they feel?"

The breeches felt superb, like a second skin. "Perfect."

"Okay, here's the jerkin. What do you do about your bosoms?"

"Oh," I said. "I should wrap them." I walked over to the armoire and took out my swathe of linen. I wrapped my chest tight, and then donned the jerkin. It too was white, and I suspected the leather was goatskin because of its softness. "I'll want a pair of gauntlets, too," I said.

"All right," Maimie said. "You want me to write you up a bill?"

"Yes, please," I said. "But could you not include the riding suit in the list, and just charge extra on the dresses to cover the cost of it?" I asked. "My husband will be checking the receipt."

She paused to think and then set to writing in the receipt book. Finally she tore out the page. I examined the receipt. She'd included the third dress in the write up, as well as a pair of gloves. All the dress prices were considerably higher than we'd discussed to accommodate the secret racing suit. I nodded. "Thank you."

Maimie beamed as she gathered up the newly-pinned clothes. "I'll have these all ready by tomorrow, and another two days after that for the third dress. You let me know when you get into the races, you hear? I'll have my man take me to see *that* race, and I won't have no for an answer! I'll suffer any elbow prods and gropes to watch a woman at the races. Fancy that," she added. "A woman in the races!"

By Venuday, I was going stir-crazy in the house. After my morning exercises I found Orson and told him I'd like the carriage to drop me off at my brother's house. This seemed to me the better approach than walking with Ben; at least I could leave the carriage and driver and have privacy once I arrived at Escot House. Orson summoned the carriage—not Everett's gas carriage, just the usual horse-drawn kind—and off I headed.

I arrived at half past eight. I knocked on the front door, and Maman answered. "Emmeline," she exclaimed, looking over my shoulder at the conveyance parked on the curb. "You should have sent a note that you were coming."

I wore my new racing duds under an ugly grey dress—the only piece of my wardrobe voluminous enough to accommodate the hidden clothes. In my pocket I'd stuffed the extra five marks I'd wheedled from Everett. I pulled out the billets, shoving them at my mother.

"What is this?" she asked, snatching the money without hesitation. Maman never saw a penny she didn't want, regardless of its source.

"I've an allowance," I told her. "I'm being frugal with my new clothing so there's some left over for you."

"Does Mr. Everett know?"

I shrugged, though I knew such a gesture would appall Maman. "I imagine he expects it."

She tucked the bills into her apron pocket. She looked weary. "Is it—is he—how is it for you, Emmy?" She sounded worried.

"It's fine," I said. "Everett's hardly ever home, just like Papan. I've only seen him on the weekends. He works all the time." I could not mention his mistress, but I saw by Maman's look that she suspected the existence of such a woman.

"Well, at least he's not being a nuisance," she remarked.

I snorted. "Is Gabriel about? I hoped he could take me walking in the park."

"He planned to go to the practice track today," she said. "He has a race on Sonneday."

"I'll go with him and watch the practice races," I said.

"I'm not sure that's wise, Emmeline. What would your husband think of such behavior?" Maman called as I climbed the stairs. I ignored her.

"No," Gabriel said, puffing atop his trainer as I walked into the room. "Don't even ask, Emmy."

I was already unlacing my dress to show him my new riding suit. I dropped the old grey dress on the ground and twirled proudly in front of my brother.

"Isn't it perfect? I finally have riding clothes that fit me!"

"It's indecent," Gabriel said. "You're crazy. How much did that cost, Emmy, and couldn't you have found something better to do with the money?"

"Like what, buy another dress? It's *my* money; I earned it by getting married. And this is what *I* wanted."

"You can't be thinking to come to the track with me today, Emmy. What if Eddings is there?"

"We'll ignore him."

"No."

"Please, Gabriel? It is so boring at Everett House. Everett's away all day; the servants do everything, and they give me dirty looks if I try to help around the house—I'm not even allowed to wash my own coffee cup. You know I've never been good for sitting and reading or doing needlepoint. I need this, Gabriel."

He sighed. "It's reckless, Emmy. I'd hate to see you shamed. Mr. Everett would be so angry, and you have to think of—"

"Damn Everett," I interrupted. The paintings of Lena in his bedroom swam before my eyes.

Gabriel stared at me. "Is he cruel, Emmy?"

"The whole marriage is a joke."

Gabriel blushed. "You mean he doesn't—"

I knew what he was getting at, but the topic embarrassed me, too. I shook my head and instead trained my best pleading look on my brother. He had no natural resistance to such wiles.

"Fine, you can come," Gabriel sighed. "But on your own head be it."

Eddings was nowhere to be seen at the practice track. Likely he was racing in the evening races tonight. Gabriel and I each had three good races on the practice course. I was thrilled to be riding in my new clothes. They made me feel bold. I showed in each race, though I had to hold myself back from winning in the last one, lest I call too much attention to myself as I had last time. It rankled that I had to sabotage myself, but for me the threat of too much notice posed as much of a risk as crashing.

Gabriel and I flew right past Everett's carriage as we rode home. I'd forgotten the driver waited out there for me. I hurriedly threw my dress on over my leathers and walked back through the house to exit from the front door. Fortunately Maman was busy in the kitchen. She would have commented on my disheveled state.

Back at Everett House I went upstairs and began to peel off my leathers when there was a knock at the bedchamber door. I had the tight breeches worked down to my ankles, but getting them off over my feet was a tricky operation.

"Yes?" I replied in a strained voice.

"It's me, Letty, ma'am," the maid's cheerful voice announced. "I've brought a fresh vase of flowers for your room."

I waddled into my dressing room and frantically worked at the pant legs. I heard the door open and Letty's footsteps moving through the room as I pulled at the stuck breeches.

"Are you all right, ma'am?" Just as I yanked the breeches off my foot, Letty peered through the dressing room doorway. I jumped about a foot off the ground. My breasts were still bound in my linen. Other than that, I wore nothing but my pantalettes.

I threw one of my new mod-dresses over my head. It billowed around me.

Letty stared at it. "Is that your new gown?" she asked. "I can see why you need to bind up the b'soms for it—it looks smoother that way. My, but it's scandalous different!"

The dress skimmed over my body, loose and light and airy, nothing like the heavy, restrictive traditional gown of a lady. "Maimie the shopgirl calls it a mod-dress," I said, using my foot to shove my breeches towards the baskets at the back of the dressing room.

"A mod-dress? Looks mighty comfortable. Don't take a corset, no?"

"It *is* comfortable, Letty. You should try one. It's so much easier to move."

The maid blushed. "Well now, I don't see as Mrs. Hoving would approve."

"At least for your days off, Letty." I turned to my cedar chest, lifting the top. I'd put my change from my bill from Maimie in there. "You go see Maimie," I told the maid. "Go and talk with her, see if she can make you up a mod-dress outside of the shop. She doesn't have to charge so much if it doesn't go through Jacquelenne." I handed Letty three marks.

She refused to even look at the money. "You know I can't take that."

"Letty, I want you to have a nice comfortable dress. How can you stand to work so hard in that heavy dress all laced up? You can't imagine how much better it is to be free to move. I insist."

Letty reached out with trembling fingers and took the proffered notes. "You want me to wear it around the house when I *work*?" she whispered.

"I want you to wear it whenever you want," I said. "I want you to dress to please yourself."

"You'll speak to Mrs. Hoving about it, so she don't go having all kinds of kittens over it? I need this job, ma'am."

"Yes, yes, I'll speak with her, and Mr. Everett, too."

Letty took the money and headed out in a daze. I finished dressing and hid my riding leathers deep in the clothing chest.

·   ·   ·

When I descended to the dining room for supper I found my husband already there, dressed in a tight-fitting black suit with tails. He examined the table, which had been set for four.

He looked up as I crept beyond the doorway, and his gaze froze on me, taking in my strange attire from head to foot. "What in God's name are you wearing?" he demanded.

I was glad indeed I'd had the good sense to don a petticoat beneath the mod-dress before coming down, otherwise I would have been standing there with my ankles exposed. Also, I was barefoot, but he couldn't see that because of my long petticoat.

I took my only recourse and behaved like a haughty lady. "It's one of my new dresses. They're all the rage. Called a mod-dress." I turned in a circle, arms outstretched.

"You look like—a—a *pixie*," Everett said. I couldn't tell from his voice if he was angry.

"I think that's part of the appeal," I invented. "It's a lighter style of dress. More *moveable*."

Everett catalogued the abnormal muscles in my arms, but he said nothing further about my attire, and he did not send me away to change with my cheeks burning from a slap, as Papan would have. "I invited two of my jockeys over for dinner," he said. "I hope you don't mind."

"Two *jockeys*?" Velo jockeys made unlikely dinner guests.

"They are the best sources of information about up and coming riders. I'm only looking to pick up one new one this season, and I want to discuss possibilities."

"Oh." Gabriel and my past due favor flitted through my mind, but I said nothing.

Everett offered his arm, and together we walked to the front entertaining parlor. I minced so that Everett would not see my bare feet. "Who is coming?" I asked as he settled me onto the settee.

"Vern and Marshall," Everett replied.

My stomach dropped. Vern? Did he mean Vern *Eddings?* Everett had been so irritable when he'd thought Eddings knew me—I rather imagined he'd invited Eddings on purpose just to see if I would squirm. And I would squirm—though not for the reasons Everett suspected.

The knocker sounded. Orson made his way to the front door, and a few moments later, the two jockeys arrived.

Everett made introductions. "Emmeline, you've met Vern Eddings at the park." *Did I detect an edge in my husband's voice?* "And this is Marshall Manton." He gestured to the taller of the two men. I recognized the name Manton. He was a well-known jockey, often placing, one of the strongest riders on the elite field. As I shook his hand, I could understand his success; he had the perfect build for a sprinter. His thighs bulged in his trousers; his shoulders and upper arms were lumpy beneath his jacket. Really, a man of such proportions should wear nothing but racing gear. Everything else made a mockery of his potent physique. His evening clothes must have felt almost as restrictive as a lady's costume. He shook my hand instead of kissing it. Manton was no prig.

But Eddings gave me a narrow-eyed look when I offered my hand to him. Instead of shaking it, he leaned over to kiss it, fawningly. "Mrs. Everett," he said. "How lovely to see you again."

He kept his silvery eyes cast down, but I feared he alluded to my day in the park. *Did he know?*

"Can I offer you drinks?" I said brightly. "A little prosecco, perhaps?" I had no idea if we even had the beverage in the house, but prosecco was the fashionable beverage of choice in mixed company.

Thankfully both men shook their heads. "We don't drink," explained Manton. "Alcohol can slow you down." I nodded.

Had these men been here before? They seemed very comfortable in Everett's house. I was an inexperienced hostess, and I felt inadequate to the job. If they had come to dinner before, it must have been Lena who played hostess. I'd bet she was the kind of woman who never had a hair out of place and always knew just what to say. She'd not have offered abstaining jockeys alcohol; she'd have known they did not imbibe. Such thoughts snuffed out my limited confidence. I curled my toes under the petticoat, praying they would not see that I wore no shoes.

"Who's in the lineup for the elite race this Sonneday?" Everett asked once everyone was seated. I had an urge to tuck my bare feet up onto the settee with me, but restrained myself.

Eddings answered, "Manton, of course. Smith, Parker, Lanner, me, Livingston, and Filips."

Everett leaned back and studied his two jockeys. "Do you have a strategy?" he asked.

Eddings scowled, but Manton replied, "The two to watch are Lanner and Livingston. Lanner, because he's got his vendetta with Vern, and Livingston, well, because he's Livingston. If I'm down the line from Vern, I could draft him at the bell."

Eddings didn't look too happy about this plan. It meant he'd be used as a tool to advance Manton's prospects. Eddings was devilishly competitive and did not like to sacrifice his own chances even for a good friend and co-sponsored racer.

"You know I won't interfere in your plans," Everett said. "Do what seems best. But we need to show in this race. One or the other of you, for the Everett Team name. A win would be nice, to follow up your last one." Everett gestured at Eddings.

Both jockeys nodded. I got the feeling they'd do whatever Everett asked of them. Having a rich sponsor was more important than individual glory.

Everett manipulated the seating so that Eddings and I ended up beside each other. I picked at my food, stirring it on my plate more than taking bites.

At first, neither Eddings nor I had anything to say to each other. The men were used to these dinners being masculine affairs. I threw a wrench into things, perhaps limiting the conversation to more conventional boundaries. I wished Everett had warned me. I would have happily remained upstairs.

"I raced against your brother the other day," Eddings finally attempted. "In a most unusual race."

"How do you mean?" I asked in a light voice.

"He assisted a young rider at the practice track—a good rider. The new kid came in third in our practice race. After the race, I went to find out about him—seemed like a rider to watch, if you know what I mean."

Everett leaned in to listen to our conversation.

Eddings went on, "Anyway, as soon as I approached, your brother and the kid took off, racing away from the track as if they were afraid of me."

I held very still as I asked, "Oh?"

"I gave pursuit, of course. I couldn't help myself. They took me on quite a chase, way up into the western hills, a punishing climb. Eventually they both beat me. I didn't know Escot had that kind of stamina."

"Gabriel's very good at longer distances," I murmured.

"You know who the kid was?" Eddings asked. "Someone who trains with your brother?"

I shook my head. "I wouldn't know. I'm sorry."

Eddings was aware of Everett's interest in our conversation. He turned to him and said, "You'd have liked this rider, Everett. He was a little too small, to be sure, but he had a real finesse about him, good control. And boy, he and Escot sure steamed me on that hill. They can really ride, the both of 'em."

"We'll have to have your brother over for a dinner, Emmeline, so I can ask him about his friend," Everett said.

I gave up on even stirring my food. I couldn't hold the fork without it rattling against the plate. For the rest of the meal, Everett and the two jockeys discussed the Arena riders on the field this season. I wished I could concentrate on what they were saying, but I was too desperately trying to suss out whether Everett's earlier statement meant he knew I was the "friend." I couldn't read the man at all.

I stood beside Everett in the hall as the jockeys departed. Again, Manton shook my hand, winking at me. "Make him take you to the races," he said to me. "I think a spirited girl like you might enjoy them."

As the men departed down the front stairs, Everett surprised me by wrapping an arm over my shoulders. "Would you like to see the Sonneday races?" he asked.

"Yes!" I leapt to affirm.

"Good," he said. "I'll take you."

"Thank you."

"Who is your brother's training partner?" Everett asked the question almost casually, even though it cast a direct aspersion upon my honesty, since I'd already claimed I did not know.

"I—I said I didn't know."

"Come now, Emmeline, I know you do. You and your brother are as thick as thieves. Who does he train with? You promised you would not lie to me." I did not fail to hear the leashed tension behind Everett's words.

"He trains alone, most of the time. Sometimes he rides out with Horace Barre and Manny Fitch."

"Eddings would recognize Horace Barre. Manny Fitch—Fitch—I don't know the name. Is he an Arena rider?"

I shook my head. "He didn't pass the trials."

"But is he good?" Everett asked. "Can he ride like Eddings said this boy rode?"

Everett's eagerness galled me. So did the fact that I could not tell him the true identity of the rider who incited such interest. I was so annoyed that I spit out the truth, though upon reflection I knew I should have maintained that the mystery rider was Manny. "No. Manny didn't pass the trial because his kilometer times weren't good enough. I hardly think he could have beaten Eddings in any forum."

Everett narrowed his eyes at me. "You seem to know very well how Eddings rides. And yet you say you did not meet him until that day at the park."

Had I been alone, I would have kicked the wall in frustration. "I don't know Eddings."

"So who was it then?" Everett demanded, switching back to his original interrogation. "Not Barre, not this Fitch boy—who are your brother's other friends?"

I threw up my hands in frustration. That Everett should have such interest in an unknown amateur rider was ridiculous. I could only think Eddings had found me out and revealed all to Everett, that my husband was playing with me as a cat plays with a mouse before he kills it.

Well, two can play, I thought. I would not declare my transgression until Everett confronted me. "I don't know! Ask Gabriel if you are so curious!" I turned to flee up the hall, but Everett caught my arm before I could escape.

"Emmeline," Everett said in a much quieter tone. "I'm sorry. Please don't run away. God, you make me feel that I've caught a fluttering, wild creature, and I don't know how to keep you. Forgive me for speaking so harshly."

I stilled my struggle to get away from him, all my suppositions about what he knew draining away as he spoke so gently. Reading Everett was like the mania of betting: not knowing his mind kept me swinging from one extreme to the other.

I cleared my throat. "I forgive you. But I cannot tell you anything more about Gabriel's friend."

"I just thought that since you and your brother are so close you would know. But you are correct. If I wish to know the mystery rider's identity I should ask your brother."

I stiffened. Gabriel would be no better at coming up with a false identity for the rider than I was. He'd be flummoxed to receive such a question, and I couldn't trust him to give a believable answer. I scrambled for a means to deter Everett. "Why do you care about an amateur rider anyway?" I said, giving the words my best haughty sneer. "I would think you'd look to established Arena riders to support."

"Everyone starts out as an amateur. I like to offer my support early if I can. For a worthy but financially-strapped jockey, it can make all the difference." He tugged on my arm. "Come sit in the garden with me. I promise I won't bore you with further racing talk."

Everett led me down the hall and out through the back door into the rear courtyard. It was a far sight more elaborate than the one at Escot House. This courtyard was well tended— the gardeners came every Moonday. A fountain with a mermaid spout burbled happily in the center of the patio, and apple trees lined the perimeter, interspersed with ceramic pots containing flowers.

Maman would have told me to make a proper conversation, but I couldn't think of anything to say. I still reeled from Everett's interrogation, bemused by this unexpected reprieve. I had worked myself up into a panic, thinking I had finally been discovered.

I headed towards the row of apple trees. More than once, while left alone at Everett House, I'd considered climbing them.

Everett followed a few paces behind me. "What are you doing?" he asked.

"I wanted to look at the apple trees," I said.

"There are no apples on them, yet." Everett grabbed one of the branches overhead and lifted his feet off the ground. The branch had been tempting me to do just the same.

"Are you going to climb the tree?" I asked, watching as Everett swung his legs forward and back like a young boy.

"Would it impress you?" he asked, swinging harder.

"No." Very little impressed me, and anything that did generally had to do with racing. "But I would like to see you ride a velo," I ventured.

Everett dropped from the branch. "You've seen me ride the touring velo at Vreeland Park," he said.

"I mean a racing velo," I said. "Like at the Arena."

"Would you?" he said. "And that's what it would take?" He stepped closer to where I stood with my hands clasped together in front of me.

I looked up at him. "What it would take?" I echoed.

"To impress you."

I shrugged. "You don't need to impress me, Everett."

"Maybe I want to." He lifted a hand and ran a finger down the side of my face; it made my spine shiver pleasantly. His finger arrived at the hollow below my throat. I held very still, uncertain how to react. He wanted something from me, but I did not understand what it was.

I fought the urge to squirm beneath his intense scrutiny. He did not move that hand—his finger crooked a little, sinking into the notch between my collarbones. He rolled his lip under his teeth.

I began to get an inkling that Everett was just as uncertain about how to treat me as I was about how to treat him. Everett did not know what to make of a wife like me.

The fact that Everett had hardly touched me since our wedding had not escaped me. Given Maman's obvious distress about the marital duty, I had expected to be put upon by my husband's wishes, but instead I felt denied. I took a deep breath. Never one to hesitate, I plunged into the discussion despite the embarrassing flush coloring my cheeks. "What do you want me to do?" I asked. "Maman said I should try to please you. I will try, but I don't know what you want to do to me."

Everett dropped his hand from my person as if I'd burned him. "I don't want it to be something I'm doing *to* you, Emmeline. I want us to do it *with* each other." He untwined my hands from each other and clasped them in his.

I frowned. "Does Lena do it *with* you?" The words were out of my mouth before I could catch them.

A wave of tension moved through Everett as he flung my hands back to my sides. "What?" he rasped. "Who told you about Lena?"

I could not answer, for I would not betray poor Letty. My question had destroyed the tender moment. Everett ran his hand through his hair and paced before the fountain. I cursed myself for an impulsive idiot.

"Who told you?" he demanded again.

I shook my head, staring at the ground in shame. "I should not have said anything."

I lifted my head, but my husband had already stalked out of the courtyard.

11

I did not see Everett the following day. It was Worship Day, and the servants were all away, so I remained alone in the house. I went to the library out of boredom, but found little to interest me. Everett's office adjoined the library. His desk was a big, heavy piece, made of expensive grenadilla just like his bedroom furniture.

I paused, hovering above the desk's wide expanse. Everett left no papers out on the desk, only a paperweight and a vase full of roses that sat on a lace doily, probably courtesy of Letty. She had an obsession with flowers—every room had arrangements that changed daily.

I bumped the roses, and petals fell. I turned away from the desk to resist the temptation to look through the drawers and discover more about my husband. I only knew he was rich, he sponsored riders, and he worked with Adon Voler. I pinched my face, trying to recall what Voler's company did. *Transport? Carriages?*

Something stuck out from behind the winged chair in the corner. It looked out of place, so I went to investigate. Hauling the thing out was difficult, for it was larger than I expected, and a little unwieldy. I retrieved a rectangular wooden frame, covered with a shredded canvas.

Then he cut up a bunch of the paintings he'd had done of 'er, slashed 'em, like, with a knife, I heard Letty say in her broad accent.

As I turned the painting so I could see the side with the image on it, I gasped. I'd seen the woman depicted in other paintings: the sensual, dark-haired woman from the portraits in Everett's bedchamber. *Lena.*

This had been a full-length portrait. She wore an old-fashioned red dress in heavy velvet, the kind of gown I'd expect an older woman to wear. Dark, heavy eyebrows gave her a rather imperious look. She smiled faintly, looking beyond the viewer, as if at someone behind my shoulder. *Everett, standing just behind the painter,* I thought.

I tucked the painting back into its corner and retreated back to the library to flop on the settee there. I admired the dainty little couch, upholstered in feminine beige brocade. Did Lena select it? "You're being ridiculous," I said aloud. "What did you expect out of a marriage forced on both parties?"

He promised he would be honest, a little voice said inside my head. *So did you,* I thought back. *But you haven't told him about the racing.*

I'd been entertaining a childish fantasy about my marriage. I'd wanted it to sweep me away, like a story in a fairy tale book. I'd wanted to believe Everett when he'd said I could have our marriage be however I wanted. But this was the reality: I was married to a man who loved someone else, while he was married to a selfish woman who loved *something* else. Maybe it was a fair trade. He could have his secret; I could have mine.

•   •   •

I padded downstairs with bare feet on Sonneday morning, finding it pleasant to wake to an empty house. Since Gabriel was racing today, I wondered if I might not sneak over to Escot House and snatch his practice velo. I couldn't race at the practice track without a companion to hold my velo at the starting line, but I could go for a ride in the hills.

I also had half a mind to try to find Maimie. She just might agree to dress up in men's clothing and hold my seat at the practice races. I only worried that she would look conspicuously female—she was much more buxom than I was.

I was so absorbed with my thoughts that I walked right into Everett as I entered the kitchen. He was coming out, coffee in hand, and the coffee sloshed out of his cup to dump down the front of my new mod-dress.

I screamed and lunged to move the hot, wet fabric away from my skin.

"Damn!" Everett cursed. He turned away and then returned with a cloth, pushing aside my hands and shoving the cloth down the front of my dress so that it rested between my skin and my clothing.

"Are you all right?" Everett asked. "Are you burned?"

I shook my head. "Not badly. I'll just—I'll just go upstairs and get a fresh dress."

"Go to my room," Everett said. "There's burn salve in my dressing room. I'll bring you a fresh gown there."

I was still so shocked by the pain on the front of my body that I obeyed without argument. In his room, I found the salve and applied it, holding the coffee-soaked dress away from my red skin. I wet a towel in the washbasin beside Everett's bed and spread the cool cloth over my angry skin. I tried, without success, to ignore the penetrating gaze of Lena, assessing me from her portrait above the bed.

Everett arrived carrying the crimson silk he'd given me. "Hurry, or we'll be late," he said, throwing the dress over the bed. He laid the black hat he'd purchased for me over it. "I couldn't find your gauntlettes," he said. "But I did find this." He waved a paper.

I froze. *He'd been snooping in my dressing room!* I knew where the gauntlettes were: in the same chest as my new riding leathers. At least he hadn't found them! I grabbed the paper. It was Maimie's receipt. I had forgotten to give it to him.

"What are all the numbers on the back of it?" Everett said, leaning to get a better look.

I flipped the receipt, concerned that Maimie might have jotted down something about the riding clothes there.

I exhaled with relief. "Those are just my measurements. She had to take them for the fitting."

"That's more measurements than we take to fit a velo. Does it hurt?" Everett pointed at my chest. "Let me have a look at it."

I tightened my arms over my chest. The last thing I wanted was Everett scrutinizing my body.

"Emmeline, let me see." Everett spoke to me in the voice he must use for business. It brooked no argument.

Awfully aware of Lena watching me from two directions, I let my arms fall. Everett peered down my bodice. I bit my lip and trained my eyes on the ceiling while he examined me. Luckily, Everett only looked with a doctorly, avuncular gaze. He clucked his tongue. "I'm afraid it might blister," he said in concern. "And it will certainly hurt for days. Are you sure you still wish to go?"

"Go where?" I asked blankly.

"The velocipede races, of course. We're going to the Arena today."

I brightened. I had thought after our argument that he would not take me. "You still mean to go?" I asked.

"I said I'd take you."

"I had thought—" I broke off when I saw the forbidding and rather pained expression on his face. My eyes flicked across the room to the painting of Lena.

Everett jerked as he realized where I stared. He put a hand on my shoulder, squeezing. "I'm sorry," he said. "I—"

"No," I said. "You don't need to apologize. I understand." I pushed away from him, grabbed the crimson dress, and darted into his dressing room.

It wasn't until I struggled to lace the dress that I felt the perusal. Everett stood in the doorway watching me. How long had he been there studying my body? What had he seen? Panic rolled through me as I thought of the incriminating shape of my thighs—only velo jockeys had such developed thighs, and Everett must know what a jockey's legs looked like. I could not meet his gaze. Instead, I smoothed the crimson silk that covered the evidence of my secret. I hoped he would think my muscles only more indication of my poverty before I married him. Perhaps he would imagine I'd gotten such legs by hauling laundry?

I turned away from his scrutiny, twisting to reach the back laces of the dress again.

"I'll do it," he said stepping in and grasping the ribbons. Everett laced the gown for me, leaving it a little loose so it would not lie tight on the burn.

"Thank you," I whispered.

"Emmeline," he began again. "I didn't want it to be like this between us," he said. "I made a mistake in not telling you about her. Can you forgive me?"

I shook my head. "There's nothing to forgive, Everett. I understand. I do. You can—you can do what you like. I wouldn't want to be a—a hindrance to your enjoyment of your own life."

"No!" he said, so vehemently I jerked away from him. "Don't think that, Emmeline, for it's not how I feel. You aren't a hindrance to anything. It's just that you've been a little unexpected."

"You have been a little unexpected for me, too, Everett," I said. "I'll go fetch my shoes and gauntlettes. I don't want to miss any of the races." I hastened towards the door.

"Cassius," Everett said from behind me. "Call me Cassius."

•   •   •

We pulled up at the Arena lot in record time. Everett, much to my pleasure, had driven like a madman to get us there on time. I'd watched his motions closely, and I began to understand how the gas carriage worked. He used the staff to change speeds and his feet to brake and accelerate. He concentrated as he drove, saying nothing, for which I was relieved. I had expected awkwardness in my marriage, though not quite of this variety. Two big secrets, circling around each other like wary dogs. I knew both secrets. That gave me an advantage.

We did not stop at the peddlers' carts or in the Arena lobby. Everett did not offer to let me make a bet. Instead he marched me through the wide space, rushing to get through the crowd of bodies and smoke. The atmosphere was charged with high spirits and anticipation. For the weekend races others besides the diehard track swaddies came. Working-class men milled about the atrium, smoking. Women—not riesen ladies, but those women like Maimie who had no social standing to ruin—gripped their escorts' arms and looked half excited and half fearful amidst the chaos of the Arena. I also saw the paid companions of wealthy men, the type of women I impersonated in my crimson dress. These women showed no fear. Some were not accompanied by a man at all, but flaunted themselves in dress and behavior as if they sought companionship. They had painted faces and wore scanty clothes that revealed the edges of their corsets on top and their ankles below. I tried not to stare.

Everett drove a line through the crowd with his fast walk, tugging me behind him. I kept looking over my shoulder to see the scantily-clad women mixing with the men. The women shocked my sheltered sensibilities.

Everett hurried me into his box, and I was again struck by what a good seat my husband commanded. "You must have one of the best boxes available," I commented, heading to the window to get a look at the track. Sweepers worked on the wood, pushing their brooms to clear it of debris.

"The best, I think." Everett hung his hat on the available hook and came to take mine.

"How much does it cost for the season?" I asked.

"A pretty penny and a significant investment in the Arena, too," my husband replied. Not for the first time, I wondered how Everett had come into so much money. Not via inheritance. I turned back to stare out the window. Everett rang the service bell.

"Would you like to have a coffee?" he called to me.

"Yes, please."

The sweepers finished their circuit of the track. The pacers then took a loop on it, surveying the ground and also loosening up their legs. None of the jockeys were out yet. I glanced into the stands below the box and was surprised to see such an assortment of people in them. Most of the women were of the disreputable type. A whole row of unaccompanied women had seats right beside the track. Everett nudged my arm and handed me my coffee.

He must have followed my glance to the women below, for he said, "Jockettes. They follow the elite racers around everywhere, hoping for a scrap of their attention."

"Why?" I wondered. I took a sip of my coffee and recoiled in surprise. I had not been expecting the burn of malt whisk.

Everett smiled at my reaction. "Malt coffee is the special at the Sonneday races," he commented, lifting his chin at my cup. "Do you mean, why do the women chase after the jockeys? I expect because they are enamored of the idea of catching a sponsored athlete. The sponsored jockeys make good money during the season, and most of them are willing to spend it on high living." He lifted his eyebrows. "In my day they used to say a jockey makes a better lover. Though I should think that pales in comparison to the monetary aspect. Your class is not alone in being mercenary to the core."

I blushed and looked away, wishing I hadn't asked. Is that what he thought of me then, that I was just like my mother, interested only in his money? I considered this interpretation. Was he really wrong? I had married him for the money. I scowled and stared down at the track. The Spug jockeys wheeled their velos up the ramp.

"Are you going to stand at the window through all the races again?" Everett asked, moving away. "I tell you, the view's no worse from the divan. In fact, it's rather better, depending on what you want to see. You get the side view better from here."

The divan, as he called it—not a Serenian word—was too cozy for my taste. If we both sat there, we could not avoid touching each other. Everett sat down, placing his coffee on the side table. He crossed one heel over the opposite knee and leaned back against the back of the sofa. I inched in his direction and perched at the edge of the settee, keeping my eyes trained on the wall of windows overlooking the track.

The Spug jockeys drew their start positions. I read through the list of names on the tote board, recognizing some from my last visit to the Arena. Each of the three tiers of racers had fourteen jockeys in it, and the lineups were rarely the same twice in a season.

"Shall we wager again?" Everett asked.

"Again? What will we wager this time?" I asked. I had not forgotten that he still owed me a favor.

"Hmmm. Since you have not yet claimed your favor, and I must admit that has given me anxiety—I'm never knowing when or how you might redeem it—I think we should be more specific about what we want this time."

"Will we wager on each race?" I asked.

"Why don't we have one wager to cover the three races? Whoever comes out best at the end of three wins the bet."

"All right. What do you want if you win?"

Everett remained silent for a moment, but then said, "I'd like to hear what you want, first."

I thought of the price of a racing velo. He'd only think me more mercenary if I asked directly for money. Yet I hated having to rely on Gabriel's approval in order to ride. The possibility of unfettered riding won out over my pride. "Bigger, regular allowance," I said.

Everett snorted. "How much and how often?" he snapped. My request did not surprise him, but it didn't please him, either.

I lost my nerve upon hearing the scorn in his voice. I depended upon his good graces. He could make my life comfortable, or he could make it hellish. Such is the life of a married Serenian woman. I cleared my throat. "I would leave that for you to decide."

Everett snorted again. "That's not the way to do it, my dear. You must be ruthless in business."

"Is that what you are?" I asked. "Ruthless?"

"When it comes to money, yes. Now, name your price."

"I'd like two marks a week." To me, it sounded a lot.

"That's it?" Everett asked. "I might have given you that already if you'd only asked for it. But now you've made it a matter of the outcome of the races."

"Sometimes asking for things is uncomfortable," I murmured. Everett did not hear what I said. I'd always hated having to ask. One of the worst things about my situation as a woman was having no recourse to get what I wanted for myself. I never had the freedom to simply make my choice and act—always, always, there were strings.

"All right. Two marks a week for you," Everett announced. "I shall have to ask more than I'd planned, if that's your bid." He paused. "What I want is more of your time. I have tried not to impose on you much, but I would like to claim your Venuday evenings. That is my bid."

"My—Venuday evenings?" I asked. "What do you want with them?"

"I'm not entirely sure. But I will want you to reserve that time for me. Shall we say from seven of the clock on?"

"Agreed," I said. I thought his wager silly. I would have given him any of my evenings gladly.

"Hurry and pick your winner for the Spug race. They're about to begin," Everett urged.

I scanned the tote board again. "Philips, Number Six," I said. I'd raced him at the practice track once or twice, before my marriage. He was a solid rider.

"I'm going with Bonatrice, Number Three," Everett said. "Shall we agree that the win goes to whoever picks the jockey that places highest?"

I nodded. Everett held out his right hand. I took it, and he shook, brusquely. Then we both focused all our attention on the track. My jockey rode a blue velo; Everett's rode a red.

The gunshot signaled the take off. The jockeys dropped into line from their starting positions.

"No one is ever bold early," Everett commented. "No one ever tries to get a different position off the starting line because—"

"It's considered bad form," I interrupted without thinking.

Everett's gaze slid sideways at me. "How did you know that?"

"Gabriel, of course. He says there is a whole—ah—etiquette— that governs the paced laps."

"It's a well-kept secret amongst the jockeys," he said. "The etiquette and honor in the races. It's a private matter amongst them."

"Of course," I said. "Their sponsors and the track swaddies just want them to win. But between jockeys, it's a different balancing act. You need friends as well as rivals on the track."

"Your brother told you such things?"

"We're twins. We'll always be close." My error struck me immediately. If Gabriel and I were so close, why hadn't he told me about his training partner?

Everett ignored the obvious implication gracefully. "I find I'm rather jealous," he murmured. "I did not have any siblings."

I made no reply, because the pacer moved off the track, and the heat of the race began. I focused all my attention on the two riders involved in our wager, red and blue. Everett's man made his move early, coming up from his third position to flank the leader. Philips, my racer, kept apace, but did not get involved in the front battle. Everett's jockey shouldered in between the first and second rider, while tracking another jockey moving up the outside. He slashed out to prevent the pass. Bonatrice was a dominating rider. He cut low towards the leader for the final lap, and both greased their wheels. I scowled as I searched for Philips, but he remained boxed in the back of the pack. Things didn't look good for my wager.

Bonatrice and the leader—riding white—surged evenly down the homestretch. The finish was so close I could not tell who crossed over first. The results came to the board slowly, for the officiators had to be consulted. Finally, they named the rider in white, Stewart, the winner.

Everett beamed. "One-zero, advantage me," he gloated. I flicked my gaze over him where he sat in the corner of the settee. As if he'd read my discomfort with the tight seating, he'd remained folded in the corner, avoiding any contact between us. My husband glowed with glory. I was no stranger to such emotions. I liked to win, too.

"Bonatrice played with fire," I commented. "If he'd been any rougher they should have disqualified him."

"Yes, yes, he's a spitfire. I like that about him."

"Are you going to sponsor him?"

"Can't. Voler's already claimed him, and he wants him all to himself. He's always a good bet, though. Places in almost every race he's in."

The tote board was being rearranged for the next race, Gabriel's race, the mid-tiers. I reflected again how unfortunate it was that the only money to be made from velo jockeying was in the Arena keir. The purer endeavors of velo sports suited Gabriel so much better than the keir. He raced the clock far better than he raced other riders. I sighed and read over the names of the other jockeys in Gabriel's group.

Part of me wanted to pick Gabriel this time, out of loyalty and hope, both. But the fact that Everett had won once put pressure on my next wager. I had to win the mid-tier in order to have a chance.

"You can pick first," Everett said. "Since you're at the disadvantage."

"Very gallant of you," I snapped, annoyed by his exultant behavior. "I'll go with Scorella."

"You're seeing the wisdom of a rough rider, I see," Everett said. "I'd better go with Horace Barre then."

As soon as Everett selected Horace, I wished I had. *Damn.* He was a skilled rider with unusual control, not to mention one of Gabriel's best friends.

The riders lined up at the line. Gabriel had the sixth wheel, while my rider, Scorella, had the fourth, riding a red velo. Barre rode white, and he started in the third wheel position.

The paced laps began. The coffee made me restless; the malt whisk made me giddy. I got up and leaned against the window. My restlessness would annoy Everett, but he deserved be to be annoyed after his little gloat session. Besides, I was too anxious to sit. I had never realized how difficult it would be to watch Gabriel race. His nerves were so apparent. I knew him so well I could sense his distress by the way he held his body on his velo. Poor Gabriel. Racing only got worse for him.

As the pacer left the track, the riders simply continued in formation, almost as if they hadn't noticed that the second half of the race, the real race, had begun. To my surprise, Gabriel made the first move. A yellow blur worked up the outside of the line, passing Scorella and the jockey in fifth wheel, easing in beside Barre.

Barre reacted, dropping back to give Gabriel space. I recalled that Horace was a big believer in having room to maneuver on the track. Scorella didn't like being passed by Gabriel. He pushed in beside Gabriel and Horace in an aggressive move that worried me as much as it pleased me. Barre moved back even further, allowing Gabriel and Scorella to inch up. Scorella kept the heat on and drove all the way up the outside into the second position. Gabriel settled into the fourth wheel position. The race progressed in the new formation.

As the gong rang to indicate the last lap and a half, Barre chased up the outside of the front pack of four, making good use of the space he had allowed himself. He came up Gabriel's outer flank, and Gabriel tried to match Barre's increased speed. Barre got in close; he knew how Gabriel hated that. Gabriel backed off, so Barre took advantage, passing him up and continuing his chase.

Barre had quite a kick; he was a fury moving up the line. He took the third- place rider on the outside, and then snuck beside Scorella into second wheel. I put both hands on the glass. A rider on an orange velo came up Gabriel's outside. The rider swerved as he tried to elbow past my brother, and he knocked into Gabriel. Gabriel and the orange jockey went down hard, crashing with so much velocity they both skidded across the track. Gabriel's legs twisted awfully beneath his velo as his helmet slammed into the track. I let out a choked breath. Other riders had crashed, too, but I watched my brother so intently that I could not see the rest of the field. I no longer cared who won, though I was vaguely aware of a rider crossing the finish line. Gabriel lay motionless on the track. Racing honor demanded that even if a rider fell, he get back up and cross the finish line. Gabriel did not move, which told me he *couldn't*.

"Emmeline!" Everett called from behind me as I threw open the door and dashed into the hall. I did not know how to get down to the track from the box. I looked right and then left, but I had no idea where each way would take me. I tore down to the betting lobby, flying down the stairs and through the slip-littered hall, following the sounds of cheers and shouts through a large double door, and found myself amidst the seats at track level. I pushed up the narrow aisle towards the track and leaned over the wall, ignoring the displeased grunts of those already there. Someone slapped a hand across my bottom, assuming by my attire that I was a courtesan.

"Don't you touch her!" I heard Everett yell from behind me. I scanned the track. Gabriel remained stuck in a sprawl beneath his velo. His coach leaned over him, working to free his feet from his pedals. I had to suppress the crazy urge to leap over the wall directly onto the track. If Gabriel hadn't tried to cross the finish line, something was horribly wrong.

I leaned as far over the wall as I dared and screamed, "Gabriel!" but he could not possibly hear me over the roar of the crowd.

An arm came around my waist, pulling me back from the wall. "Emmeline," Everett whispered urgently in my ear. "Come away. There's nothing you can do for him right now."

"He's injured!" I cried. "There's something really wrong. I can tell."

Everett guided me back up the narrow aisle. I could see we were attracting stares from the nearby audience, but I did not care. "Come back to the box. I'll send an Arena footman down to enquire about him. This is no place for you." Everett sounded so calm, so rational. I wanted to scream. But as I looked up, I saw upsetting expressions on the faces of the nearby crowd. The men had hungry looks, raking my body up and down, settling on the low-cut bodice of the dress. The women's looks were just as bad, the looks of annoyed rivals, as if I'd cut in on them in their own races. Their stares were as sharp as elbows on the track.

I let Everett lead me back to his box, where I collapsed onto the settee. They finally freed Gabriel from his velo, but they had to carry him off the track. That could mean any number of injuries. My hands clutched at my skirt so hard I almost tore it.

Everett spoke softly to a footman in the doorway. After the footman left, he came and sat beside me, taking one of my hands into both of his. I tried to pull free; I was embarrassed by how wet and sweaty my fingers had become.

"I've sent someone down," he said soothingly, trapping my hand. "He'll report back to us on Gabriel's condition."

I nodded and bit my lip. In retrospect, my impulsive reaction looked like the kind of hysterical display that men cited as an excuse to keep women away from the track. *Riesen women cannot help but get emotional about the crashes,* I could hear Papan say. *It's in their nature to be sensitive. It is better that they stay away from such scenes of excitement. Their temperaments are too delicate.*

I ground my teeth, annoyed with myself for acting without thinking. "I'm sorry," I hissed in Everett's direction.

"Sorry?" he asked, clutching my hand harder. "Whatever for?"

"For making such a display."

"He's your brother, Emmeline. You're worried for him. How could you not be?"

Once again, my husband's favorable interpretation of my behavior relieved me. The knock on the box's door sounded ominous. I leapt up and followed Everett as he opened it.

The footman gave a short bow. "The jockey Escot is unconscious. They said he hit his head, and there may be a problem with his knee. They won't know until he wakes."

"Thank you," Everett said. I pulled at my skirts frantically. Concussions were bad enough, but a serious knee injury could sideline Gabriel for the rest of the season. I gnawed at my lip. *Who was I kidding?* Gabriel would have a hard time returning to the Arena after this, no matter what. He was already too cautious a rider. This could destroy his mind for racing.

Everett closed the door on the footman and took my hand again. "Would you like to leave?" he asked.

I looked up into Everett's gaze. "What about the third race? What about our wager?"

Everett looked uncomfortable, shifting his weight from foot to foot. Finally he pointed out the window to the tote board. *First: Barre, #3; Second: Scorella, #4,* the sign read. All the other jockeys in the race had crashed. Everett had already won our bet. I crossed my arms over my chest. My upset for Gabriel far outweighed my frustration at losing the bet, but the one on top of the other was too much. Yet I refused to give into another hysterical urge. If I ran home with Everett, I'd only prove that women really were too delicate for the Arena.

"No. I want to stay and watch the final race."

As if to showcase the sloppiness in the mid-tier race, the elite jockeys ran one of the cleanest, tightest races I'd ever witnessed. They made no contact, no uncertain jostling, not even a scramble at the finish. Everett's two riders, Eddings and Manton, placed first and second, respectively, with Lanner showing a distant third. I tried to hold the memory of the clean race in my head rather than the chaos of the crash. Gabriel was not the only one who would have trouble recovering from the carnage of his race. I had been shocked, too, to witness how bad it could get.

Everett led me back to the gas carriage. As he helped me enter the vehicle, he said, "We'll go to Escot House later today to see how he fares."

"Thank you." I had planned to go alone, but I did not mind the idea of Everett's company.

12

Maimie's mod-dresses had excited me so much that I had ordered nothing more traditional. Maman would be horrified if I wore a mod-dress to visit Gabriel, so I opted for the dress I'd been married in, though I had a feeling Everett would disapprove. I hissed through my teeth as I dressed. Unbelievable what occupied my mind at a time like this—why did anyone give a damn what I wore? But they did. To Maman the mod-dress would reflect poorly upon her, signifying that she had failed to bring me up properly. But the shabbiness of my old dress would signify that Everett had not outfitted his new wife well, and that would reflect on him. My clothing signified little about *me*—as if I only existed as a reflection of others. My clothes wrote the story of what I was— owned by other people. I wanted to put on my riding leathers, but I shunted aside the reckless, rebellious urge.

Everett waited in the front foyer, hat in hands, pacing. He seemed almost as anxious about Gabriel as I was. A show of solidarity or another mistaken read on my part?

"Why are you wearing that old thing?" he demanded.

"I'm just going to see Gabriel," I snapped. "It doesn't matter what I wear. It's not a social call."

"Your mother will think I have not been generous," he argued.

I thought of the five marks I'd given her recently and her surprise to receive them. "She knows you've been generous enough, Everett," I said.

"You've given her money, have you?" he demanded as we walked out to the gas carriage.

"Is my allowance not mine to do with as I will?" I was in no mood for being treated like a child.

"I gave it to you so you could outfit yourself in a manner that befits my wife."

I yanked open the carriage door myself and slipped into my seat before Everett could assist me.

"I'll do what I want with it," I bit out. "I can make my own decisions. I'm not a *child*."

Everett entered on his side of the carriage and leaned across the seats to glare at me. "Then don't act like one," he said.

I wanted to ask him what he meant by that, but I did not know if that would qualify as "acting like a child," so I did not. I ground my teeth during the drive west towards Escot House. *How was I supposed to avoid acting like a child if everyone always treated me like one?*

As soon as we pulled up to the curb, I opened the door and flew up the front stairs of my old home. I rapped on the door, ignoring the broken knocker.

I heard Maman's footsteps shuffling along the hall from inside. "Emmy!" she said as she threw open the door. "Thank goodness you've come." Dark circles ringed her eyes.

"Maman! Is he very bad?" My nerves twitched as I wondered if the Arena footman had not given us a full report of Gabriel's injuries. Everett came up the steps behind me and wrapped an arm around my waist. Maman looked up at him and tried to put on her social mask to hide her worry.

"Mr. Everett," she murmured. "Forgive me; I have been distraught all day. I have nothing prepared for visitors."

I knew she meant she had been unable to buy any refreshments this week. She had no tea, no brandy, nothing to offer him.

"We just came to see how Gabriel fared," Everett said.

Maman's face fell. "He does very poorly."

"I'm going up to him." I pushed into the house past Maman. "I want to see him."

"He's upset, Emmeline," Maman cautioned. "He and your father had words."

I took the stairs two at a time up to Gabriel's bedroom. He was tucked into bed and looked rather bleary. His right leg sat elevated on a stack of pillows, and a block of ice squeezed his knee, attached with towels.

"Gabriel, how are you?"

He winced. "I busted my knee pretty badly."

"Did a doctor look at it? Did he say how long it would take to recover?"

Gabriel shook his head. "Maman cannot afford a doctor," he said. "Papan was in fine form today at the races. He lost a bucket of money."

"You must have a doctor." I pushed at the block of ice. His knee was definitely swollen. "I'll speak to Everett."

"Oh Emmy, you don't have to do that." Gabriel looked away from me, and he flushed across his cheekbones. "I hurt everywhere," he added, as if to better explain his tears. I knew they were not due to physical pain.

I patted his hand. "You'll feel better soon."

Gabriel scowled. "I doubt it. The worst is my head. I hit it so hard. My coach said I'm not allowed to sleep for long periods of time. Maman has to check on me every hour and wake me."

"Maybe you should come stay with me," I ventured.

"And how will your husband feel about that?" Gabriel asked.

"He's never home—"

"Of course he must come stay with us," Everett said from behind me. I had not heard him arrive—the man moved like a cat. "We'll take him in the carriage right now. I'll send for a doctor, too."

Gabriel writhed on his bed, displeased to accept Everett's charity. I put a hand on his arm to settle him. "You're coming. That's all there is to it." Gabriel knew the tone in my voice. He knew better than to argue with me.

Everett put his shoulder under one of Gabriel's arms and I put mine under the other. Together we managed to assist him down the stairs, past Maman at the door looking half-relieved and half-worried, and into the back seat of the gas carriage, where Gabriel could raise his bad knee up again.

Once at Everett House we got Gabriel situated in one of the spare bedrooms. I made up the bed while Everett helped my brother from the carriage to the house. I tucked a large pillow beneath Gabriel's knee and probed his swollen flesh with a finger. He winced when I touched it. "It's scraped up pretty bad," he said. "Maman gave me stitches where my velo hit my leg. And my whole right side is all burned up. I tore my leathers."

I nodded. I'd seen him skid along the track. Riding leathers were cut thin so they were not heavy, but this meant they tore easily. Gabriel's had ripped along his leg and torso. I'd seen it when I went down trackside. That meant Maman would have to figure out how to get him more racing leathers. If he'd had a sponsor, replacement leathers would have been provided. I thought of my new white leathers and wondered if they might fit Gabriel. But no, he was too large in the chest and shoulders, and his thighs were wider and longer than mine. They would never do.

"I'll get you new leathers," I said to Gabriel, continuing the conversation as if he had heard my thoughts. "I know a girl who can make them very well for cheaper than Voronson."

Gabriel shook his head. "Don't bother, Emmy. I'm done for the season."

"Wait until the doctor has a look at you—"

"I don't care what the doctor says," Gabriel said heatedly. "I'm done, Emmy. I can't do it anymore. I don't want to."

"Did you tell Papan that?" I asked. "Is that why you argued?"

"I told him I wouldn't race anymore. He gave me the usual guilt speech, 'After all we've done for you, after all the sacrifices your mother has made, and so on,' and I said, 'What about you making a sacrifice for once, Papan?' He told me he didn't know what I meant, and I said, 'Stop wasting all your money and time at the track!'"

"Oh Gabriel, you didn't," I gasped. The one thing that could rouse Papan's temper was commentary about his gambling. He believed every gentleman had the God-given right to bet at the Arena, and he would hear no judgment of it. Nothing sent him faster into a fury than to be criticized for "his pleasures."

"It's time he took responsibility for his family," Gabriel said darkly. "His gambling forced me to race when I never wanted to, and it forced you to marry when you didn't want to, Emmy. We've been sacrificed for his goddamned pleasures for too long. I won't do it anymore."

"Emmeline, let the doctor have a look at your brother now," Everett's voice said. I whirled around to stare at my husband in the doorway—creeping up on us again! The doctor in his black suit stood behind him. How long had they been standing there, listening to our personal conversation? I hurried up off the bed and darted around my husband into the corridor. The doctor went into the room with Gabriel, and Everett shut the door on them.

"Emmy," he said. I looked up, surprised that he would use the nickname to address me. "He calls you Emmy. Do you prefer it?"

I shrugged. "Maman only calls me that when she's upset or worried. It's Gabriel's name for me."

"Is what he said true?"

I did not reply, hoping to avert the annoyance I could see in Everett's eyes.

"Is it true, Emmeline? Were you forced to marry me by your family? Would you have called it off if they had let you?"

"It doesn't matter now, does it, Everett?" I hissed. I lifted my left hand and shook it at him. "They tied us up, and we said our vows. It's done."

"It matters to me."

I stalked away from him. "Thank you for sending for the doctor," I called over my shoulder as I descended the stairs.

Everett and the doctor came down almost a full hour later. I accosted the doctor in the foyer, asking, "What do you think? Will he be able to race again this season?" Though Gabriel had said he would not race even if he could, I couldn't imagine he'd continue to feel that way after the shock of the crash wore off.

The doctor exchanged a glance with Everett. "The boy will never race again," he said reluctantly. "I believe he's torn at least one ligament in his knee, maybe more, and those do not heal. He'll always lack strength in the leg. He'll ride again for pleasure, but not for profit."

My stomach dropped. It was as if the doctor had put his sentence on *me* as well as Gabriel. *Never race again. Never race again.* I stood, speechless in shock.

Everett took the doctor out the front door while I remained motionless in the foyer. If Gabriel couldn't race, what would he and Maman do for money? Without sponsorship, Gabriel didn't make much, but he *was* paid a stipend for every race he rode, and I knew Maman had been living on that money since the start of the season. My dread mounted as I considered the circumstances. If Gabriel couldn't race, that would mean *I'd* have to look after them. And I'd lost my wager with Everett, so I had no guarantee of a regular allowance.

I would have to try harder to please Everett. I didn't know how I'd manage it, since I'd made a muck of it so far, but I had no other option.

I returned to the room where Gabriel rested. He stared blankly at the ceiling. If he noticed me, he made no expression of it until I sat, and he said, without looking at me, "Did the doctor tell you?"

"That you can't race? I'm sorry, Gabriel."

"I'm not sorry. The more I think about it, the freer I feel, Emmy. I'm free of it. I don't have to do it anymore. You can't believe what a relief it is!"

My first reaction was envy, followed by the slow unfolding of a senseless, raging hopelessness: everything my brother had been given, he hadn't wanted. I wanted it all—but had none of it. I pressed my lips together to compose myself.

When I thought I could speak without a shaky voice, I said, "What will you and Maman do for money?" I sounded just like Maman.

Gabriel sighed and lifted his head from his pillow only to drop it again. "I don't know. Once I'm allowed up I can start looking for work."

"Gabriel, you're only eighteen. You haven't any schooling except for your Arena training. What will you do?" I did not mention that riesen men did not work unless they were fallen very low, because it seemed the Escot family was indeed that far gone.

"Maybe I can coach a young man who aspires to be a jockey."

"Without first proving yourself in the Arena? It's unlikely."

"But not unheard of. I'm not ready to hear all the reasons it won't work, Emmy. If you can't say nice things, go away."

I felt ashamed. But then, out of the stew of longing and despair and frustration in my mind, an idea came to me. "I could take your place. I could pretend to be *you* in the races, Gabriel, if you don't tell them your injury is so severe."

"You're crazy, Emmy." He patted my hand as if I were the one in need of comfort.

I snatched my hand away. "Why not, Gabriel? You know I'm as good a keir-racer as you are. Maybe better. We are of a similar size. If anyone notices, we can say you lost weight while you were injured. It's what, five or six more races until the season is out? Think about it, Gabriel. If I finish the season, you'll have a full record on your resume. If I finish it out well for you, it will be that much easier for you to get a coaching position."

"Emmy. You know it's impossible."

"No, it isn't! It would be easy. You'd have to stand in as the coach. We'd have to disguise you a little bit. We could say you fired your regular coach after the crash—"

"Emmy—"

"But with a hat and a haircut, no one will recognize you. You could wear shaded spectacles. Most in the Arena will have only seen you in your velo gear—"

"Emmy, look at me!" Gabriel spoke so sharply it finally cut me off. I did as he asked, looking searchingly up into the golden eyes that were so similar to my own. *We could easily pull this off,* I thought.

"If you crash, the ruse will be up, and everyone will know your secret," Gabriel said slowly, deliberately, as if speaking to a particularly wayward child whose misbehaviors had mounted past the point of cuteness. "You cannot risk it. Your marriage, your reputation—"

"Damn them!" I shouted. "I don't care about them! This is what I want, Gabriel. Look, you've finally gotten what you want—a nice restful life, is it? What about me? What about what I want? No one's ever asked me what I want!"

I dared to throw such a tantrum because Gabriel was my only audience. I had expected sympathy, but instead he shared a dark look with me and said, "No one gets what they want, Emmy, least of all someone like you, whose dreams are so far out of proportion to the possibilities! Only a child expects her dreams to become reality."

Then he closed his eyes in a clear dismissal. He did not want me in his sick room anymore.

Back in my own room, I was too distracted to do anything but pace and think. I stood by my window overlooking Vreeland Park. The race in progress was clearly for amateurs; in fact, it looked as if it consisted of people riding Rovers. I turned away. If Gabriel would only agree to my plan, I knew I could pull it off perfectly. I could race his yellow velo—I'd always wanted to—and wear my new leathers. I'd be careful and avoid crashes. I tapped my fingers on the glass of the window. Gabriel *had* to agree.

·   ·   ·

To my surprise, Everett waited downstairs to dine with me that evening. "I took a tray up to Gabriel," he said. "He was sleeping."

"Oh. I should go wake him. He's not supposed to sleep for long."

"I already did. Now he's eating. Sit, Emmeline, and have something yourself. You look quite exhausted."

I didn't feel exhausted. I'd been thinking furiously all afternoon about how to sway Gabriel to my plan. My cheeks were flushed, and I could not settle.

I picked at my food, and Everett noticed that little of my dinner actually went into my mouth. "Are you well, Emmeline?"

"I want to go check on Gabriel," I murmured, standing. I fled back upstairs.

Gabriel looked happily ensconced in the bed, pillows piled up behind him so he could sit up. He kept his leg elevated, so I leaned over his knee to examine it. The swelling was prominent. He'd truly injured himself.

"Have you come to your senses, then?" he asked me.

I did not reply.

"Look at that, Emmy," my brother said, pointing at his knee. "This could happen to you in a race, and then you'd be in a world of trouble. I know you want it, but think of the consequences."

"I'll be careful, Gabriel, so careful. You know I hardly ever fall. You know that's my talent, control."

He snorted. "I know *you*, Emmy. You're rarely careful once you're strapped onto a velo. And it's different in the Arena. You can be as careful as you please, and someone might knock you over just for spite."

"I won't get into it with anyone. It's a good plan, Gabriel," I argued. "It will help you get a job, and it will let me—"

"Oh, Emmy. I know that look in your eye, and it scares me. I'm not going to be able to talk you out of this, am I? Are you going to do it whether I agree or not?"

"One way or another, I'm going to do it."

Gabriel groaned.

I shook my head. "It's my chance, Gabriel. I've dreamed of such an opportunity my whole life. I won't just pass it up. You cannot expect that of me."

He wavered. His golden eyes grew more and more uncertain. Instead of pushing with more words, I waited in silence. I knew best how to convince him.

The sigh he gave sounded as if he bent metal in his soul. "All right," he moaned. "One race. I'm scheduled next Venuday in the evening races. I will tell them I want to try to race, that my knee isn't so bad. What will you tell Mr. Everett?"

I leapt from the bed and twirled in a circle. I wanted to scream with my excitement, but I feared such antics would attract Everett. "He's never home evenings during the week. I'll just tell everyone that I'm visiting Maman."

Venuday morning I rose early, unable to sleep because of my exhilaration. I did my stretches twice. The hours of waiting loomed before me; Gabriel and I agreed he'd set out for the Arena in a rented cab at four of the clock. I would ride the racing velo over at the same time. I tried to read, but I could not settle. I found Gabriel still asleep in the guest room upstairs. He was much better, but he would stay at Everett House through the end of the week, the better for my plan to come to fruition.

I brought my brother a tray with coffee and cinnamon buns. He wouldn't mind waking for that. He must have smelled the treats, for his eyes flew open upon my arrival. "Emmy," he said. "Good morning." He took one look at me and knew I was brimming over with excited tension. "You'd better try to relax," he advised. "You're too wound up."

I set the tray down on his lap. "I can't help it. I sent the footman over to Escot House to collect your velo and gear. I wish I had my own velo. Yours are always just a little big for me."

"I'll help you adjust it when it arrives," Gabriel offered. "You know you'll have to wear all the gear on your ride over."

"That's fine. Did you try on your disguise?" I had raided Everett's closet to find passé moleskin breeches and an old leather jacket for Gabriel to wear in his role as my "coach." While sneaking around in my husband's closet, I'd also found not one, not two, but three sets of utterly flash racing leathers, as well as riding boots, gauntlets, goggles, and a grenadilla helmet—all professional grade, all too big to be of use to me. Everett would have such things in his wardrobe only if he continued to ride. Where did he keep his velo? I wanted to see it.

"I think they will work," Gabriel said as he examined the purloined clothes. "But you know I'm the weakest link in the plan. People will wonder why Gabriel Escot hasn't got his regular coach."

"I've spread it about that you had a falling out with Kersey over whether or not you should race with your injuries. I told Everett and he told his jockeys. I'm sure everyone's heard the tale by now."

Gabriel frowned. "I suppose. But that may make all the jockeys target you in the race. They'll think you're weak and vulnerable."

"They'll think that after your fall, anyway, Gabriel. Stop fretting and eat your breakfast."

Gabriel and I whiled away the day together. It had been most enjoyable to have his company all week in lonely Everett House. I would miss him when he left after the weekend. At three of the clock, I went to my rooms to prepare. I stripped, bound my chest with linen, and squeezed into my white racing leathers. My hair was the trickiest thing to organize. Normally, I wore an old practice helmet with a fabric cap inside to hold my hair. Gabriel's racing helmet had no such cap. The day before, I'd written to Maimie asking her to make me something that could fit beneath the helmet and secure my hair, and she had quickly produced a perfect moleskin-lined leather cap. Luckily my blond hair was not thick; I could still fit into the helmet comfortably. Maimie had included a note saying she would attend the races this evening, *No matter what.*

Hair stuffed away, leather jerkin laced closed, breeches hauled over feet, I worked on Gabriel's too-large racing boots. I stuffed lamb's wool into the toes, for I thought it would be more comfortable than my usual socks or handkerchiefs. I drew on my goatskin gauntlets, courtesy of Maimie, and I was ready. I went for inspection by Gabriel.

"Nice leathers," he commented as he looked me over. "They're very soft." He rubbed the hem of my jerkin between his fingers, assessing. "That's really good leather. Thin yet durable."

"I told you I could have my friend make you new ones."

"I hope I won't need any," Gabriel retorted.

"I mean for when you're coaching. You'll have to ride if you coach, at least a little. You'll want leathers for that."

"Maybe."

"She'll give us a good price," I said.

Gabriel did not reply. Instead, he checked the fit of helmet and goggles, adjusting the straps on both to better suit my head. "There," he said when finished. "I think you're set. How do you feel?"

"Ready," I affirmed. "More than ready."

"You must have nerves of steel, Emmy. I'm a wreck."

I shook my head. "I had my nerves this morning. Now, I'm just ready." Despite the fact that his knee remained swollen, Gabriel moved well. His gait had only the faintest limp. "I'll meet you in the Arena parking lot?"

Gabriel nodded. We had agreed that it would be best if we entered the Arena together, since only Gabriel knew the pre-race protocol for the jockeys.

I beat the cab to the Arena, as I could weave in and out of the carriages, gas and horse-drawn alike, on the velo. Venuday evening races were the most popular at the Arena, and the traffic around the building confirmed that I'd be making my first-ever race in front of a large and eager crowd.

I used the ride to the Arena to reaccustom my body to the new velo. Gabriel had let me ride it once or twice at the practice track, and often in the trainer at home, so the new posture wasn't entirely foreign. It felt fantastic: smaller, lighter, and faster than what I usually rode. The handlebars were slammed as low as they could legally go, giving me the strongest and most aggressive possible body position for the race.

I loitered near the area where cabs dropped off their passengers in the Arena lot. When Gabriel stepped down from his cab, I darted over to his side. He wore a pair of Everett's shaded spectacles. My husband had a large collection of shaded spectacles—along with the best racing goggles I'd ever seen. I'd discovered them when searching his closet for Gabriel's costume. I had been tempted to steal a pair of those pricey goggles for my race, but caution held me back. Jockeys were fussy about their gear. What if I cracked the goggles, or what if Everett somehow noticed they'd been used? The stolen shades—also risky, but necessary—concealed Gabriel's face from those at the track who might know him. We were arriving as late as possible in order to decrease any interactions with others, though Gabriel said the jockeys and coaches never conversed with each other before races—etiquette did not permit it. After the race was when we would have to be careful.

My brother led me around the Arena to the jockeys' entrance on the west side. We passed through it, Gabriel striding ahead, me wheeling the yellow velo a few steps behind him. Gabriel gave curt, distancing nods to everyone we passed. I watched the ground.

Gabriel paused, surreptitiously pointing at a line of jockeys and velos off to the right. "Go get in line to get the velo checked," he said. "I'll meet back up with you over there." He pointed to a row of benches near the big double doors that must lead to the track itself. I nodded. The jockeys' area was quiet of voices, but loud in mechanical sounds. Some of the jockeys were making last-minute adjustments to their velos before being assessed for conformation. Cleats clacked loudly on the wooden floor. The crowd beyond the double doors murmured in an increasing crescendo.

Gabriel had carefully assessed the velo earlier in the day, and it passed the conformation check without incident. We reconvened. I placed the yellow velo in one of the authorized racks where approved ones could be stored before the races and took a seat with Gabriel on a bench. We had to wait through the Spug race before mine began. Part of me wished I could race with the Spugs for my first attempt, but I pushed that lily-livered thought away.

The Spugs lined up to make their entrance. When the doors opened, the roar of the Arena crowd blared through, almost deafening. I winced at the noise. The Spugs filed out, followed by their coaches. Then the doors closed, and the relative quiet was a relief.

"It's loud out there," I commented to Gabriel.

"Very," he said. "Try to ignore it, or it will seep into your soul and wreak havoc on your nerves."

We sat quietly as the Spugs raced. From back here, we could not see the race, but we did hear the changing sound wave of the crowd, rising and falling in reaction to the race's events. I kept my eyes closed, breathing almost musically to help tune out all the other sounds.

Gabriel patted my leg. "It's time," he whispered. "Are you all right?"

I nodded, but I found my voice had disappeared. Excitement coupled with anxiety washed through me. My head was as light as it had been when I wore the Whittler. I forced myself to stand and follow Gabriel into the line of mid-tier jockeys. We gave the others space. None of them had seen Gabriel since his accident, but even so no one spoke. Racing etiquette held.

I assessed the field of competitors I'd be facing. I'd seen three of them race in the Arena on my visits with Everett: Scorella, Barre, and Samuels. I did not recognize the others.

"Huston," Gabriel whispered, jerking his chin at the jockey just in front of me. "He's reckless, and he hasn't got good control to match his speed. Avoid him. And behind you is Borge. Don't look," he admonished as I turned my head. "He's big, heavy for a jockey. You'll want to avoid him, too. If he pushes on you, you'll go down."

I nodded. Then the double doors opened, and the deafening roar of the crowd washed over us. I followed Gabriel like an automaton. The din took on a cadence; the entire crowd clapped in unison as we marched along the tunnel that led onto the expanse of the track. Riding boots met glossy track; I had to adjust my steps to prevent a slip. Gabriel pulled up short, and I almost ran into him. The young man with the number bowl offered it to the jockeys in front of me. When the number man paused at my side, I didn't dare look at him as I jammed my hand in the glass bowl and grabbed the first bit of fabric that I touched.

"Two," I read aloud. Not a bad starting position. Gabriel took my number flag with shaking hands and pulled the two pieces of fabric apart. The first, he pinned to the back of my jersey. The other he attached to the side of the helmet on hooks made for that purpose.

We headed to the starting line. I checked my flanks: to my right, in third wheel position, stood Borge, the man Gabriel had suggested I avoid. Tough Scorella stood in first wheel position on my other side. Horace Barre had picked sixth wheel, a nice place for a jockey who had plenty of kick, and conveniently far from Gabriel and me. That was a relief—he was the jockey most likely to recognize us. I mounted the velo, and Gabriel bent to batten down the leather bindings that held my boots on the pedals. His white, drawn face told me he was experiencing nerves almost as bad as when he himself raced. I tried to give him a reassuring smile, but my cheeks felt frozen. I dropped down onto my handlebars, took a deep breath, and forced every worry from my mind. I stared down the shining wooden floor of the track and narrowed my vision into a small tunnel—straight ahead and few degrees to each side to monitor my neighbors. Scorella and Borge crouched atop their velos beside me, muscles tensed for firing. Their sharp breaths reminded me to modulate my own.

Gabriel steadied the velo from behind, holding me upright. His hands gave me strength. I raced not only for myself but also for *his* prospects.

The pacer approached in a whirring of wheels. I inhaled. The starting gun fired. My legs obeyed the signal and pumped. I dropped down into the line behind the pacer with the other jockeys. Beneath my wheels the slick track felt as slippery as ice. I matched the churn of Scorella's thighs in front of me to keep apace. These men were experts at maintaining the set pace; I had less experience, so I had to concentrate.

Like a herd animal, I was aware of the bodies behind me, particularly Borge's so near. The pace steadily increased with each lap we turned, until, going into the fourth lap, we moved at a brisk sprint of 50 kilometers per hour.

The pacer faded off the track into the center ring.

For several pedal strokes, everyone sped up at once. I matched the collective surge. Scorella checked his shoulder and cut wide to discourage passing. As he did so, I inched forward on his inside to maintain my position. I did not see it, but I felt a move coming from behind, a rush of air and energy. A cyclist in white flew past both Scorella and me on the turn. *Barre.* He had kicked early, well before the gong. He took the lead, a full velo-length ahead of Scorella.

Scorella matched Barre's taunt as the gong rang. I knew I had to stick with them, so I did, leaning down and sending my legs into an all-out frenzy. I stayed tight on Scorella's wheel. I sensed Borge behind me, but he was not yet trying to pass. He'd wait until the last moment.

On the homestretch headed toward the finish line, Borge kicked. First he tried to get on my inside, but I blocked him. Then he moved on my outside. Instead of blocking, I focused and kicked, calling forth every last drop of strength in my legs. Borge was gaining, but I managed to cross the line half a tyre in front of him.

I took my braking lap in shock. *Third place! I'd showed! Gabriel would be so pleased!* Gabriel waited for me near the last corner on the top end of the track, and I slowed further so he could come catch me. I was grinning; he was not.

He hurried to my side as I brought the velo to rest. "Damn it, Emmy," he hissed. "You could have used a little discretion!"

I cocked my head and wondered why he was fussing.

Gabriel continued, "People are going to want to talk to you afterwards with a performance like that! We'd better get out of here as quick as we can. Come on." He practically yanked me off the velo, grabbed it, and wheeled it quickly to the jockeys' double doors. I followed. My legs quivered like aspic, and the racing boots' slick soles made walking tricky.

Gabriel cut a swathe through the backstage excitement. Someone offered congratulations from afar: "Nice race, Escot! That injury did you wonders!"

"Way to get right back up on the velo!" called another voice. Gabriel and I ignored the congratulators.

The elite jockeys waited to enter the Arena. We passed right beside their line as we exited. One of the waiting jockeys caught my wrist. I gasped in surprise, a foolish, girlish sound I should have repressed.

"I know you," Eddings hissed, squeezing my wrist. "You're that kid who rides with Escot."

My heart almost stopped. I twisted my arm from his grip and whispered, "I don't now what you're talking about." I hurried after Gabriel, glad he hadn't seen Eddings hold me up. It would have made him frantic. But the knowledge that Eddings suspected us made my palms go clammy.

I didn't have time to consider what Eddings might do. Gabriel pushed through the crowd at the exit to the jockeys' area and forced our way outside. Then he turned to look at me. "You'd better get out of here," he said in a low voice.

"You, too," I countered. He glanced around, but there wouldn't be any cabs for rent until the end of the elite race.

"Damn," he said.

I gestured at the velo. "Can you ride?"

Gabriel nodded. "Lord, Emmy, this has to be the craziest thing we've ever done." He leaned over and unbound my feet from the pedals.

I took a seat on the saddle and brought my feet up to let Gabriel mount the velo pedals in front of me. We'd often ridden like this years ago; we still knew how to do it. Gabriel stood up on the pedals and rode, while I sat on the seat and balanced, hands clutching the front of the seat, legs dangling. We must have looked ridiculous, like two children on a professional's stolen velo.

Gabriel pedaled painfully all the way back to Escot House.

"Don't you want to come back to Everett House?" I asked.

He shook his head. "Your husband—ah—intimated that I would not be welcome there tonight."

"He did?" *How annoying!* When had Everett spoken with Gabriel, anyway? *I* hadn't seen my husband in days.

Gabriel and I stood in the back courtyard of Escot House. He pushed his velo against the crumbling stone wall, looking uncomfortable. "He hinted that you and he...had plans for the evening," he added.

I blinked at my brother in horror. I'd forgotten. I'd lost the wager and committed my Venuday evenings to Everett. My mouth gaped. I had to be back at Everett House and ready to entertain Everett by seven of the clock! "What time is it?"

Gabriel fumbled in the pocket of Everett's leather jacket and pulled out his timepiece. "Quarter past six," he said.

"I need the velo. I have to get home and get changed. I forgot he wanted to see me tonight!"

"Not the racing velo," Gabriel said. "Take my old one. If anyone sees it you can say I left it there after my time staying with you." He ran into the house and returned in a few moments with the other velo. I wasted no time mounting it and tearing out of the courtyard at a full sprint. I was exhausted, but anxiety gave me new energy to get home.

I flew past the front of Everett House and darted into the back alley to the mews where Everett kept his carriages, though I'd never been there. I was relieved to see the gas carriage was gone. That meant Everett had not yet returned. Had he gone to watch the Arena races? Had he seen my race?

Inside the mews, I peeked into one of the stalls and gasped. *Three* gorgeous racing velos hung from hooks on the rafters. Professional quality, each slightly different, only one of them conformation for the Arena—the others looked more modern. I wanted to look them over, even try one out, but I knew I had no time. *Later*, I promised myself. I stowed Gabriel's old velo in the same stall, along with riding boots, helmet, and goggles. Now I had to figure how to get back into the house in my riding leathers, for I had been so intent on my anticipation for the race that I had not thought of this aftermath at all—I had no other clothes.

The front door was not an option. Orson would be haunting it. The servants' entry at the side of the house was chancy as well, since they used that hall for getting back and forth from the kitchen and downstairs to the formal rooms above. That left the kitchen door or a window. As I departed the mews, I heard the characteristic rumble of a gas carriage. Despite my exhausted legs, I broke into a run towards the back courtyard. Everett's black carriage turned the corner into the alleyway. I scrabbled over the retaining wall into the back courtyard, lunged for the nearest window, and pushed frantically at the sash. It opened, and I heedlessly dove through it, recalling as I sprawled on a lovely Basilean carpet that someone could easily be in the room I'd just entered.

Thankfully, I'd fallen into Everett's empty library. I stood up, closed the window, and crept over to the closed door. Now I had to find my way upstairs to my bedchamber without being seen. I cracked the door and peered down the hall. To the left, at the end of the hall by the front door, Orson hovered, awaiting his master's return as I'd expected. He smoothed the lapels of his jacket. If I tried to exit the library now, he'd catch me. My only hope was to wait until he was distracted by Everett's imminent arrival, and dart upstairs then. I would be cutting it close if Everett came looking for me right away. It couldn't yet be seven of the clock, though. I waited, and each moment felt painfully long and desperate. Each breath that I heaved echoed loudly through the house. I was sure Orson would hear me.

Boot heels clacked up the front stairs. Orson turned to the door. Now was my moment. I slipped from the library, thankful for my sock feet, and raced up the stairs two at a time. I didn't dare look back over my shoulder or take a single breath. I kept expecting to hear Orson cry out, but I made it around the bend in the landing with no commotion. I wasn't safe yet. I threw open the door to my bedroom and thrust it closed behind me, leaping into my enormous dressing room. My hands fumbled on the leather laces of my breeches. Racing leathers were not easy to remove. After I pulled the breeches as low as I could get them in one swoop, I sat down and worked at the ankles, wiggling the pants in small increments to get the damned things off my feet, where they inevitably got stuck. Finally, I was free, and I tossed the breeches into the chest. Then I squeezed out of the equally difficult jersey, contorting to get it free from my shoulders. Just as I unwound the restricting linen on my chest, I heard my bedroom door creak. Frantic, I ripped the linen in two, tossing half of it onto the floor while the rest fell away from my chest. I stood naked in my dressing room as the door opened, and Everett said, "Emmeline, are you in here?"

The linen wafted over my ankles. I looked guiltily over my shoulder. Everett stood framed in the doorway in a black suit, hat in hand, looking uncharacteristically dashing.

I muffled a scream in the back of my throat. I had to be thankful I'd gotten out of my racing clothes, but it was hardly better to be caught *naked*. I looked around the dressing room desperately, but I must have left my robe on the bed earlier. I reached for my new silk mod-dress.

Everett did not step out of my closet's doorway. My hand wavered above the mod-dress. He stared at me. He must know my secret, for his gaze roved my body, taking in my legs with the veins popping from exertion, my firm abdomen, my arms with such scant flesh: all the musculature no riesen lady ought to have.

My hand yanked the dress from the hanger. I lifted it, though I knew the damage was already done. *Should I explain now?* I wondered. How angry would he be at my deception? I looked at his face. *Pretty angry.*

"Wait!" he rasped as I stuck my arms into the dress. I froze. The confrontation I dreaded was at hand.

Everett took two steps into the dressing room. I glared at him. He seemed taken aback by the look and inched back.

"I'm sorry," he said. "I've disturbed your privacy." But he did not leave.

"I'm trying to dress," I said, hoping I sounded suitably haughty, though all I could hear was the tremble in my voice.

"I wish you wouldn't."

His words startled me so much that I dropped the mod-dress. Everett moved faster than I could, bending and snatching up the dress. He ran it through his hands, the thin, delicate fabric narrowing to fit easily through his circled thumb and finger. The gesture transfixed me. I stared at the silk as it ran through the aperture he'd formed with his hand, nearly forgetting my own vulnerable nakedness.

He watched me watching him. "Emmeline," he whispered. "Can I—would it be too much to ask—"

His words snapped me from my immobility. I held out a hand for the dress. "Of course not," I said, "I'll dress and be ready in a moment."

I met his eyes. His look was one of dissatisfaction that I did not comprehend. He made no move to give over the dress, so I reached for it. He snatched the gown away, turned and threw it out the closet's door.

"What—" I began. Everett grabbed me, snaking an arm around my waist, restraining me. The wool of his coat was itchy against my bare skin.

With his one arm still holding me, he lifted his other hand to my cheek and turned my face up to his. "Do you hate me?" he asked. "Do you hate me because of Lena?"

His mistress's name caused my concerns to overwhelm me: my nakedness, my fear that Everett would see from my body the secret I had hidden, my embarrassment about his mistress. Fatigue from my race made my legs waver.

"No," I said, trying to wriggle away from him. He kept me clasped against him.

"Thank God," he said. And then he did it again, the thing I'd been longing for in the most secret corner of my heart: he kissed me. He tasted strongly of smoke and malt whisk. His hand tightened on the back of my head; his fingers pulled in my hair. I did not care if he was intoxicated. I wanted this.

But I had no strength left in me; I'd given it all to the Arena race. Despite their telltale muscles, my legs could no longer hold me up. I hung from his hands, and he supported me.

He carried me out of the closet and placed me on my bed. Then he pulled away and unbuttoned his jacket, shrugging it off and letting it fall to the floor. I sat watching him, curious what he was doing. After his jacket, he removed his white shirt. He glanced down at himself, and looked annoyed for a moment. I followed his gaze and saw that it rested on his boots.

"Shall I help you with them?" I asked, pointing at the boots. They would be almost impossible for him to remove on his own.

"Do you mind?" he said, looking down at me beneath eyelashes I'd never noticed were so dense and long.

I slipped from the bed as he sat down, coming to my knees to grasp one boot with both hands. I pulled. The boot did not budge. I couldn't help myself; I giggled. It reminded me of trying to get out of my racing leathers. Everett smiled, too. "Ridiculous, isn't it?" he said. It struck me that in some ways men were just as tightly laced as women.

I bore down again, and the boot came sliding off in one go. I felt the trick in the angle and removed the other shoe easily. Everett tucked his hands beneath my arms and pulled me into his lap.

This intimacy with Everett was almost too much to layer atop my heightened emotions after the race. I would break apart into a hundred pieces. And yet for the first time in my life I believed that someone *saw* me: Everett admired me for what I truly was, not for how I had forced myself to be. He had not chastised me for my muscles; in fact he touched them with an interest bordering on longing.

I wished I weren't so exhausted. I wanted to fully participate in what Everett showed me, but I was so tired that I could only let him lead. I followed willingly, and perhaps it was better that I was so passive, closer to what he expected.

"I want...I want..." I murmured, too tired to find words.

"I'll give you anything you want," Everett replied as he lowered me onto the bed. "Haven't you seen that yet?"

•   •   •

I woke with one cheek pressed into Everett's arm. My entire body ached. Yesterday's extremes had tired me in a way I had never experienced. I lifted my head to study my husband's sleeping face. I remained concerned over the secret I kept from him, and the one he had tried to keep from me. He would not be forgiving about my racing, of that I was certain. No one would be. Even Gabriel was losing his patience; only a lifetime of loyalty prevented him from curbing my inappropriate behaviors, but the strain was beginning to tighten him. Everett, so touchy about matters of honesty, would never understand. He did not know me as my brother did.

I pushed the bed covers from my body. I had been a little frightened by what Everett had wanted of me last night—it hurt at first—but Everett had given me silent reassurance with his hands. Now I understood that this act, this joining of our bodies, was the "duty" to which my mother had referred. She had spoken of it distastefully, as something to be endured. I had not found it so, though it came as no surprise that Maman and I had differing opinions. I could only imagine that Maman disliked the physicality, but to me, I felt as if my corset had been unlaced, and I could finally breathe.

I left Everett sleeping and went to make coffee. It was Worship Day, so the servants were off. I poured two cups of coffee and went back to my room. Everett blinked sleepily as I arrived.

Everett's face wrinkled with confusion. He did not know where he was or who I was. "Coffee?" I asked, lifting the cup.

"Emmeline," he said, placing me. His lapse of memory estranged me. "Are you all right?" he asked, not meeting my eyes. "I'm sorry. I think—I must have behaved very badly last night."

I placed the coffee in his hands. "Badly?" I said. "I wouldn't know, as I've nothing to compare it to."

"Oh my God," he said. "I'm a perfect lout."

Having my husband react to our first intimacy with such chagrin was lowering. "Was I very...bumbling?" I asked. I couldn't think of a better word.

"Was *I*?" he retorted. "I can't remember a thing. I was that drunk. I should not have come to you. I should not even have driven home. I drank too much. The races were so exciting! Your brother came in third, by the way, riding on his injury. Amazing."

Balancing my coffee, I slipped under the covers beside him. His eyes widened. I took a sip and watched him.

"You don't seem so upset," he said. "My head is killing me." He pulled at one of his eyebrows.

I shook my head. "I'm not upset. Why would I be?"

Everett tried to smile. "I think I could have been more gentle. How do you...feel?"

"I am happy," I said. I was more than happy. I was elated. I was delirious. I'd *raced* in the Arena yesterday.

14

Everett had invited Eddings and Manton to dinner again. He held me by the waist as we greeted the two men, and I basked in his touch, despite the fact that Eddings still made me nervous.

Everett served our guests lemonade and took a malt whisk for himself. I opted for lemonade. Like the two jockeys, I'd be racing on Moonday evening. We sat in the entertaining parlor, and the first thing Manton said was, "Escot had a good race on Venuday. Did you see it?"

Everett nodded. "Very unexpected. I thought his injury would set him back more. The doctor told me he would never race again."

"Physically, he looked recovered, though he surely lost some weight," commented Manton. "But his kick was stronger than ever."

I squirmed in my seat. I *had* always had a better kick than Gabriel.

"His control was good, too." Everett said. "He rode bolder than I've ever seen. He was confident. Unlike himself in every way."

I flushed. I couldn't help it.

"I don't think it was him," Eddings interjected.

"What do you mean?" Everett asked sharply as my stomach lurched.

"I told you how I saw Escot at the track with some fast kid a while back?" Eddings said. "I watched that race and saw what you saw. The only similarity that rider had to Escot was that he was a runt, too. But in style and tactics—nothing like Escot. I went to speak with him after the race, and I'm almost certain it was the kid I saw with Escot that day at the practice course. Escot told me the kid was his cousin when I asked him about it a few days after they dusted me in the hills. I think Escot got his cousin to take his place in the races."

"That's ridiculous!" I snapped. Had they forgotten that they were speaking of my brother? "Gabriel wouldn't do something like that. Nor would my cousin." I thought of Randal Finchley, my only male cousin, Helen's older brother, and had to repress a most inopportune giggle. He didn't have a race-worthy bone in his body, the stuffy old swaddy.

Eddings turned to me. "If that kid wasn't your cousin, who was he? He had the same eyes as you and your brother."

"You don't know Gabriel," I argued. "He's always had potential. I've known it. He struggled with anxiety, it being his first year at the Arena. Maybe now that he's crashed, now that the worst has happened, he's gotten over his nerves. Now he can race as he has always been capable of racing."

"Very loyal of you," Eddings said. "I still don't buy it. I got a good look at that jockey, and I don't think it was Escot. He was smaller than your brother, for one thing."

"He's due to race again Moonday, is he not?" Everett said mildly. "Perhaps you'd like to come to the Arena and observe for yourself, Emmy? You'd recognize your brother in a heartbeat."

Said heartbeat pounded in my chest. I retreated into convention. "No. I don't think so," I said coldly. "The Arena is no place for a lady."

Everett narrowed his eyes. "You liked it well enough the other times I took you."

"Not after Gabriel crashed," I invented. That Everett admitted to taking me to the Arena in front of his jockeys surprised me. Jockeys did not have the same stringent social rules as people of my class, but even so.

Everett looked taken aback. "I'm sorry," he said. "I forgot you had witnessed the crash. Of course that would repel you."

I exhaled. I thought I was safe, but Eddings pressed, "Who's your cousin? I want to know his name."

I couldn't give him Randal's name; he'd never ridden a velo in his life and he wasn't the sort to lie for us. I got the feeling Eddings asked about him because he meant to interview him. "I think you are too forward," I snapped, rising from my seat. "I find your commentary rude. Gabriel is my brother! He would not seek another to replace him in the races!" With that, I stomped from the parlor, shaken. *Damn Eddings. Why was he so interested in Gabriel's performance, anyway?*

A soft knock roused me. I'd fallen asleep on my bed without changing from my dinner clothes. I got up and went to the door. I figured Letty had come to warm my sheets or bank the fire, but it was Everett, still in his dinner jacket, looking severe.

"May I come in?" he asked.

I allowed the door wider and stepped aside so he could enter.

"I wish you could have curbed your temper before our guests," Everett said as he closed the door behind him.

I glowered and regretted giving him entry. I stalked back to my bed, sat down, and crossed my arms over my chest. "I didn't like what they said about Gabriel."

"You are too sensitive about him—"

"He's my brother!"

"I know, but you weren't there to see what we saw. He was utterly transformed, and I cannot help but agree with Eddings; he raced like a different person. But you over-reacted to our idle speculation and conjecture."

Maybe I had over-reacted, but I had good reason for my response. My own anxiety fueled my distress. I couldn't quell it. "You don't understand," I hissed. "Gabriel is—he's my best friend.

I couldn't listen to them say such things about him. He's the only person who really understands me." He knew my secret.

Everett stared at me. "*I* want to understand you." He approached as if to sit beside me on the bed and then seemed to think better of it.

"You can't," I blurted. "You won't."

An irritated look crossed Everett's face. "Why not? If your brother can know you, why can't I? Is it because I'm not riesen?"

His words stymied me. Such a thought had never occurred to me. Did he really think me such a snob? My mouth opened, but I got no words out before my husband stalked towards the door and said, "I know you have secrets, Emmeline. I only hope some day you'll share them with me. I might not be of your class, but I am your husband." He left.

I bit my knuckles and wondered how I could fix matters between us. I should have kept my mouth shut, right from the beginning. I should have never argued with Eddings. No good riesen lady would have done it, and it had likely only roused his suspicions more. Once again, I'd alienated Everett.

•　　　•　　　•

I didn't see Everett at all on Sonneday, so the entire house was empty and echoing. Though tempted to visit Gabriel at Escot House, I feared if I gave him the opportunity, he'd force me to back out of the Moonday race. It wasn't just the risk of being caught that displeased him—he hadn't liked that I'd performed so well. I would never have thought Gabriel could be envious of *me*, but I had recognized that particular look of displeasure on his face after the race. I'd been trying to conceal just such a look on my own face for years.

I remained at Everett House and pondered all the possible places Everett might have gone on a day when he could have no business to do. At first, I tried to think positive thoughts: he'd gone to his office in Seren's financial district or to an East End club with his friends. Maybe he'd even taken one of his lovely racing velos for a ride. But I'd noticed his tendency to disappear after our spats, and I couldn't help but think he'd probably gone to *Lena*.

I plopped down on the settee in the library and examined my emotions. I had no good reason for such jealousy. I'd entered this marriage knowing my husband's hand had been forced. I could not blame him for loving elsewhere. Lena and Everett had a history I could not touch. That thought only made me more jealous.

I was competitive by nature. I wanted to be first in Everett's affections just as I wanted to be first in any race. And yet in a velocipede race, the parameters of the competition were clear to me—all I had to do was go the fastest and strategize around the various players on the field. But in this circumstance, I did not know how to compete. Every time I thought to let down a wall, every time I grew comfortable beside Everett, it seemed I set him into a sulk just by being myself. I sighed. I should have known better. Maman had forever been warning me that my behavior would not be tolerated in a marriage. How many times had she said, *"Emmeline, you mustn't speak like that. It's childish and unbecoming. Keep such thoughts to yourself, or better yet, don't think them at all!"*

My restlessness and curiosity got the better of me. Or perhaps I succumbed to temptation. I went out to the mews to get a better look at Everett's racing velos. To my surprise, one of them was missing—he *had* gone for a ride. Crippling, irrational envy caused me to smack a fist into the side of the stall, stinging my hand. I stared up at the two remaining velos hanging from the rafters. I wanted to take one down and ride, viciously, but I feared I'd get caught. Gabriel's practice velo still leaned up against the wall. I wondered what Everett had made of it. After a thorough investigation of the remaining velos—they had so many modifications from the Arena standard that I could not anticipate how they would feel to ride except *fast*—I returned to the house. I needed to settle myself before my next race.

·   ·   ·

After ogling Everett's lovely velos, I itched to race on Moonday. Gabriel and I planned to meet at four of the clock at Escot House. I had to force myself to wait for the hour, knowing I'd face an argument with Gabriel that I didn't want if I gave him any time for lengthy conversation. He wasn't going to want me to race; I knew it already, before I even saw him. When I did see him, waiting in the back courtyard, I took one look at his face and braced myself.

"Emmy, I'm going to withdraw from the race," he announced as soon as he saw me slipping through the gate with his old velo.

"Oh no, Gabriel!" I cried. "You can't. It's too late, and I'm ready—"

"It's too risky. I can't condone it. Have you imagined how upset Maman will be if we are discovered? Have you thought about what would happen to *you*? You'd end up a perfect pariah, or worse. Emmy, you'd be utterly ruined. Mr. Everett would surely forsake you, and then where would we be? This is folly on a grand scale, and I cannot let it continue." Gabriel sounded uncharacteristically firm.

"Just one more race, Gabriel," I wheedled in my best pleading voice. It had worked on him thousands of times. "Just tonight, and then I promise, you can withdraw from the season. Think how it will improve your chances of a coaching position if I do well tonight. What if I could show again?"

Gabriel scowled. I might have rubbed my success too much into his face. "You know it will improve your situation, Gabriel." I spoke the truth, little as he liked to admit it. It would be better for him if I finished out the season entirely. One good race proved little. Anyone could have a lucky race. He needed at least two to have any sort of reputation upon which to build a coaching career. Gabriel would be an excellent coach—he'd never shown anything but calm patience to my endless demands for information and advice.

"Damnation, Emmy," he muttered. "How do you always talk me into things I know are wrong?"

I patted his arm. "Just because I always choose the risky route doesn't mean it's the wrong one." When we planned long rides in the hills, I always picked the more precarious but direct route; Gabriel always argued for the safer but slower roads. I usually won.

"Just tonight," my brother whispered as he turned to go fetch his yellow velo.

•   •   •

The Arena was in its usual state of bustle and hustle before the races began. Gabriel and I were careful to stay against the back wall in the shadows to avoid other jockeys. I worried. I wore my helmet, goggles, and leathers, and it was truly difficult to tell one jockey from another once we were decked out in racing apparel, but Gabriel was vulnerable.

We stayed out of everyone's way until the time came for the mid-tiers to enter the Arena. The crowd's collective gaze raised the hairs on my arms as we lined up and marched through the wide doors, but I kept my focus. I had far less stage fright than I'd had the first time. Now that I knew what to expect, I was eager to race again.

I drew the sixth wheel position, so I'd be at the back of the pack during the paced laps. Gabriel offered no advice, but I could see on his face that he thought my position a bad omen. Jockeys were a very superstitious lot; most wore a good luck charm or had a ritual they performed before each race. Gabriel's friend

Horace Barre, who had drawn the second wheel starting position, wore a blue ribbon around his upper arm. Huston, directly in front of me, had what appeared to be a wedding binding ribbon wrapped about his wrist, shimmering gold in the sun. Many married jockeys wore their binding ribbons for luck. I wished I had mine, but I couldn't have worn it anyway, since Gabriel was not married.

My race contained Mabry, a famous jockey I'd never raced against, as well as others I recognized: Barre, Borge, Huston, and Samuels. Scorella had the race off, and for that I was glad. He was one of the fiercest competitors in the mid-tier group.

I mounted Gabriel's velo as he held it for me. He leaned close, I thought to whisper something encouraging in my ear, but instead he said, "This is it, Emmy. After this, no more. I can't take the tension of it any better when it's you out here. In fact, I think it might be worse."

"Shut up," I told him. "I'm strategizing."

Gabriel snorted. "Get out from behind as quick as you can. If you let them get too far ahead you'll never be able to catch them and cut through the pack. Sixth wheel position means you'll need at least two separate kicks."

I nodded, thankful for the coaching. I'd do as he advised. Now that I had a plan, I mounted my seat and curled my body into position. Nothing ever felt so right to me as settling onto a racing velo. My body came home with an animal satisfaction, instinctual and natural. *How could they deny me this?* I was born to ride. I knew it, had always known it. Nothing compared.

When the gun fired, my muscles unfurled in their trained habits. I went through the paced laps in a comfortable clockwork that composed my mind, dropping into that place where I could hold my concentration finely but not tightly. I heard the sound of my breath; I absorbed information from my eyes and reacted. I imagined this was how most animals lived—in the moment, without concern for past or future.

The pacer left the track, and I galvanized, driving up the outside of the line in a daring move. I almost reached the front before anyone checked me. Horace Barre sliced sideways and tried to slow my progress, but he moved a second too late. I took the first wheel position with Horace pinched in close behind me. I could sense movements in the pack, but I did not check my shoulder for details. Barre stayed glued to my back wheel as we entered the final two laps. The pack tightened. Though Barre rode dangerously close, I trusted his precision. He was a careful rider. I was not so confident in the others. As the bell rang, Barre squeezed me. He knew Gabriel's style; he expected me to back off under such dicey conditions. I did not, kicking again just as Horace did. The rest of the pack did the same. This race would be close all the way to the end.

Horace Barre gunned past me. I reined in my thoughts and just *pedaled*. I stuck to his wheel even as I felt another jockey moving on my outside flank. I sallied to maintain my position for the final stretch, leaning low to keep second place as we crossed the finish line.

My performance left me annoyed. I didn't like a race where I held onto my position by such a small thread, but I had no time to celebrate or be disgruntled, for Gabriel hurried to my side as I slowed the velo, reaching to hold the seat to get me down.

"C'mon, c'mon," he hissed. "The faster we get out of there, the better." He and I had made a sound plan for our escape this time. We rushed off the track well ahead of the other jockeys in the mid-tier race. No one would look for us if the other jockeys were still on the track. We dashed through the doors into the waiting area.

Once off the track, we both broke into full sprints. Gabriel had parked the practice velo just outside the entrance to the jockeys' waiting area. We made a beeline for the door.

"Escot!" A voice called out. Both Gabriel and I checked our shoulders, but did not stop our run.

Damn! It was Eddings! At least this time Eddings couldn't follow us. He had a race to ride.

Just to the side of the jockey's waiting area, a posh little sitting balcony had been arranged for privileged fans or sponsors to converse with the jockeys and coaches after the races. I happened to glance up at the sitting area as Gabriel and I rushed by.

What I saw almost stopped me in my tracks.

Everett sat upon a settee with a dark-haired woman in his lap. She wore a gown of rich red, black lace gauntlettes *just like mine*, and a jaunty red and black striped cap with a veil that covered most of her face. Even so, I recognized her. *Lena, the woman from the paintings.* My heart stuttered. Gabriel pulled up short as he recognized Everett. I threw out a hand as I passed him, yanking on him to keep moving.

"Escot," Everett said, gently removing the woman from his lap. Gabriel was about to answer him. I could tell it upset my brother to see Everett here so brazenly with another woman, and he'd forgotten he wasn't supposed to answer to his name at all—he wasn't supposed to be Escot!

I hauled on Gabriel's arm before he could do anything foolish. "Now!" I cried, hoping to snap my brother into awareness. Good grief, he was wearing Everett's own clothes! We had to get out of the Arena, fast.

Gabriel and I rushed outside. I launched myself onto the yellow velo that I'd been wheeling, and Gabriel mounted the one he'd parked outside.

"Did you *see* him, Emmy?" Gabriel snarled as he pedaled to my side. "The gall! I could just kill him! Flaunting her in the jockeys' area like that!"

"Shhh! Gabriel!" We weren't far enough away from the Arena yet. I glanced behind us to be sure no one had followed us out.

Eddings stood just outside the jockey's entrance, helmet and goggles in hand. He wore a wide smirk on his face, and I couldn't help but think he must have heard Gabriel call me by my nickname.

Fear fueled my ride back to Escot House with Gabriel. We pulled into the back courtyard, and I leapt from the velo. The childish part of me wanted to throw the thing against the wall and scream.

"He heard us! Gabriel, he heard you call me Emmy!"

"W—what? Who heard? Everett? I don't think so—"

"Eddings!" I screamed. "Eddings heard! He followed us out of the Arena. He heard, and now he'll tell Everett! Oh my God, what am I going to do?"

I collapsed against a tree trunk, squatting to catch my breath. Gabriel panted and leaned into the wall at my side.

"Maybe he didn't hear," he protested. "I didn't say it very loud."

"I saw the look on his face. He heard."

"Well…we'll have to get to him before he can tell Everett," Gabriel said. "There has to be a way we can convince him to stay quiet. Most jockeys want more money. We're a pretty mercenary bunch."

"Everett's his sponsor," I said glumly.

"Damnation." Gabriel heaved himself off the wall and paced. I pressed a hand to my head to quell the ache behind my eyes. I was in trouble. Eddings didn't strike me as the type to keep quiet. He'd be outraged that a woman had pushed into the races. He'd be even more indignant that I'd performed well in them.

"I'm going back to the track," Gabriel announced. "I'll find him after his race and talk with him." He made to pick up his practice velo from where he'd left it.

"At least change your clothes and ride your own velo," I said, gesturing at the yellow racing one I'd almost tried to ruin. "Don't give me away to everyone just yet."

Gabriel flushed and turned towards the house, presumably to go change. While he was gone, I pulled my dress over my racing leathers. My stomach roiled; the thought of returning to Everett House terrified me. What if Eddings had gone directly back in and told Everett what he'd heard? Everett had been *right there.*

But Everett had been with Lena. Not even Eddings would be so uncouth as to bring up a man's wife in front of his mistress. *Would he?* I took small comfort from the idea that Lena might have saved me from immediate exposure.

Gabriel returned wearing a pair of loose breeches and a pullover sweater, the kind of attire a jockey might throw on after a race to cover up his leathers.

"I'm coming with you," I said.

"Absolutely not," Gabriel barked.

I reached for the practice velo. I'd already tied my dress up while I waited. "I have to speak with him, too, Gabriel. It's *my* disaster. I can convince him it's in his best interest to stay quiet."

"Emmy, it's not a good idea."

"I don't care. I have nothing to lose—if he exposes me, I'm ruined anyway." I tried not to care. Indeed I thought I didn't care, except for what it would do to Maman. She'd never live down the fact that she'd raised the girl who dared to enter the velocipede races.

"I think you should let me handle this," Gabriel said.

"I can't, Gabriel. Besides, I know Eddings. He comes to dinner at Everett House. I think I can soften him. He has to understand what it will do to me if he lets my secret out—what it will do to Everett. He'll listen to me. I'm the wife of his sponsor."

Gabriel capitulated. "All right then. Let's hurry."

We parked the velos a ways off from the Arena, for already we could see the crowd spilling from the building. The elite race had finished. I untied and smoothed down my dress, the loose-fitting grey one I always wore over my leathers. Maman had once admonished me never to wear it out of the house. I would have preferred to be looking a little finer for this confrontation. A picture of Lena in her bright fashionable clothing flashed through my mind.

Gabriel took my arm and led me back towards the jockeys' entrance. A crowd had gathered outside the door, fans eager to catch a glimpse of the elite jockeys or get an autograph on a jersey. A group of the track women that Everett had pointed out to me recognized Gabriel as we passed, and they cooed and screamed.

Gabriel and I pushed through them to the guard manning the door.

"Escot," the man said in surprise. "I heard you'd left after your race."

"Just to go and change," Gabriel said. "This is my sister. She'd like to go in and meet a few of the elite jockeys." Gabriel's request was utterly unorthodox, but the doorman made no comment, simply gesturing us inside.

Gabriel's hand tightened on mine. "Let me do the talking," he advised. We both knew I'd be unlikely to stick to that advice. Gabriel gestured me towards the stairs that led to the sitting balcony for the sponsors and guests of the jockeys. "Wait up there," he said. "I'm sure Everett's gone back to his box. I'll go find Eddings."

I climbed the stairs and pushed aside the curtain that covered the entrance to the sitting area. To my dismay, a red skirt peeked from the back of the high-backed settee directly in front of me. I gasped and turned to flee. Everett and Lena were still here!

But I was too late. "Emmeline?" I heard the question from behind me and slowly turned, my cheeks blazing. I reflected, just briefly, how perfect the day of my first race had been—the very pinnacle of my life. And how awful this day of my second race was turning out!

"What are you doing here?" My husband sounded more than a little angry.

"Gabriel brought me." I chanced a glance at the back of the settee, and saw that all evidence of the red dress had been tucked away. *Everett had hidden her in the sofa!*

"You and your damned brother," he muttered. "This is no place for you! What could Gabriel be thinking?" Despite the increasing desperation of my situation, part of me wanted to rail at Everett: why could one woman be taken here—Lena—but not another—me? The senseless injustice of everything felt like a burden I could no longer shoulder.

Any moment now Gabriel would arrive with Eddings in tow and my world would come crashing down.

"It was just a lark," I muttered at Everett. "I'm leaving now." I pushed aside the curtain and darted back down the stairs, praying Lena's presence would prevent Everett from following me.

I ran into the thick of the jockeys and coaches milling below, cringing at the loud clack that my riding boots made on the floor. I'd forgotten I still wore them—had Everett seen? I bit my lip, scanning for Gabriel and Eddings. I finally saw them, furrowed in a corner, speaking heatedly.

I rushed over to them. Eddings saw me first and glared at me. Gabriel gave me a tired look, his unspoken wish that I could have stayed away visible in his wince.

"Well, well," said Eddings. "If it isn't the *manotte* freak herself." Manotte was a Serenian insult for a woman who behaved too much like a man.

I recoiled. Well, he clearly knew I'd raced. And disapproved wholeheartedly. This would be the response I faced from most everyone if my secret got out.

In all the years I'd dreamed of racing in the Arena as a professional jockey, I'd never quite understood how others would see my dreams if I shared them. To me, my aspirations were as natural as breathing; racing was all I'd ever wanted. It had never mattered to me that others would see it as unnatural, improper, or even immoral. I'd discounted their opinions as stupid and unsympathetic, closed-minded. But now Eddings gave me a taste of what it truly meant to have broken out from the box. Serenian society would not forgive me my transgression.

"I'm not a freak," I hissed.

"What other female does what you do?" Eddings said. "I call it freakish. Unnatural."

"Listen, Eddings," Gabriel began. "You cannot tell anyone. She's my sister—"

"More importantly, I'm your sponsor's wife." I had to use the main leverage I had over the man.

"All the more reason I should tell him what you've been up to," Eddings said. He had a nasty edge to his voice.

"Then I'll tell him he shouldn't sponsor a man who'd spread such rumors," I retorted. My temper ranged beyond my control already.

"I wonder which of us Everett will listen to?" Eddings pondered.

"Which of who, about what?" My husband's voice said from behind me. Once again, he'd crept up without any sound.

Eddings grinned evilly. "I've discovered who's been taking Escot's place in the races."

Everett turned an enquiring look on Gabriel. My brother stiffened. "I'm not discussing this with you," he asserted to Everett. And then he turned from my husband, giving him a direct cut. He stalked away from our little gathering with all the haughty presence of a riesen gentleman. Gabriel rarely used his birthright status to such effect. I stared after him, oddly pleased. *What had gotten into him?*

I chanced a peek at Everett and understood. Lurking behind Everett stood Lena in her red dress. She looked irritated and also uncertain, but she sidled up to Everett's side and laced her arm through his.

Everett jumped about a foot into the air. He hadn't known she'd approached. He tried to shake her off. I debated whether to follow Gabriel. But if I did, I knew Eddings would immediately reveal my secret.

I turned to Eddings for one final plea. "Please, don't do this."

The man lifted his nose at me. Lena had distracted Everett; he hissed something in her ear, too low to hear. I stepped back from our circle. *Would it be better to run?*

But no. Everett was bound to find out. I might as well face the music all at once. In entering myself into the Arena and competing in the velocipede races, I had made an agreement. I'd taken on the varied consequences of racing, all of them: crashing, losing, shaming. I'd accepted the possibility of scandal, exposure, and scrutiny. I would not slink away now. It wasn't what an Arena jockey would do.

Eddings huffed impatiently and spoke, though Everett remained in his whispering match with Lena. "Your wife has been taking her brother's place in the races." His words had the finality of a bell tolling a death at the Worship Hall.

Everett dropped Lena's arm and whirled to face me. "*What?*"

I stared at the ground. I refused to feel ashamed of what I had done. Racing in the Arena had been the fulfillment of my soul's promise. If I let them dress me up in shame, I'd lose all the joy my races had given me. *I couldn't let them do that.*

I lifted my chin. "Yes, I took Gabriel's place because it was the only opportunity I'd ever have to race. And I don't regret it. I raced, and I placed. I was good enough to compete, but they would never have let me try. The only way was to disguise myself as a man."

"*What?*" Everett said again.

"I'm going to take the matter to the Arena officials," Eddings announced.

"Your wife?" Lena said. She stood a little behind Everett, scowling. "That scrawny thing is your wife? *She's* why you kicked me out of your house? She's nothing but a—a bloodless *manotte!*"

Everett put a hand over his face and pulled down, squeezing his skin into a grimace.

At least Lena's outburst had shut Eddings up for the moment. "I hope this was what you wanted, Cassius," she said to Everett. "But ask me no such favors again! Oh, I could just kill you!" She gathered her skirts into her fists, turned on one dainty heel, and stalked away.

"Eddings, I require your forbearance for a few hours. Come to my house at seven, and we can discuss the best way to proceed. Please?" Everett added this last as an afterthought, perhaps surprised to see mutiny on his jockey's face.

Eddings wavered. "I don't like it, Mr. Everett. I don't like it at all."

"I don't like it much myself. But I'd like to speak privately with my wife before—before we take any action. Come to Everett House at seven."

"Very well." Eddings nodded curtly. "I'll see you then."

Let Eddings reveal me, I thought darkly. Let them heap down their scorn and shame. At least then I'd be free of the need for secrecy. The whole world would know me. I'd accept infamy so they'd know what I had been capable of doing in the Arena.

"Emmeline," Everett said softly. "You'd better come home with me." He offered his hand.

I did not take it. "I don't care," I said. "Let the world hate me. I don't care. It was worth it to race."

"Come," he said, walking towards the exit. I didn't know what else to do but follow him. Much as I longed to be free of all of it, the trappings of society still tied me down. What did I have if I didn't have Everett? Nothing. No money, no prospects. What would I do if Everett turned me out?

I gritted my teeth as I followed Everett to his gas carriage. "What about Lena?" I asked as he opened the door for me. "We can't leave her alone at the Arena. And how will she get home?"

Everett passed his hand over his face again. "I don't know." He looked truly miserable, and I felt accountable for it.

"You'd better go find her," I murmured. "You can't just abandon her here."

He gazed at me for a moment. "Get in the carriage. I'll be back. I'm sorry about all this."

Everett departed. After a moment in the front seat, I made up my mind and crawled into the back.

Maybe I could leave Seren, I thought as I waited in the carriage. *Go to another city.* Maybe Everett would give me the money to disappear quietly. I didn't know much about other cities. Did a city exist where a woman could race velos? My limited research in the encyclopaedia had not seemed hopeful on that front. But if such a place existed, perhaps I could make enough money to live, especially if I had only myself to support. I thought of Maimie and what she'd said about the working-class women using velos to get to and from their jobs outside the home. Things were changing in Seren. Maybe I could just find work here and disappear in this new culture of working, velo-riding women.

Everett and Lena approached. "I won't ride with her," I heard Lena say. She crossed her arms over her ample bosom.

"Dammit, Lena," Everett said. "I need to take you both home. Just get in. You don't have to speak to her. I doubt she's happy to see you, either."

"I knew this was a bad idea," she said. "You never fail to make a mess of things, Cassius. I can't believe I let you talk me into this."

"I'm beginning to feel the same way. But do stop making a scene and get in the carriage."

Everett jerked the door open and peered in at me in the back seat. "You should sit in front," he admonished me.

I shook my head. "I'm fine back here."

"Emmeline," he urged.

"Really," I said.

Lena slid into the front seat and glared at me over her shoulder. "I'll never understand why the Serenians favor such pale coloring," she said out of nowhere.

"Where are you from, then?" I asked.

"Alora. Dark eyes are considered most beautiful there." Her own eyes were like pools of rich coffee.

I had only a vague notion of the city, down on the coast further east, south of the great sprawling city-state of Murcia.

"If you like it so much in Alora," Everett snapped to Lena as he ignited the engine, "why don't you go back?"

Lena turned away from him and tried to burn a hole in the window with her eyes. Suddenly hungry for information about distant places, I asked, "What's it like there?"

"There are miles and miles of beaches," Lena replied without changing her gaze. "You can walk along the shore for hours."

"Can women walk alone on the shore?" I blurted. I wanted to know what women had the power to *do* there.

Lena said nothing.

"No, they cannot," Everett answered. "High-born women go nowhere unescorted in Alora. Only very rich and very lucky women ever walk along the beach, and then only by the grace of their husbands' permission. You wouldn't like it in Alora, Emmeline. A woman's situation there is very desperate; she's considered a man's property throughout her life. And Lena knows this."

I scowled. *Well, cross Alora off the list,* I thought.

I pursued the topic of far-flung places. "Have you been to any other cities?" I asked, not caring who answered.

"I was raised in Murcia," Everett said. He'd never told me where he was from. "But I went to Alora to compete in their velodrome. Murcia has no velodrome—they prefer horse-racing. But the men of Alora are mad for velocipede races."

Lena turned her well-coiffed head and looked at Everett. "Did you not tell her why you'd left Alora?" she asked, chuckling.

"You can hardly be angry with the girl for having her secrets, Cassius."

Now it was Everett's turn for sullen silence. He steered the carriage through unfamiliar streets in the southern side of the city. It was an area a lady of my class would be horrified to go, but the houses were quite fine.

He pulled up at a modern townhouse and parked at the curb. He got out of the car, walked to Lena's side, and opened her door for her. She accepted all his courtesies with grace, never seeming to feel, as I so often did, that such gestures infantilized her, as if a woman could not open her own door or did not have the muscles to push herself out of her own seat. *Was I overly sensitive?* Or was it just that I so relished any opportunity to make use of my muscles that such assistance felt stifling? Or perhaps my opposition was a general resistance to the prescriptions "good manners" wrote for us all?

Everett walked Lena up the stairs to her house. On his arm, she seemed all things feminine and delicate. I had a sudden mixed up rush of emotions, ranging from envy to sadness to rebellion to impatience. She accepted his attentions so willingly, and he gave them so easily. *Why shouldn't they be together?* I wanted to kick the back of the seat before me, but I restrained myself.

I was an odd peg. I didn't fit in anywhere. I felt hugely guilty for making Everett marry me. My motivations, desperate at the time, now felt painfully shallow and self-serving.

Everett descended the townhouse steps and returned to the carriage. He opened the back door and peered in at me. "Won't you sit up front now, Emmeline? I hate feeling like a chauffeur. I did that job for long enough."

"Very well." I scrambled out, hurriedly snatching open the carriage door before Everett could.

As he started the engine again he said, "I can only imagine how this all looks to you, Emmeline. But I want to assure you, it isn't what you think."

I almost laughed. "It doesn't matter, Everett. When Eddings reveals me, you can go back to her openly, and no one will even judge you for it. Not that they would anyway. It's perfectly acceptable for a man to have a mistress in Seren."

"I won't let Eddings reveal you. I'll pay him what it takes. I'll protect you."

"No," I said. "No, it would be a relief to reveal myself. I'm tired of lying about it. I'm sick of it. I'm sick of all of it. I *want* to tell. Everyone."

"But Emmeline! The censure! The judgment! Your peers will be very cruel. You'll be ostracized."

"Ruined," I agreed. "But I won't have to hide anymore, do you see? This is what I am. I'm a jockey. I ride velos. I ride velos as well as a man. If I stay quiet, if I keep it a secret, I'm just being a coward. Don't you see how it is? Someone has to break the box. If I don't show them what I can do, if I pretend to be a man forever, the box isn't broken. But if I say, *yes, I'm a woman, and I did this thing that no one believed I could do,* then I've made room for someone else to do it, too. I have to make space where there is none, just like in a velocipede race."

I took a deep breath and forged on. "No one's ever believed a woman could compete in the Arena. But I showed them, Everett. I showed them! And I mean for them to know it. Let Eddings tell everyone. Let him announce it to the world."

"Good lord, Emmeline."

"You can divorce me," I said. "I understand."

"I don't want to divorce you. I'm sorely tempted to sponsor you."

Everett's proclamation left me speechless. I sat and stared at my hands. He must be mocking me.

It took me several moments to realize the carriage engine was dead, that we had stopped moving. Everett had parked the vehicle behind our home. He watched me watch my hands.

"You can't. They'd shun you, too. You can't, Everett."

"I don't care what Serenian high society thinks of me," he said. "I've never been all that high in their regard in the first place. If we can get you a place in the races, let me do this for you, Emmeline."

I shook my head and opened the carriage door. "It's not what I want," I explained. And that was true. Everyone would say I'd only gotten sponsorship because I had an indulgent husband. It would become a great farce, and whatever point I had made would be diminished.

•   •   •

Everett and I sat silently side by side on the settee in the entertaining parlor as we waited for Eddings to arrive. Everett looked worn and dismayed, and I fretted that my pursuit of my dream had brought him such discomfort. I did not feel sad at all; ever since Eddings had told Everett my secret, a creeping triumph had been rising in my chest. My body tingled; my thoughts raced. I sat still only because of my upbringing.

Orson opened the parlor door and announced our guest. Eddings strode in, still wearing his racing leathers. I wondered what drove him to race—was it money, need, or passion? I could not tell by looking at his face.

"Vern," Everett said. "Sit down. Would you care for refreshment?"

"I'll take a malt whisk," he said. Everett glanced at him in surprise, but did not question his choice. He poured one for each of us and then resumed his seat at my side. I found his presence there oddly comforting.

"Well?" Eddings asked after sipping his malt whisk. "Are you agreed? I shall go to the Arena Council tomorrow?"

Everett and I spoke at once.

"No," he voiced.

"Yes," I affirmed.

Eddings stared at me, more perplexed by my response than Everett's.

"Emmeline, you haven't thought this through," Everett said.

"But I have." I rolled my eyes at him. "I told you! I told you I needed to come clean, and I told you *why*." I turned to Eddings. "I'll go with you. Tomorrow, what time?"

Eddings frowned. "You'll come *with* me?"

"I think I ought to speak with the Arena Council, too."

Everett leaned back into the settee and put a hand over his face.

"Fine," Eddings said. "I'll meet you at the Arena at nine of the clock." He stood and bowed at his sponsor, who did not remove his hand from his face. "Mr. Everett," he clipped. "Mrs. Everett. I bid you good night."

I finished my malt whisk while Everett continued to pull on his eyebrows. My life was about to get turned upside down. I rather looked forward to the change. Everett did not seem so optimistic.

I got up to go to my rooms, and he did not lift his head. I would have left him without speaking, but one question would not excise itself from my mind. I couldn't bear that I did not know, when Lena did. "Why *did* you leave Alora?" I asked.

That snapped Everett's head right up. He stared at me. "What?"

"Lena laughed at you for not having told me. Why did you leave Alora?"

"Scandal," he clipped. "I left because of a scandal. It became...too difficult to live there. And Lena *had* to flee; we had no choice. For Aloran women, the punishment for adultery is death by stoning. We came to Seren because we had heard it was a liberal place, and its velocipede track was one of the best. So I know, Emmeline. I know how bad a scandal can get. Don't underestimate the damage it can do to your life. That's what I want to spare you. They may not stone you here, but if it's bad enough, no one will acknowledge you. It will be as if you were a ghost."

"What kind of jockey were you when you raced?" I wished again I could see him ride. He wasn't one of the really famous jockeys, or I'd have known his name. But his wealth and prestige at the track told me he couldn't have been only a Spug, either.

"I was fast." He smirked. "I didn't need to throw elbows very often. I did well enough in the Arena."

"Sponsored?"

"Yes. But Emmeline, listen to me—you can't—"

"I am resolved, Everett. Just tell me, will this hurt your business?" The only reason I doubted my decision was that I didn't want to hurt Everett.

He waved a hand. "I doubt it. Oh, maybe a little, but Voler's influence is great enough that it will be but a passing bump, if anything. You never know—it might even help my business. I have been considering manufacturing a new velocipede built just for women. I see more and more women riding them on the city streets."

"You make velocipedes?" *Why didn't I know this?*

"Velocipedes and gas carriages. They're my two passions. Voler invested in my efforts after injury put me off racing. The business took off immediately."

"How long did you race in the Arena?" I felt strange, asking these things of my husband. I ought to know.

"I spent two seasons at the velodrome in Alora and three seasons here. I took a bad crash, broke my arm and my collarbone. The arm, badly. That's when I began making designs with Banksy, who I met while jockeying. My arm never recovered. Even once I could use it for most things, it didn't work right for competitive riding. Banksy knew Voler and introduced us. That's when Voler gave me the job as his chauffeur. Only Banksy and I knew how the gas carriage worked, so Voler was happy to get me."

"But that must have been years ago," I mused. "Gas carriages have been around, why, ever since I can remember."

Everett sighed, wearily. "Yes, my dear. I probably gave up racing just as you were learning to ride a velo."

"Your Lena," I said. "She's been with you all this time?" I felt more awful than I had already—the marriage to Everett seemed worse, knowing that he'd loved Lena for half as long as I'd been alive.

"She isn't *my* Lena. Never has been, not even back then, much as I would have wished it so."

"But you love her." The words ought not to have hurt me as they did.

His hand went back to his eyebrows, pulling, pulling. "If only it were so simple." He paused. "Lena saw me as a means to an end. I don't think she ever *loved* me. She used me to escape from an unhappy marriage and a restrictive life."

Knowing what I did about Alora's punishments, I couldn't help but say, "But why would she have taken such a risk if it wasn't for love?"

"Because she could. Because I was available, and I did not fully understand the consequences of what I did. I was a foreigner from Murcia, where personal lives are free from such strictures. I had no idea what I was getting into, becoming the lover of one of the wives of an Aloran magistrate. But Lena knew."

"She used you."

"I don't blame her. I'd have done it in her shoes. She wanted out. She got out. I was her escape hatch." He waved a hand as if to dismiss himself.

"You should have told me," I said, knowing how ridiculous that sounded in light of all that I hadn't told him. "I might have released you from the obligation to marry me, if I had known about her."

"I didn't want to be released," he said. "I thought—I felt you were a chance to start over. I wanted to make myself new." He looked up at me. "You are so fresh and different, Emmeline."

I didn't understand. "But you didn't start fresh, Everett. You were seeing her the whole time!" Now I sounded like a scolding Serenian wife. "I'm sorry," I said. "It's none of my affair."

"But I wasn't," he argued. "I hadn't seen her until tonight, not since we were married. I'd kicked her out—and not for the first time—before I'd even met you. I only took her to the Arena tonight to startle your brother. I didn't believe it was Gabriel racing. I'd noticed his new coach had a limp. I suspected Gabriel posed as the coach for a confederate, and I wanted to catch him out. I meant to use Lena to shock him into revealing himself—and she certainly did that."

I did not quite understand what Everett was saying. I backtracked. "I found a painting, all cut up. Letty said you slashed all the paintings of her, but I saw the two in your bedroom."

"She betrayed me again, and I found out," Everett said darkly. "We argued. I was so sick of it all—sick of the lies. She simply can't do it. She can't help herself; she lies and she's unfaithful, and I'm exhausted with it. When he caught us—her husband in Alora—he laughed at me. I told him we loved each other, and he should let us go in peace. I begged him not to report her crime. He said: never trust a woman. A faithless creature does not change, a cheater will cheat again, a liar is always a liar."

I could not tell if he said such a thing to judge me for withholding my secret from him, or because he remembered the past. I walked to the door. Before I left, I said, "Neither of us lied, Everett. We only withheld pieces of ourselves."

15

I could not say I woke feeling refreshed and ready to face the irate Arena Council that morning. I'd spent a fitful night chasing odd dreams. In the one I remembered, Everett told me I was not welcome in his house anymore because deceivers never changed. I'd left Everett House by the back door and stood in the courtyard with the row of apple trees along the wall. A two-headed bird flitted down from the trees, red-breasted, each head looking in opposite directions. The ungainly creature managed to land at my feet and hopped along without tripping, as if its two heads had found a magical concord about how to direct its single body. I had woken wondering what to make of the bird. A golden ribbon girded its two necks, binding them together.

Everett was waiting for me with a fresh carafe of coffee at eight of the clock, looking grim. "What can I do to convince you not to go?" he said, filling my hand with a cup.

"I am determined," I said. "And when I feel this way, there is no swaying me. Just ask Gabriel."

"I believe you," he said. "Though I wish you'd heed me when I say the Council will not be sympathetic. I'd better come with you to the Arena."

I shook my head. "You needn't, Everett. You should keep your distance from this. Tell the truth. Say you were trapped into our marriage; say that you never wanted it. You'll get the divorce more easily that way, and public opinion will be on your side." I finished the coffee in two gulps and set the cup down.

"B—But I don't—" Everett sputtered at my departing back.

I planned to walk to the Arena despite the distance. I wore my silk mod-dress in honor of Maimie and rebellion. I left Everett looking forlorn in the kitchen in his bathrobe and marched out the front door, arranging my hat and gauntlettes as I departed.

I'd walked for about a quarter of an hour when the shadow of a black gas carriage pulled beside me and slowed. I looked up. Everett parked the carriage at the curb and leapt out to catch up with me. He wore one of his finer suits, as if dressed for work.

"Emmeline, at least let me drive you over there. It's too far to walk."

"All right," I said in an uncharacteristic capitulation. He seemed so unhappy, and if allowing him to drive me might cheer him, I owed him at least that much. Relief eased a few of the creases in his forehead as I got into the carriage.

We sat in silence as he drove to the Arena. I could not say if Everett felt as relaxed as I did—I rather doubted it. I waited while he opened the door for me because I knew he liked to be chivalrous.

We stood in the parking lot for a moment, regarding the Arena, so ominously quiet and empty. I thought of the first time he had brought me here, how kind he had been, buying me the hat and gauntlettes, concerned for my reputation and disguise.

I turned to him and threw my arms around his neck. "Thank you," I murmured. "Thank you for everything. You were a good husband to me, and I didn't deserve it."

Everett wrapped his arms around me in response. "Don't act as if it's over. I'm still your husband."

I pulled away from him to walk through the large double doors guarded by marble jockeys. I knew I was leaving him; once I passed those large doors, it would be over. He'd have no other choice.

Everett followed me, crumbling my attempt at melodramatic leave-taking. "What are you doing?" I asked.

"I'm going to the meeting."

"I told you not to—"

Everett's eyebrows drew together. "Oh, I'm not going on your account, my dear. I'm on the Arena Council, you know. I've every right to be there whether you like it or not."

With that, he broke into his natural long gait and went through the doors without me.

Without the noise of spectators, swaddies, and bookies, the Arena atrium was an empty shell. Though the wide hall must have been swept after the evening races, old betting slips still papered the floor, thin and white like the residue of old dreams.

I took a deep breath.

"Mrs. Everett," someone said from behind me. I turned. Eddings looked unlike himself—I'd only ever seen him in racing attire or formal dining clothes—and now he wore a brown tweed jacket and pressed trousers with a cap. He glared at my mod-dress in a judging manner, and my shoulders tightened in instant resistance. I wished it could be someone else who would reveal me, someone who might have had just the faintest speck of understanding for what I had done.

Eddings and I crossed the slip-laden floor. He seemed to know where he was going, for he pulled open a door at the east end of the hall. I followed him through it to find another large room, this one occupied by six men at a table. One of them was Everett, looking as distant and stern as all the others. A short, stocky man stood up and held his hand out. "Mr. Eddings," he said in an unexpectedly sonorous voice. "Thank you for your message of the evening."

"You're welcome," Eddings said. He gestured with his hand in my direction. "This is Mrs. Cassius Everett, formerly Emmeline Escot. She's the jockey Gabriel Escot's twin sister."

A few sideways glances fell on Everett as Eddings spoke, but most of the Council members turned to me.

"After Gabriel Escot's crash, he was diagnosed with torn ligaments in his knee and advised he would not race again," Eddings continued. "Instead of withdrawing from his remaining races, he let his sister take his place. Escot did not ride in his last two races; his sister competed in his stead."

Silence met these words. Of the six council members, only Everett remained stoic at the news. Two of the men scowled; two went wide-eyed with shock, and the little one who'd addressed Eddings earlier wrinkled his entire face in consternation.

The Arena spokesman finally clarified, "You're telling me Mrs. Everett—Mrs. Cassius Everett—raced and placed in those two races? Disguised as—as Gabriel Escot?"

Eddings gave a clipped nod. "Yes. And I'm petitioning for Escot's permanent disqualification from the Arena."

I gasped. I had not considered that *Gabriel* might be held to account for *my* behavior. "It wasn't Gabriel's fault!" I cried. "Gabriel had nothing to do with it—it was my plan from the outset."

Six heads swiveled towards me. Everett wore a pained expression, as if he'd known all along it would come to this.

"Of course Escot knew about it," Eddings snapped. "You couldn't have pulled it off without his complicity."

I clasped my hands in front of me. I had no way of defending Gabriel because Eddings was right. My brother hadn't withdrawn from his races; he'd let me ride instead. All my noble intentions of exposing the prejudice against women at the Arena and in Serenian society fell away. They weren't going to punish me— society would do that—but they would blacklist Gabriel and destroy his chances of ever working in the world of velocipede racing again. I wanted to cry.

"You admit to this deceit then," the Arena spokesman said. "You do not deny that you raced in your brother's stead?"

How could I deny it now? I gave a short, jerky nod, like a puppet on a string. Eddings smirked.

"Very well," the spokesman said. "Escot must be disqualified from the Arena. It is flagrant cheating and breach of contract to replace himself with any other jockey, regardless of whom it is. And as for you, Mrs. Everett, I think we shall do best to remit you to your husband's care. Mr. Everett?" He looked enquiringly at Everett, who stood up, and to my surprise, spoke.

"Do you not find it interesting that Emmeline showed in the races?" my husband said in a casual tone.

The spokesman blinked up at Everett. "Are you telling me you knew about this, Mr. Everett?"

"Of course I did not," Everett said. "I respect the rules we set. But she was good, gentlemen. She rode stellar races."

"That's beside the point!" cried one of the other men at the table. "She and her brother cheated. That's the matter at hand, not whether some *manotte* can ride a velo. They cheated."

"Cheating seems not quite the word," Everett said. "I see it more along the lines of a deception. But imagine, gentlemen, if *you* were a female jockey with talent. How would you race? Emmeline had no forum for her talent."

"Talent," scoffed the man beside Everett. "Females don't ride. Good lord, Everett, the quality ones don't even spectate! It's scandalous!"

"But what if there are others out there with a talent like Emmeline's?" Everett said. "Think about it. You all know we've been seeing greater and greater numbers of women at the races. And not just the usual jockettes—working-class women, even middle-class women. I know for a fact that some ladies disguise themselves and sneak in to watch incognito. These old-fashioned notions about a woman's place are costly to us—why, imagine if we had a division of female jockeys with their own races! We'd make a bundle! People would come for the novelty of watching such a race. Women would come to watch out of interest to see what their sisters could do. I'm telling you, women's racing is a fortune waiting to be made."

How my heart expanded as Everett argued for my dream. And he so cleverly tried to lead them into it with the temptation of money—an argument they might understand. But I could see that the rest of the Arena Council would not bite. They were shaking their heads and muttering.

"It's an idea, Everett," the little spokesman said generously. "It's an idea for the future. For the moment, we've got this mess to address." He waved in my direction. "I suggest you take your wife home forthwith. This news is bound to get out when we announce Escot's disqualification. You're going to have a scandal and a half to weather."

I stood as panic pressed through my limbs. This wasn't how I envisioned it happening! They weren't supposed to punish Gabriel, only me. "Wait!" I cried, but the men of the Council had already risen, and three of them had already donned coats to depart. All of them ignored my plea.

Everett gave the Council and Eddings a clipped bow, strode to my side, and took my arm in a grip that brooked no argument. He escorted me back into the empty betting hall.

"I—I have to go tell Gabriel. I didn't think of him," I whispered. Two tears slid down my cheeks. "I didn't think of him, and now they will destroy him."

Everett squeezed my arm. "I'll drive you to Escot House," he said.

•　　　•　　　•

I flew up the steps of Escot House and rapped on the door. Everett remained in the gas carriage parked at the curb. His face looked worn and gaunt when I left him. The guilt was starting to get to me. Not only had I destroyed Gabriel's prospects, I'd likely given Everett a fair share of headaches, too.

The door swung open to reveal Maman. As she broke into a pleased smile, I realized Gabriel had not yet told her what had happened. "Emmeline," she said. "You'll never believe it. We've had the best news!"

I could not imagine what news could be good at a time like this. "What?"

"Come in," she said, gesturing. "Gabriel's gotten a sponsorship offer! Did you hear he won second place in his race last night?"

"*What!*" I nearly shrieked. "Who? Who made the offer?"

"Voronson," she said. I froze in the hallway. To get a sponsorship from the renowned velo designer conveyed instant prestige.

"Voronson?" I echoed. "Voronson wants to sponsor Gabriel?"

Maman beamed. "He wrote a letter that came by special delivery last night. He said he wanted to design a special velocipede for Gabriel, a new, lighter design. And he offered a stipend of 50 marks a month."

Fifty marks alone was a solid sponsorship offer. Add a custom velo to it, and the offer was pure gold. The irony ate at me—I wanted to kick the wall, scream, slam doors, anything to release my frustration.

"Emmy." Gabriel stood at the top of the stairs, staring down at me. He could tell by my stricken face that I brought bad news.

"Gabriel," I murmured. "I need to speak with you."

"Why, Emmeline, no congratulations for your brother?" Maman scolded. "I swear, I sometimes think you were raised by someone else. You have no courtesies, no manners at all. Nothing I taught you ever stuck."

"Gabriel," I pleaded. He was already down the stairs, steering me into the front parlor. Maman must have detected that something was amiss, for she followed us. I spoke despite her presence since she was bound to find out anyway. Perhaps it would be best that she hear it first from me.

"Eddings went to the Council," I told Gabriel. He looked nauseous; I hesitated. "Oh God, Gabriel, I'm sorry. They're going to disqualify you."

He nodded woodenly as Maman shrieked, "Disqualify! Emmy! What are you talking about? He's just won a sponsor!"

Perhaps because we'd perpetrated our greatest and most thorough deception against Maman, the words stuck in my throat as I saw the dismay on her face.

I forced myself to speak. "I took Gabriel's place in these past two races, Maman. His knee was far too injured for him to ride. I raced in his stead. The Council discovered our deception, and they will disqualify Gabriel."

Maman's hands batted the air helplessly as she stared at me in horror. Her mouth opened and closed, but not a sound came out.

"I'm so sorry," I said. "Gabriel, I'm so sorry."

My brother leaned back into the settee, placing his injured leg up on the seat in an action that normally would have brought down a tirade from Maman. She was too distraught to even notice.

"I thought it might come to this," Gabriel said. "I hoped it wouldn't, but I thought it might. If I move quickly, we'll be able to stay ahead of the gossip." He looked at my face, and I think he must have known I was about to cry. "Emmy, it will be all right."

I wanted to sit, but only the settee remained, and Gabriel took up the entire seat. Maman paced by the mantle, her hands still fluttering in anxious reflex. "But Gabriel, what will you do?" I asked.

He put an arm over the back of the settee. "I haven't been idle while I've been injured. I've set a plan in motion, and if I can just stay ahead of the rumor that I've been disqualified, all will be well. I got a position in Basile. They want to build a velodrome, and I've been hired as a jockey-consultant. I am to travel to the city tomorrow to sign the contract. Once it's signed, even if they learn I have been disqualified, there will be little they can do. They'll be stuck with me for a year—and I can prove to them in that year that my knowledge is worth a bit of infamy."

"Gabriel!" Maman gasped. She looked about to swoon, her face was so pale. "What are you talking about? You're planning to leave Seren?"

"Yes, Maman, and I want you to come with me. You can't stay here with Papan, especially not if they disqualify me. Imagine the scandal! It will be brutal. You must come, Maman. We'll rent a townhouse together. The rents in Basile are cheaper, and the salary they promised me is generous. We'll do fine, Maman."

"Your father cannot manage on his own," Maman said weakly. "You know he can't keep track of money."

I went to Maman's side to support her. "Gabriel, move your leg. Maman needs to sit."

Grimacing, Gabriel obeyed. I settled Maman beside him. He patted her shoulder. "We're going to be fine, Maman. I have it all arranged. Come with me to Basile, and we'll find a house to rent together. I have the coach fare set aside."

Maman nodded shakily. "All right, Gabriel. I'll come and have a look. It sounds—why, I've never seen you so—so organized. I'm proud of you, Gabriel, I truly am."

Gabriel flushed, but it was from pleasure rather than embarrassment. He so rarely got any kind of attention that wasn't about his athletics.

Looking at Maman and Gabriel, I felt very lost. I wanted to go to Basile with them and start over, too, but I had been extended no invitation. What would I do without Gabriel? He'd been the reflection in my mirror for my entire life. "I want to come with you, Gabriel," I said.

Maman narrowed her eyes at me. "No," she said. "If you come, Emmeline, the scandal will follow us. I will not have you ruining things again."

"You can't, Emmy. You know you can't," Gabriel added. "Everett would never allow it. But you have him, Emmy. You'll be all right. Everett will look after you."

Gabriel tried to offer me comfort, but I could not take any from his words. I nodded. "When will you go?"

"As soon as possible," answered Gabriel. "Today."

I followed Gabriel like a duckling as he went upstairs to his room and began to pack a bag. "Go help Maman," he directed, sounding like a different person than my complacent brother. I obeyed, though I found that Maman had rallied and was fully capable of packing her own satchel.

"Emmeline, you'll need to come check on your father. He is likely to be quite distraught by our leaving." She tied the drawstrings of her bag and frowned at me. "You'll do that, won't you? Otherwise I will worry about him."

I sighed. Looking after Papan was next to impossible; he did what he wanted to do, and nothing I said would deter him. But the tide of my guilt pulled me along; I'd agree to anything they asked of me. It was the least I could do, given that my own actions were forcing them to leave.

I'd entirely forgotten that Everett awaited me in the gas carriage on the curb. He stepped out as I descended the stairs of Escot House and opened the passenger door for me.

"Thank you," I said.

We drove in silence. Everett did not ask what had happened, and I did not offer an explanation. I was a curse; I dragged down everyone around me.

A commotion at Everett House greeted us. "Damnation," Everett muttered as he peered out the window. "The news has already broken."

I turned on my seat to look at the people gathered on the steps of Everett House: mostly reporters and Arena swaddies who hung on every bit of news and gossip about velocipede racing.

"We can go through the back," I whispered as he pulled into the mews. "Everett, I'm afraid it's going to be very bad."

He glanced over his shoulder at me as he threw the parking brake. He shook his head. "And this is just the beginning. Come."

Though we tried to be inconspicuous, a straggler from the crowd saw us as we crept along the street.

"There she is!" came the shout from behind us.

Everett gripped my arm and hurried me towards the house. But the mob moved quickly too, surging around the corner en masse. The reporters shouted their questions as they flailed their notebooks in the air.

"Mr. Everett, do you care to comment on your wife's behavior?"

"Is it true Mrs. Everett rode in two velocipede races last week?"

"Mr. Everett, what will you do with her? Are you planning to seek a divorce?"

This last question was perhaps the most scandalous of all. Serenian divorces were almost impossible to get, unless it could be shown that one partner had acted in bad faith. Everett, I had already considered, might have a chance with that argument.

The crowd closed in around us. Everett tried to shield me with his body, but so many people pressed in—young men flapping notebooks and stabbing pens, track swaddies hooting and whistling, and others, perhaps passersby from Vreeland Park who had seen the growing scene and attached themselves to it— that I was jostled and pushed. I would have fallen in the crush if not for Everett's steadying body at my side.

Anger flared hot and immediate in my stomach—that they should do this, that they felt they had a right to do this, because I had dared to shatter the glass box that trapped a Serenian woman.

Someone shoved me. I shoved back. I created an opening in the crowd before us, and Everett and I made it to the servants' entrance. One more push, and the door opened. Everett hauled me through and slammed it. He threw the lock and leaned against the door, breathing hard. "Are you all right?"

I nodded. "But it's going to be like that all the time, isn't it?"

Everett lifted himself from the door as if his body weighed a thousand kilograms. "For the near future, I imagine so. I'm afraid they'll make it impossible for you to come or go without that sort of attack."

I scowled to hide my urge to cry. "How will you manage?" I said, knowing Everett had no choice but to leave each day for his business.

Everett shrugged. "I guess I will find out."

He went upstairs and I walked deeper into the house. In the main hall I could hear the crowd still shouting on the front steps. Orson stood looking pained in the foyer. His glare told me all I needed to know: he loathed me, and he blamed me for this disaster that marred his master's life.

I turned from his reproach and went into the front salon. At the window, I flicked the curtain to get a glimpse of the crowd. As if they had been searching for any motion in the house, the mob shifted towards the window. They trampled the flowering groundcover to get closer, destroying the carefully-designed landscape under the window. I yanked the curtains closed and moved back. The tenor of the crowd's shouts seemed to change.

"That was her!" I heard someone call above the din. "That was Emmeline Everett!"

The roar intensified. Shattering glass crashed through the salon. The curtains bulged inwards. Noises blared through the broken window.

"Mrs. Everett! Mrs. Everett!"

And then, a woman's scream: "How dare you! You give a bad name to Serenian women!"

"Shameless!"

"Unnatural!"

"Mrs. Everett, do you think you are a man?"

"*Manotte! Manotte! Manotte!*" the crowd chanted.

Thankfully the curtains were closed as I backed away from them. They wanted to cow me back into the box through fear. But fear wasn't what I felt; no, this uplifting burn in my belly was rage. Rage at the crowd that they would try to intimidate me from their own small-mindedness, that they would dare to break any part of Everett's beautiful house to achieve their ends.

A cord snapped inside me. *How dare they! How dare they!*

I ran to the broken window and threw the curtains open. I brushed away the worst of the glass shards as the mob screamed, and then I leaned out the window.

"Yes!" I cried. "Yes, I did it. I raced. I dared to race at the Arena, and I showed both times. I'm a woman, and I—"

The first rock was just a pebble, a small thing, likely plucked up from amongst the cobbles in the street. It stung me across the cheek and stopped the angry flow of my words. Another stone, larger, sailed at me, but I ducked in time. The horde had taken to this new humiliation with zest, and something splatted onto my dress even as I stood: horse dung, collected off the street.

Something hit the side of my head, and I fell backwards into the salon. My ears rang with shouts and screams. Booted feet flashed past me. My head hurt unbearably, and the noise was so loud and intense, the screams so frenzied in their pitch, that I finally began to cry.

"Emmeline, Emmeline. Can you stand?" Everett knelt over me, a deep furrow between his brows. I felt awful. I had brought all this trouble upon him. I sat up, despite the fact that my head spun.

"There's dung on my dress," I muttered. I did not want to face his concern or be forced to acknowledge what I had done to him. "I must go change."

I scrambled to my feet and flew up the stairs to my bedroom, locking the door behind me. I peeled the mod-dress over my head, tossing it into the corner, and put a different one on. Even in this dark moment, I appreciated Maimie's design. Had I been squashed into a corset while having to endure this, I would have lost my mind.

I heard the footsteps on the stairs, the soft knock on my door. "Emmeline?" Everett's voice murmured from the hall. "What happened?"

The last thing I wanted to do was explain my foolishness. "Go away, Everett," I said. "I need to rest."

I had the impression that he stood silently outside my door for a very long time.

When I finally determined that Everett was gone, I went to the little writing desk in the corner of the room. I had lately avoided it because I couldn't get the notion out of my head that it had been Lena's. I imagined her sitting at it to compose her correspondence. I could see her so clearly with my mind's eye, her richly-colored skirts sweeping gracefully, her back held in a perfect curve. I imagined that her handwriting would be slanted, embellished with ladylike flourishes.

I pulled out the middle drawer to reveal a stack of fresh cream-colored stationery, one sheet of which I withdrew. The right-hand drawer produced pen and ink. The left-hand drawer I opened only for curiosity, and in it I found two stacks of letters.

Hands shaking, I brought them out. I knew already who had written the first stack—that was Everett's bold hand; I had seen it more than once on the notes he'd written to me.

I pulled the top letter from the second stack. Her penmanship was not quite as I'd envisioned: instead of flourishes, she favored clean, elegant strokes. I frowned. Why had the letters been left here? Surely Everett would not have been so careless? It must be that Lena had collected the letters as a memento of their times together, and she had left them here when she departed.

I stared at the letter in my hand. It would be so easy to open it, to see what they had written to each other in their private love. I knew it would hurt me, and it made me feel a void inside, an emptiness and an awareness of a love I would never have. People like me didn't get that. I pressed the two stacks of letters back into their drawer.

Then I took up the pen and ink to compose my own letter.

Dear Everett, I wrote. I wondered if he would think *Cassius* when he read that, but I continued.

> I'm grateful for everything you have done for me, and everything you tried to do. You are too good a man for someone like me. I wish you happiness. You deserve an undivided love.
>
> After the events this afternoon at Everett House, the only way forward is for me to leave Seren. There is not room here for a woman who wishes to race velocipedes. I hope, in my leaving, that your own circumstances are bettered. I think you will find that a wife's abandonment can be leveraged to achieve a divorce. I have heard of such a thing before, and I hope you will pursue this course for your own happiness. It will be better for you to entirely distance yourself from my disgrace.
>
> You know you owe me one favor, and I must ask you to do something for me even though I know you will have no taste for the task. My brother and mother have departed today for a new life in Basile. They have left my father to his own devices. They asked me to check up on him, as they fear for his welfare without anyone around to curb his destructive habits. Will you send someone to Escot House on occasion to look in on him? I promised Maman that I would see it done.
>
> I never meant to cause you any shame. I only wanted to race. I knew it would be bad if I got caught, though I did not quite imagine it could be this bad. I hope you will forgive me for chasing my own dream at your expense. I wish it could have been different—different for my racing dream, different between us.
>
> Thank you.
>
> > Yours,
> > Emmeline

The lie in the letter was necessary. Everett might come looking for me if he knew I meant to remain in Seren.

I waited until the dark morning hours, packing a satchel with my mod-dresses and my racing leathers, my black lace gauntlettes, and the scant money I had left from the shopping allowance Everett had given me. I left my letter in the middle of the writing desk. Before I departed I shoved my too-identifiable hair into an ugly house cap.

Then I looked sadly around the lovely room. I would miss Everett House. I would miss *Everett*.

The mob had broken up around midnight, but even so I slipped from the house using the servants' entrance. In my shabby dress, most would have mistaken me for a servant, anyway. I walked down the street, away from the fine abodes that housed the wealth of Serenian society. I walked away from all of it.

Saville Street was deserted at this hour. I leaned against the entry of Jacquelenne's dress shop and watched the street change with the sunrise. Working men rode Rovers to their jobs, pedaling along at a decent clip. Others walked on the sidewalks, as did the working women, dressed in their sack-like dresses in subdued colors.

Then I saw the girl. She was young, my age or even younger. She sailed down the middle of Saville Street, sitting tall on her fat-tyred velo. She wore a dress, but she'd altered the thing, cutting it up the center of the skirt and sewing the two halves into wide-legged trousers that did not interfere with her pedaling.

I moved out of the shadow of the dress shop to watch her progress up the road. Something inside my chest began to dance as I watched her cutting a swathe through the men on their velos. She moved faster than any of the others because she rode with more purpose. The feeling in my chest intensified into a familiar rebellious urge, the old one born when I'd watched Gabriel soar into the distance on a racing velo for the very first time.

My dream was still alive.

"Why, what are you doing here, Mrs.—"

I turned to Maimie before she could say my name, lifting a finger to my lips. "Don't say it," I said.

Her brow wrinkled in concern. "What is it? What's wrong?"

"Have you not heard?" I asked incredulously. Surely the whole city knew now of my notoriety. "Can we go inside?" I added, looking anxiously around the street for people who might overhear us.

Maimie brought out her keys and jerked her head. "Miss Jackie doesn't arrive until noon," she said. "And the shop doesn't open until nine of the clock."

"I'm not here to shop," I said.

"Well, come on in then," she said, pushing open the door. She set her bag on the table and gestured to a seat. She pulled out pamphlets from the shelves, arranging them on the table in neat stacks.

"What do you think of this?" she asked, shoving a pamphlet under my nose.

I studied the pattern. It depicted a willowy woman wearing a loose-fitting blouse and what at first I thought was a narrow, straight skirt. I looked closer and saw that the skirt was actually split into a pair of trousers like what the girl on the velo had been wearing.

"These are your designs?"

Maimie laughed. "You don't think Miss Jackie would think of such a thing, now, do you? You want me to make you a set? I'm going to call them *trousettes.* Clothing for the velo-riding gal."

I shook my head. "I can't, Maimie. Listen, I came to talk to you. They caught me at it—my racing. They found out I raced at the Arena, and the scandal is out. I have to go into hiding." Asking for help did not come naturally to me, but I had no other option. "I hoped you could help me? I need to find a place to stay, some work. I don't know where to begin."

"What?" she exclaimed. "You left your fine man and that pretty house? Are you crazy?"

I shook my head. "I couldn't stay. They're going to vilify me."

Maimie still stared at me, aghast. "But you had it so good. Money to buy whatever you wanted. Didn't have to get up early to work, nothing. You had it so good. Mrs.—"

"Call me Emmy." I hastened to curb her tendency to use my married name. "Please, Maimie, I need this help."

She shrugged. "Well, all right then. You can stay with me, I suppose. But you'll have to pay your share on the rent. Can't say as I mind having help with that. I pay five marks a month. You can split it with me. As for work, well, what can you do?"

I frowned. My skills weren't many, truth to be told. Riesen ladies were not prepared for anything but ornamentation and marriage.

But Maimie showed me that I had more than I imagined. "You can read and write real pretty, I bet," she said. "What d'you think about being a secretary? Most men don't want to hire a female, but there're some who will. A friend of mine got herself a real posh position with a merchant down near the docks, doing his writing for him. We'll go and see her tonight after I get off."

I helped Maimie around the dress shop until eleven of the clock, when she told me I had to go because Miss Jackie would be coming soon. She gave me directions to her flat, and I walked though an area of the city I'd never seen, searching the street signs to find my way. At first being alone on unfamiliar streets caused me anxiety. It was one thing to walk unescorted in Vreeland Park or around Escot House—I knew those parts of the city so well—but Seren was different here in Maimie's world. The streets I walked had not been swept in days, and the people who traversed them did not meet my eye. It took me a while to realize that the people I passed didn't look at me because they did not know I was a riesen. I didn't look like one. No one made any assumptions about me at all; I blended into the scenery. Casting off my social status granted me freedoms that I'd never imagined. No one gazed at me with hungry scrutiny, as if I were a treasure to be hoarded. No one believed I was in any way precious or vulnerable. I could almost feel that old perception of a woman being a weak and fragile thing slipping away like linen on the breeze.

Maimie lived in a tiny walk-up apartment within an old mansion that had probably once belonged to a riesen family. The huge, dilapidated house had been converted to flats. The landlady, Maimie had told me, lived off the premises, which was a lucky thing, because if she found two lodgers occupying Maimie's apartment, she'd likely double the rent.

Maimie had given me the key with the warning to "keep scarce," so I let myself into the room. It was sparse, furnished only with a single worn wing chair—the kind of cast-off item my family had sold piece by piece to generate funds to live on—and a narrow, cotlike bed. She had a tiny stove in the corner where she could boil water. I sat in the chair, curled my legs beneath me, and slept.

•　　　•　　　•

"What, ho? Ready to go, Mrs. Emmy?" Maimie woke me as she bustled through the door with a loaf of bread, still warm from wherever she'd picked it up. I realized I was ravenous as she handed it to me.

"Where are we going?" I asked through mouthfuls of bread.

"Why, to see my friend, Jane, the secretary. If you're serious about this hiding from the scandal, Mrs. Emmy, the best thing you can do is find a job and blend in with us working girls. It ain't a posh life like what you're used to, but if you work hard, you can make ends meet and stay out of worse situations. Ain't easy, mind you, and lots of girls end up on Rouge Street 'cause the money's easier."

I wrinkled my nose in distaste. "Let's go meet Jane."

I followed Maimie down the road a few blocks, where we came to another house of flats similar to Maimie's. "Jane's got a top-floor situation," Maimie said. "Real nice, and no footsteps overhead keeping her awake at all hours."

We climbed the stairs.

Jane expected us, for she opened the door directly after our knock and said, "There you are, Maimie. I wondered if you'd make it before dark."

Jane was a pretty girl several years my senior. She oozed competence. She made us weak tea and brought us into her "sitting area," which consisted of two uncomfortable wooden chairs and a battered settee. Several of Lavinia Beau's radical pamphlets lay strewn over the tea table.

"Emmy's looking for work," Maimie began. "She has a pretty hand, and I thought she should go for a secretary like you."

Jane studied me. "Have you worked in this capacity before?" she asked.

I shook my head. Jane bit her lip. "Well, there's not many who would hire a female, let alone one with no experience. But why don't you write down a few samples of your penmanship, and I'll see what I can do. The man I work for has contacts, and it can't hurt to put the word out that you're looking for a position."

Jane brought cheap paper and even cheaper ink, and I wrote out the alphabet in upper and lower cases. Jane looked over my work. "That *is* pretty," she said. "Almost too pretty. Well, I'll take these in tomorrow and drop by Maimie's if I find any leads for you."

I gave Maimie three marks from the remaining five I'd taken from Everett House to cover a month of rent and additional expenses such as food. Then I waited for four days with my fingers crossed, hoping Jane would bring me encouraging news. Meanwhile, rumors of Emmeline Everett and her scandalous rides flew through the city, causing outcries everywhere. Riots raged outside the Arena. I heard that two people were trampled to death in the rampage.

I wondered how Papan was faring, but I could do nothing to find out. I had found a safe haven, a place where no one would ever look for me. I was riesen, and however low I'd fallen, the upper class of Seren did not mix with the working classes. I was known now only as Emmy Cassius. I took Everett's name for lack of ideas, and because it reminded me of him. Strangely, I missed him more than anyone else, even Gabriel.

Jane finally came by, brimming with excitement. Maimie had not come back yet from her day at the dress shop. Miss Jackie worked her until the last drop of daylight was gone.

"Well, it hasn't been easy," Jane said in her businesslike way as I offered her the lone chair. "I've searched and searched, but no one wanted a girl with no experience—it's a tricky thing. But I found someone who just might take you on. He's new to the city. He does metallurgy and metalworking—high-end stuff. He's known as a real artisan, trained in Murcia. He needs an office girl to keep track of his books and correspondence. He can pay four marks a month. What do you think?"

"Yes!" I cried, happy to have any offer at all. "Yes, of course I'll do it." The money wasn't much, but it would keep me out of debt to Maimie.

"Very well," Jane said approvingly. "Here's the address. You're to be there by eight of the clock tomorrow."

17

I wished I had a velo to ride as I trekked halfway across Seren in the dark to my new job. The address was in the warehouse district, far from Maimie's apartment. Maimie had convinced me it would be fine if I wore one of my mod-dresses to the interview, though I still heard Maman's voice in the back of my head, squawking about immodesty and bare, muscular arms. I was soon glad I'd taken Maimie's advice, for I could move my legs in a brisk trot. Even so, it took me nearly two hours to get to the destination Jane had given me.

The warehouse had a rolling door that stood wide open, and as I peered inside I saw a man bent over a project on a table. He wore a heavy leather apron and goggles to protect his eyes. He did not notice me as I crept inside.

When he lifted his metalwork from the table, I gasped. I recognized the diamond shape of a racing velo frame. He heard the sound escape my lips and glanced over his shoulder.

"You must be the girl, eh?" he said, looking me up and down. He had a hard face, grooved with lines, and few of them seemed to be from smiling.

"Yes," I said. "I'm Emmy. Emmy Cassius."

"George's girl said you could write and keep things organized," he said. "That true?"

"Yes," I said again. I longed to look closer at the velo he was building.

He set the frame down. "I guess I'd better show you my office. I'm Micheux. Mr. Micheux to you."

I followed Mr. Micheux into a little side room off the main space of his workshop. I couldn't help myself. I said, "You make velocipedes?"

Micheux grunted. "Amongst other things. But yes, that's what brought me here. Whole city's mad for 'em. I've been commissioned to produce a new bike for one of the professional jockeys."

He pointed at several disorderly stacks of paper on the desk. "That's your task for the day."

I nodded and slipped behind the desk. "But I thought only a few makers were allowed to make racing velos?" I asked, risking exposing my excessive knowledge of velocipedes. Maybe in this circumstance he'd be pleased with an informed employee?

"It's not to be used yet in the races; it's a prototype. Designs are always improving, you know."

I glanced again at the table where the frame lay. I wondered which lucky jockey had a sponsor willing to go to such expense for a velo that would not even be used in the races.

I wanted a specially designed new velo, one made just for me, custom for my needs. I'd only ever ridden Gabriel's hand-me-downs. But I knew a new velo was another useless dream. I had to learn to curb these desires. I settled down to try to make sense of Mr. Micheux's papers.

I had not considered whether I would like work when I went seeking it, only that I had to find it as a way to keep myself. Unlike most young women of my class, I had not had a life of comfortable leisure. Maman had given me chores every day around the house, the kind of chores any respectable riesen family would have had servants to perform. I was accustomed to work, so labor didn't bother me. But the way I was treated *did*.

Micheux felt that having a female as his secretary gave him license to take advantage. He demanded that I come to work an hour earlier than the usual, eight of the clock instead of nine, and stay an hour later. Yet he paid me less than what a male secretary would get for the same work. I'd asked Jane about the typical pay for a secretary, and she'd told me most made eight marks a month. I earned half that while working longer hours. The injustice rankled, but I could do nothing about it. I was desperate, and work was not easy for a woman to find.

My days were exhausting, not in the way of good exercise, but rather in a tight, unhealthy manner. I had the curious sensation that my body was not my own. Without my riding, I felt tight, achy, and strange to myself. Riding, I understood only when it had been taken away, had carved out a space for me in the world. The physical act of it had given rise to most of my rebellious urges. Doing office work for Micheux, my body felt almost as tamed as when I'd had to wear corsets. I went dull again; my life lost its color.

I did not get enough sleep, and I barely crossed paths with Maimie, for I arrived home at nine in the evening and collapsed into restless sleep, only to wake seven hours later to dash back across the city to work. I was a cog in a machine, and I had no free time. I could see how having a velo could open up a working girl's life—the time it would save me in transit might give me an hour to myself each day. An extra hour would have offered me the space to think or plan or dream. A ride to work would have given me rhythm and energy that my drudgery for Micheux sucked away. But even a secondhand slug cost too much for me, and I had to constantly push my desire to ride out of my head.

Over the weeks, I designed a system of filing for Micheux's office, wrote out his correspondence, and entered the details of his expenses in his ledger. The man was hopelessly disorganized, however brilliant he might be as a metallurgist. Every morning I had a pile of papers to sort through, all carelessly strewn over his desk. I cleaned his workshop after he departed for the day. Even in there, the man made a mess. He extruded metal shavings, dust, and debris of all kinds wherever he went.

I often tried to peek out the office door to watch him at work on his prototype. He'd built several frames of various shapes and sizes, all based on the traditional diamond of a racing velo. Most of the time he seemed annoyed with his work, cursing and throwing things in temper.

One day I heard him crow in triumph: "I got it! This is the one!" He often made outbursts, but this one had such a tone of excitement that I poked my head into the workshop.

"Look here, Miss Cassius!" he hollered, waving me to his side. He was so pleased with himself that he forgot to be gruff with me in his usual manner. He had told me more than once to stay out of the workshop while he worked. "Look at this!" He lifted the frame and brandished it as if it weighed nothing. "This is the latest and the greatest: the Micheux racing bike."

I was surprised he was so certain that he'd gotten it right without having tried to ride it. Every velo has a unique feel. How did he know, once this frame had tyres, gears, and handles, that it would be *the one*?

My jubilation matched his, except mine was, as ever, tainted by longing. I wanted the velo for my own. I missed riding more than anything. If those men of the Arena Council only knew— exile from my sport was the most severe punishment they could have inflicted upon me. Maybe they did know. Most of them were ex-jockeys themselves, pushed out of racing by age and injuries.

The following day when I arrived at work, I found a fully assembled racing velo sitting alone in the shop. I peered around the warehouse. Micheux was nowhere to be found. I checked the office and saw no sign of the leather bag that he carried everywhere with him. It was unlike him to be late. Perhaps he had taken the morning off to relish the completion of his project.

I tried to concentrate on filing the receipts that had piled up the day before. Micheux had bought several components from Voronson's: tyres, rims, gears, chain, cables, brakes.

As I looked over the receipts, my mind refused to let go of the velo. It called to me with a siren song, a song I knew I must ignore, no matter how enticing the music. I had no leeway for getting caught riding it. I *needed* this job.

But after an hour passed and Micheux had not appeared, I got up and went back into the warehouse. The rolling door stood closed. No one would ever know if I rode the velo only around the warehouse.

I tucked the skirts of my mod-dress into the waistband of my bloomers. The velo stood upright in a rack. I lifted it and set it on the ground. Then I mounted, getting settled. This little velo demanded an aggressive position, more so even than Gabriel's racing velo. The lucky jockey whose sponsor had paid for this jewel must be small like me. It was the first time I'd been on a velo that truly fit my size, and the difference was palpable. It felt *right*. My arms trembled as they bore weight; I'd lost strength in the past weeks not riding or doing my exercises.

I began to pedal, taking a lap of the warehouse. It was good. Really good. Smooth and silky. I wanted to push the velo to see what it could do, but I had no space inside the warehouse to ride.

Micheux might not even come in today. Just a few turns around the block, I told myself. It was still early; no one would see me. Three laps.

After only three laps, I remained unsatisfied. Oh, the velo fairly flew—I wasn't even using cleats and I was out of shape, yet I felt as fast as ever.

I wanted a straightaway to really put the velo through its paces. I pedaled down the road toward the long jetty by the docks. It would be the perfect place for a straight sprint.

I flew along the jetty. The air seemed to part and give around me. I sliced it with my speed, grinning from ear to ear as I tore down the narrow lane, heading back towards the road. Oh yes— this was a good velo. The best. I wanted it as badly as I'd ever wanted to ride in the Arena.

I was so enraptured by the ride that I almost missed a pedestrian approaching through the morning mist. I barreled along at such a speed that the only thing I could do was swerve to avoid him. I veered on the narrow jetty, almost taking the velo's tyre over the edge to plummet into the bay. I managed to balance, barely, passing the figure in a blur.

Shaken by my near miss, I came to my senses and pedaled back to the warehouse.

Something was wrong. I had been so careful to shut the rolling door after I brought out the velo, but now it stood wide open. Frantic yelling emanated from the workshop.

My stomach lurched. Micheux had arrived while I rode the velo. Dear God, how would I explain?

Dreading the confrontation, I dismounted and wheeled the perfect velo back inside. Micheux's back was turned to the entrance, and he waved his hands broadly as he shouted, "It was here! I've been sabotaged! Sabotaged, I tell you!" He spoke to a tall figure who also faced away from the rolling door.

"It's here," I squeaked.

My employer turned to glower at me. "Why, you thieving little runt!" He launched himself at me, briskly wrestling the velo from my hands. "For whom are you working?" he snarled.

"You," I said stupidly.

"Not me, you vixen. I know you're a spy! Who sent you?" Micheux snarled. Even in his anger, he moved the velo delicately, placing it with utmost care back into its rack.

"There must be a misunderstanding," a cool familiar voice said from behind Micheux.

My vision blurred and my breath shortened as if I were wearing the Whittler corset again. *Everett.*

"No misunderstanding," roared Micheux. "That girl was my secretary—ain't anymore, I'll tell you that, the right scheming little spy. I guess she's been spying for one of your rivals, Mr. Everett. You little wretch, Emmy Cassius. I'll kill you, I will!"

Everett emerged from behind Mr. Micheux to stare down at me. "Emmy Cassius?" he squeezed out. He sounded rather breathless. I gazed up at him, not knowing what to do or say.

Mr. Micheux lifted his hand as if to strike me. I flinched, but Everett caught his wrist to prevent the blow. "That's enough, Mr. Micheux. You misunderstood. The girl is mine."

"You sent a spy to watch over my work?" Micheux still sounded outraged, but Everett only shrugged.

"Did you ride it?" Everett asked me, casually, as if any girl secretary would naturally snatch a velo from her employer and take it for a joyride.

I couldn't help the smile that broke across my face. I was fresh from the ride, and it had been glorious, right down to the near miss on the jetty. The thrill lingered. "It was splendid."

"Excellent," he said, even as he turned towards Mr. Micheux, who gaped at us as though we'd gone mad. "Will you send me a bill, Mr. Micheux? I'll take the velo with me today. Along with my...secretary...of course."

"You'll take it today?" Micheux whined. "But I wanted to draw up plans—"

"There will be no plans," Everett said. "This velo is one-of-a-kind." He jerked his head in my direction. "Come," he commanded as he took the velo from the rack, wheeling it towards the open door.

I stood frozen for a moment, not knowing what to do. Everett glared at me over his shoulder. "Mrs. Cassius," he barked. "Come at once!"

I scrambled to his side. I couldn't remain working for Micheux, after all.

Everett strode down the street, wheeling the new velo and moving at his typical high speed. I jogged to keep up. A few blocks down, he stopped, whirled on me, and demanded, "Where in God's name have you been, Emmeline? I've had three private investigators on your trail, and none of them found a clue!"

My mouth opened and closed several times. I shook my head. "I was working for Mr. Micheux," I finally managed.

Everett snorted, shoved the velo in front of him, and began to walk again.

I hurried to his side. "Has it been very bad?" I said in a small voice.

"Very bad? Very bad? Of course it's been very bad!" He waved a hand expressively. "I had no idea where you were!"

We kept walking. I matched my stride to his. "I meant for you to divorce me so you could avoid the scandal," I said.

"I'll make up my own mind about that, thank you," Everett snapped. "Scandals die like storms, and I'm willing to wait it out. And given the fact that you disappeared, it has all died down sooner, rather than later. The crowd dispersed outside my house weeks ago."

"They'd be back if I returned."

"The reason they left is that I threatened them with a lawsuit for what they did to you. Stoning may be permissible in Alora, but it's considered assault in Seren. They won't be back."

"Who's the velo for?" I hoped very much it wasn't for Eddings. I couldn't bear the thought of him getting such a gift. It was too small for him, anyway.

"Damnation, Emmeline, don't you understand anything? It's for *you*. I had it made for you."

"For—for me? How? How did you know what dimensions—"

"Your measurements. They were on the receipt for the dresses you bought."

"But why, Everett?"

Everett seemed as angry as he'd yet been. "I thought if I found you, I could use it to lure you back to me." He flushed. "Don't you miss me? You—you used my name. You called yourself Cassius."

I put a hand up to my chest, almost breathless. I *did* miss him. Almost as much as I missed riding a velo. But they were two different longings.

"I wanted you to be free," I whispered.

"I am free with you. Free in the right way. I'd rather compete with a sport than other men." He gazed at me. "I meant my vows, Emmeline, every word. Didn't you? "

A flash of memory and dream—my clammy bare hand in his, the tight bind of the golden ribbon around our wrists, and a two-headed bird learning to fly in one direction despite itself.

He leaned over the perfect velo and cupped my cheek. "Come back to me, Emmeline. I'll buy you as many racing velos as you can handle, if only you come back to me."

I couldn't help it. I giggled with the image of me, frolicking in a glut of racing velos. With one hand, I grasped the handles of the new velo. With the other, I reached up and mimicked him, putting my own palm against his cheek. "But I can handle a lot of velos, Cassius Everett," I said. "Are you sure you are up to it? If you ride with me, it's bound to be a wild race." I released the velo as we walked again.

Everett laughed. "I've been wanting to ride with you since the moment I saw you on the track. I didn't know it was you, but even then, you dazzled me. Come with me to Basile. A—ah—contact told me Basile is building a velodrome, something even larger than Seren's Arena. I've agreed to be an investor."

"Gabriel told you!"

Everett just smiled. "The Basile velodrome is going to be a very good investment," he said.

"Why? What makes it so special?"

Everett stopped walking and rested the new velo up against the side of a building. He leaned over a second velo locked against a metal pole just behind us.

"It's going to be the first velodrome in the world to have a female jockey racing on its track."

I stared at him as he mounted the velo he'd unlocked. "That's one of yours," I said, recognizing the velo as one of the collection I'd seen hanging in the mews behind Everett House.

"So it is." He jerked his chin at me as he clipped into his pedals. "Let's go for a ride."

"Together?" I asked.

"Of course, together." he said. "Together to ride, together to race, together to Basile." As he pulled down his goggles, I saw his right wrist. He'd wrapped a golden ribbon around it several times and knotted it tight. It was the ribbon from our wedding.

Before I could comment, he kicked off the ground and took off. I snatched the new velo—*my own velo!*—from the wall and raced after him.

Epilogue

Dead silence greeted me as I stepped onto the track at *Velodrome Basile* and wheeled my custom velo to the starting line. You could have heard a stomach growl or a cat sneeze. Gazes—some malevolent, some eager, all curious—burned my skin. Racing in Seren had never been like this. I relished and loathed the exposure. No matter how they felt about me, everyone wanted to catch a glimpse of Emmeline Everett, the world's first female velo jockey to ride in a professional arena.

I trembled, imagining the whispers: *There she is, the bloody manotte, the damned freak! Who does she think she is, riding with the men? Doesn't she know her place?* Leading up to this day, the papers had been full of opinions both for and against my inclusion in Basile's first race. Cassius had laughed at every negative article. "That's what I think of such drivel," he'd said, after shredding a particularly virulent diatribe and throwing the pieces into the fireplace in our new townhouse in central Basile.

The other jockeys fussed on the starting line, adjusting their dark goggles, smoothing their leathers, yanking their gauntlets into place. My hair—newly bobbed into a modern cut—stuck out from my helmet, free from the restriction of a concealing cap. No more hiding for me.

Basilean women occupied an entire row near the front of the stands. Dressed in comfortable mod-dresses rather than corseted gowns, they waved banners stitched with my name.

I lifted a defiant hand and waved at them. En masse they rose and cheered wildly. Boos and hoots answered the women's support. The earlier silence gone, it now appeared everyone needed to express views about my presence on the track. Pressure thickened the air. If I won, if I even placed, this velodrome would raise an uproar no keir-track had ever seen. I understood the possible repercussions, but nothing would prevent me from racing full out. Nothing. Fear of public censure had forced me to sabotage myself too many times in past races—I'd held back, afraid to win lest I draw attention to myself. Afraid to win lest I be discovered. Not today. Today, I'd race with everything I had. I was free to do it.

Jockey Number Two hissed and spit on the boards in front of my tyre. I clenched my fist and suppressed the urge to raise it at him. They would use any excuse to disqualify me. My position was tenuous at best. Cassius and Gabriel had managed to convince the Velodrome Council to let me ride—the money Cassius provided made a powerful argument, I'm sure—but just because they'd permitted my participation didn't mean they were happy about it.

"He's Aloran," Gabriel muttered, holding my velo as I clipped into my pedals. My brother had agreed to serve as my coach. "Ungallant bastard."

"It doesn't matter." I dropped down into my handles. Cassius had designed the velo so that I could ride lower than ever, slung between handles and seat in a horizontal line. I'd never been able to get into such an ideal position when I'd raced in Seren on Gabriel's velo.

I had practiced over the past days to get a feel for Basile's unfamiliar track with its steeply-raked curves and aggressive design. How good it felt to ride a velo that fit my form with cleats that fit my feet! For so long I had made do with Gabriel's leavings, seat too high, handles too wide, socks stuffed in my toes.

I looked up from my starting position, scanning the stands for Cassius. He had a box seat here in Basile that was as posh as the one he'd had in Seren, but he'd promised me he'd sit in the stands so I could see him. I spotted him in the front row near my contingent of women. He lifted one gloved hand in a small wave as he caught me looking. Our gold wedding ribbon flashed as his jacket sleeve rode up, exposing his wrist. I wore the other half of the ribbon on my left wrist. "Thank you," I murmured, mouthing the words so he could see them.

"What's that, Emmy?" Gabriel asked.

"Nothing."

Number Two snorted beside us. "Quiet, bitch," he hissed from the side of his mouth.

I could do nothing but glare at him, for the officiator called, "Jockeys! On your marks!"

I crouched low over the handles.

"Set!"

Screams and stomping shook the floor beneath my velo.

Bang!

My thighs sprang to action like a wildcat's. Screams of "Freak!" and "Knock the bitch over!" came from the stands, but no insult could touch me. Governed by the keir-race code of honor, I pedaled behind Number Two for the requisite initial laps instead of dusting him at the starting line as I wished.

Before we turned the first paced lap, Number Four broke formation, surging up my outside.

"Boo! Boo!" shrieked the women's row at this flagrant disrespect for the keir code. But elsewhere, cheers greeted Four's breach of etiquette. Everyone understood the gesture: a woman didn't deserve a keir-racer's respect.

Concentrate, Emmeline. With one jockey breaking form, others would, too. The race would be a free-for-all. I drove my legs, pushing on Two's outer flank. Four and One pulled ahead.

Two and I rode neck and neck, no more than a finger's breadth of space between our elbows.

I accelerated into the curve. The Aloran jockey, instead of dropping towards the lower line, swung outwards, jostling my arm and cursing. I swayed but managed to control the velo by leaning into the Aloran to counterbalance. He snapped an elbow at my face. I ducked, glad for the perfect union of body and bike provided by my new custom velo.

Ahead, Number One flagged. The Aloran and I sprinted together, overtaking One on the straightaway though he flung out an arm to foil me. I flew past the treacherous limb, determined to beat the Aloran cretin.

We took the second and third laps in tight formation, the Aloran's breath a hiss of derision as he tried to knock into me again.

The bell rang for the final lap and the race ignited further. I held nothing back, spinning until my thighs screamed, crouching to present minimal body to the air. I rode as I had in my childhood dreams, instinctively, with animal awareness. I inched past the Aloran and moved onto Number Four's wheel. When he threw a glance over his shoulder, he allowed his velo a tiny swerve, first towards the line and then away from it. I took the chance, pushing into the gap between his velo and the line.

Control, Gabriel admonished in my head. *Risky moves require control.* Just as I passed the leader, his front tyre tagged my back one. I wobbled, but increased my speed to hold firm. The crowd's shrieks told me Number Four had fallen.

The boards flew by in a glittering blur. Spectators screamed, "Manotte! Freak!"

I galvanized, dropping to the line to prevent an inside pass from the Aloran. He tried my outside. I blocked him again.

I thought of the way Papan once pinched my cheek and said, "Pretty little things don't ride, darling," after I'd begged to have a go on Gabriel's red velocipede as a child.

Anger fed my legs as they churned a furious burn.

I crossed the finish line with my legs on fire. The velodrome erupted into chaos: shrieks, roars, applause, smashing glass. My women's contingent stood on top of their seats as they screamed and leapt and waved their flags.

The din rang in my ears. Bottles and debris flew from stands to track, smashing around me in a rain of glass. A siren blared through the velodrome to attempt to calm the crowd. Gabriel leapt and spun like a wind-up toy in uncontainable excitement. All the other trainers stood in a silent circle marked by taut, furious faces.

I searched for Cassius in the undulating crowd. He vaulted over the wall that divided stands from track and ran across the shiny boards, heedless of the track rules.

"You won, darling!" he shouted. "You *won!*"

I lifted both arms, shaking my fists in time to the cheers and the taunts. I turned in a full circle to scan the crowd, waving and smiling. The row of women burst into a fresh round of applause at my gesture. Velodrome guards formed a wall with their bodies to prevent more people from leaping onto the track as Cassius had done. Cassius caught me and kissed me madly, ignoring the angry roar of half the crowd.

He released me as the Aloran jockey, Number Two, wheeled past. I stepped toward the jockey and held out my hand. He only glared at it and refused to shake.

Shattered glass crunched beneath my riding cleats as I turned back to Cassius. The uproar in the stands intensified. I grabbed Cassius's hand and squeezed.

I had known it might come to this. I didn't care. Sometimes winning is everything.